VIRAGO
MODERN CLASSICS

Vera Brittain

Vera Brittain (1893–1970) grew up in provincial comfort in the north of England. In 1914 she won an exhibition to Somerville College, Oxford, but a year later abandoned her studies to enlist as a VAD nurse. She served throughout the war, working in London, Malta and the Front in France.

At the end of the war, with all those closest to her dead, Vera Brittain returned to Oxford. There she met Winifred Holtby – author of *South Riding* – and this friendship which was to last until Winifred Holtby's untimely death in 1935 sustained her in those difficult post-war years.

Vera Brittain was a convinced pacifist, a prolific speaker, lecturer, journalist and writer, she devoted much of her energy to the causes of peace and feminism. She wrote 29 books in all, novels, poetry, biography and autobiography and other non-fiction, but it was *Testament of Youth* which established her reputation and made her one of the best loved writers of her time. The authorised biography, *Vera Brittain: A Life* (1994) by Paul Berry and Mark Bostridge, is published by Chatto & Windus.

Vera Brittain married in 1925 and had two children.

Also by Vera Brittain

Testament of Friendship
Testament of Youth

The Dark Tide

VERA BRITTAIN

*With a Preface by Vera Brittain
and an Introduction by Mark Bostridge*

A *Virago* Book

Published by Virago Press 1999

First published in Great Britain 1923

Copyright © Mark Bostridge and Rebecca Williams 1923

Introduction Copyright © Mark Bostridge 1999

A CIP catalogue record for this book
is available from the British Library.

ISBN 1 86049 769 1

Typeset by Palimpsest Book Production Limited,
Polmont, Stirlingshire
Printed and bound in Great Britain
by Clays Ltd, St Ives plc

Virago
A Division of
Little, Brown and Company (UK)
Brettenham House
Lancaster Place
London WC2E 7EN

To
W. H.

*This book was dedicated to my beloved
friend and fellow-student Winifred Holtby,
who died on September 29, 1935*

CONTENTS

Introduction

When *Testament of Youth*, the book that made Vera Brittain famous, was published in 1933, one American reviewer went so far as to describe this memoir of Brittain's First World War experiences as 'a novel masquerading as an autobiography'. Brittain herself probably took the remark as a backhanded compliment, for she had set out to make her 'Autobiographical Study of the Years 1900–1925' as 'truthful as history, but as readable as fiction'.

Indeed, it was only after several failed attempts to tell her story as fiction that Vera Brittain had recognised that an autobiography was the most satisfactory way of presenting her experience of the war. As early as 1918, a few months before the Armistice, she had completed her first war novel, based partly on her time as a Voluntary Aid Detachment nurse at the 24 General Hospital at Etaples, not far from the Western Front. But this, like several other novels either planned, or written but not completed, from the immediate postwar period through to the mid-twenties, foundered because she was still too close to the events she described for them to be made the subject matter for imaginative reconstruction. By late 1929, Brittain had resolved 'to tell my own fairly typical story as truthfully as I could against the larger background . . .'.

While her works of autobiography and biography were consistently to employ novelistic devices, each one of Brittain's five published novels contains strongly autobiographical elements. In varying degrees they are all *romans à clef* in which identifiable persons from real life are presented as thinly disguised fictional characters. But Brittain's autobiographical impulse was even stronger than this term suggests. For, in all her writing she was intent on promoting the values associated with her own social and political activism. In 1925 she wrote that her literary and political work were closely interrelated, and that 'The first ... is simply a popular interpretation of the second; a means of presenting my theories before people who would not understand or be interested in them if they were explained seriously.'

This approach would be at its strongest in the novels she wrote from the thirties onwards, after *Testament of Youth*, where her feminist and pacifist ideals were disseminated within the framework of the novel of traditional forms and allusions, and in which the influence of the moral tone of the favourite novelists of her youth, George Eliot and Olive Schreiner, is sometimes discernible. She remained a steadfast believer in the 'power of ideas to change the shape of the world and even help to eliminate its evils', and argued that writers, whether of fiction or non-fiction, 'have the important task of interpreting for their readers this present revolutionary and complex age which has no parallel in history'.

Certainly, none of Brittain's subsequent novels ever quite equalled the impact of her first, *The Dark Tide*, which appeared in 1923. The book caused a minor sensation through its portrayal of an Oxford women's college (a thinly veiled Somerville College, where Brittain had been an undergraduate in 1914–15 and 1919–21), and because it came dangerously close to libelling a number of Oxford dons, and of causing offence to Winifred Holtby, Brittain's most intimate friend, who was caricatured as Daphne Lethbridge (in the event, Holtby accepted the characterisation with good humour). *The Dark Tide* received a total of seventy-three reviews, and established Brittain as a young writer of promise. In her next novel, *Not Without Honour* (1924), published the following year, Brittain turned to a treatment of the provincial society of her upbringing. The main action of the novel is set in the years just before the outbreak of the First World War, and the fictional market town of Torborough, with its narrow-mindedness and social snobbery, is recognisably the Buxton of her own 'provincial young ladyhood'. Christine Merivale is a self-portrait of the author, and the plot, which centres on the heroine's infatuation with a charismatic Anglican curate of unorthodox views, the Reverend Albert Clark, carries clear echoes of Brittain's own preoccupation with Buxton's Reverend Joseph Ward which she had described in her 1913–14 diary. Although *Not Without Honour* is in some ways a more coherent novel than *The Dark Tide*, it overall lacks the vitality of its predecessor.

Following the success of *Testament of Youth*, Vera Brittain planned a work of fiction which in its themes and expression might match the range and power of her autobiography. *Honourable Estate*, published in 1936, was the result, and today the novel is generally recognised as Brittain's most ambitious and sustained piece of fiction. In her foreword to the book, she explained that *Honourable Estate* 'purports to show how the women's revolution – one of the greatest in all history – united with the struggle for other democratic ideals and the cataclysm of the War to alter the private destinies of individuals'. The novel covers the period from the late-Victorian era through to 1930, and its narrative thread is composed of the stories of three marriages in which Brittain explores developing attitudes to women in the decades before and after the attainment of the vote.

Honourable Estate sold well, but its contemporary reception, especially when compared with the acclaim that had greeted *Testament of Youth*, was muted. In the immediate aftermath of its appearance, Vera Brittain worked on an idea for at least one other novel, based on the life of Mary Wollstonecraft, but her time was now increasingly taken up with her campaigning work, as a Sponsor of the Peace Pledge Union, to prevent another world war, and with the research and writing of *Testament of Friendship*, her biography of Winifred Holtby.

When Brittain did return to writing novels in the midst of the Second World War, it was perhaps inevitable that a pacifist theme would predominate. In *Account Rendered* (1945) and *Born 1925* (1948), she dealt with the effects of another war on two individuals, both of whose lives have already been irretrievably altered by their experiences in the 1914–18 war. In *Account Rendered* (inspired by the real-life case of Leonard Lockhart), the protagonist, Francis Halkin, who was shell-shocked in France in 1918, still suffers from periodic loss of memory, and is sent to trial when his wife dies suddenly, and he is suspected of having either murdered her, or of having been part of a suicide pact. *Born 1925* (which Brittain actually started writing at the end of 1944) is based on the conjunction of two plot elements: the story of Robert Carbury, the pacifist vicar of a West End church, clearly recognisable as a portrait of Dick Sheppard, the founder of the Peace Pledge Union, and of his son Adrian, whose conflict with his father represents in some ways Brittain's own generational clashes with her son John.

Vera Brittain considered *Born 1925* to be the most

important of her five novels, but although the book enjoyed strong sales in Britain it was not the triumph that she had hoped for. Like *Account Rendered, Born 1925* is too dominated by Brittain's pacifist convictions, and it is tempting to go some way towards agreeing with a reviewer of *Account Rendered* who commented that the novel marked 'the final collapse of the artist and the emergence from the novelist's ashes of the unapologetic propagandist'.

But to subscribe too heavily to this point of view would be to overlook the other pleasures which, at her best, Vera Brittain offers as a novelist. *Honourable Estate* is undoubtedly a major achievement of a conventional, non-modernist type of fiction, while *The Dark Tide* is a thoroughly diverting novel of strong biographical and historical interest. Both deserve to be read and revalued by a new generation of readers.

'Daphne', as *The Dark Tide* was originally called, was written between Easter 1920, while Vera Brittain was still up at Oxford, and the late spring of 1922, by which time she was sharing a studio flat in London at 52 Doughty Street with her college friend, Winifred Holtby. In the preface that she wrote to the 1935 edition of *The Dark Tide*, reprinted by its original publisher, Grant Richards, in the wake of *Testament of Youth*'s success, Brittain criticised the 'crude violence of its methods and the unmodified black-and-whiteness of its values', but believed that it did represent 'fairly accurately' the type of life led by women students in the Oxford of 1920.

Like *Gaudy Night* (1935) by Dorothy L. Sayers, in which Somerville appears as Shrewsbury College, and Rosamond Lehmann's first novel, *Dusty Answer* (1927), in which the heroine Judith Earle goes up to Cambridge, *The Dark Tide* portrays the enclosed world of an Oxbridge women's college at a time when postwar social changes were encouraging the fashionable, educated, self-determined 'New Woman', and when, at Oxford at least, women were about to be admitted to degree courses on the same status as men.

What made *The Dark Tide* particularly controversial at the time of its publication in the summer of 1923 was the way in which the author appeared to have betrayed her Alma Mater by poking fun at its institutions and customs, and by caricaturing several well-known Oxford personalities. Somerville was outraged by the novel's presentation of the world of 'Drayton College', and according to Brittain, vetoed the circulation of the book.

The major characters of *The Dark Tide* are not so much imaginatively redeveloped as simply transferred direct from fact to fiction, and moreover to increasingly unflattering and melodramatic situations. Thus, Alexis Stephanoff, the witty Polish, History tutor, is Lewis Namier, at that time a Modern History lecturer at Balliol; Patricia O'Neill is Somerville's own History don, the distinguished Medievalist, Maude Clarke; Raymond Sylvester is C.R.M.F. Cruttwell, the Dean of Hertford, who tutored Brittain and Holtby; and Miss Lawson-Scott bears a striking resemblance to Emily Penrose, Principal of Somerville.

To Somerville it seemed bad enough for Brittain to portray herself as Virginia Dennison, rich, small, dark-eyed and pretty, 'one of those individuals of whom other people are always aware'; but what about Daphne Lethbridge, Virginia's tutorial partner and rival, who is unmistakably modelled on Winifred Holtby? As Marion Shaw remarks, throughout the novel 'the character of Daphne-Winifred lurches between buffoonery – she is gauche, masculine, clumsy, dresses badly, is always late, and is unfortunate in her dealings with men – and pathos as she becomes the mother of a disabled child and the abandoned wife of the tutor who has all along loved Virginia'. The portrait is a cruel one, and it remains something of a mystery why Brittain should have risked ruining her friendship with Holtby – the relationship that had rescued Brittain from the deep despair of the first years after the war – by such a ruthless lack of tact.

In mitigation, it should be admitted that as the novel progresses, the two main female characters become increasingly representative of the different sides of Vera's own personality, with Daphne exhibiting her insecurity and desire for recognition, and Virginia her more autonomous, intellectual side. 'Poor Daphne!' Brittain had written to Holtby in November 1921, while struggling with the latter part of the novel. 'I get more & more cruel to her. The chief consolation is she gets less & less like you.' But the need, above all, for Brittain to exorcise the public hurt and humiliation she had suffered at Holtby's hands during the famous Somerville debate in which Brittain's championing of her own war service was held up to ridicule, meant that she was willing, as Marion Shaw says, 'to settle old scores in the public arena of fiction'. Throughout her novel-writing career, Vera Brittain would rarely be able to resist appropriating real-life characters and situations with no apparent thought for the sensibilities of the individuals concerned.

Towards the end of her life, Vera Brittain looked back on *The Dark Tide* as a 'wild little novel, full of undergraduate cleverness, ruthless, even savage', and admitted that she should have been ashamed of her caricature of 'my beloved W.H.'. Today it reads as an amusing period piece in which the main feminist theme of a woman's right to independence and self-empowerment is damaged only as the novel ends by a reversion to ideas of a woman's self-sacrifice in the cause of duty. For Vera Brittain's more sustained attempt at an explicitly feminist novel, readers would have to wait for *Honourable Estate*.

Mark Bostridge
London, March 1999

Select Bibliography

Paul Berry and Mark Bostridge, *Vera Brittain: A Life* (London: Chatto & Windus, 1995)

Deborah Gorham, *Vera Brittain: A Feminist Life* (Oxford: Blackwell Publishers, 1996)

Jean E. Kennard, *Vera Brittain and Winifred Holtby. A Working Partnership* (New Hampshire: University Press of New England, 1989)

Susan J. Leonardi, *Dangerous by Degrees. Women at Oxford and the Somerville College Novelists* (New Brunswick: Rutgers University Press, 1989)

Marion Shaw, *The Clear Stream: A Life of Winifred Holtby* (London: Virago Press, 1999)

Britta Zangen, *A Life of Her Own. Feminism in Vera Brittain's Theory, Fiction and Biography* (Frankfurt: Peter Lang, 1996)

PREFACE

To *the Reprinted Edition of*
The Dark Tide

'The Dark Tide' was my first novel, published in 1923. Its publishers are issuing a reprint in consequence of a renewed demand for it which can only, I imagine, be due to my references, in Chapter 11 of 'Testament of Youth,' to the writing of this early book, to my difficulties in placing it, and to certain unexpected consequences of its publication. These prefatory paragraphs represent a response to the somewhat embarrassing request made to me by the publishers to contribute a foreword to the new edition.

The original notes for 'The Dark Tide' were made between 1919 and 1921, when I was still an undergraduate at Oxford, and the first ten chapters describe conditions at the women's colleges as they then both were and were not. Needless to say, the Oxford of 1935 is not the Oxford of 1921. The chaperone rules to which reference is made in my story have long vanished, and a measure of freedom in which, I have been told, the strength of reaction against former ludicrous repressions was at first intense, has now taken its place. Doubtless there are other changes of which I am unaware. One that does occur to me is the cheerful detachment of the modern woman undergraduate compared with the naïve and emotional loyalties of us who belonged to the era in which Degrees for Women were won from the war-smitten university.

A present-day student from my own Oxford college was introduced to me at a party not long ago.

'I hope you're not going to talk to me about the "dear old college"' she observed immediately, and plunged gaily into another topic before I had recovered from this unexpected relegation to the ranks of those who canonize the 'old school tie.'

On the whole, in spite of the indignant chorus which arose, full-throated, from certain sections of the Press just after its publication, I still think that 'The Dark Tide' – notwithstanding the crude violence of its methods and the unmodified black-and-whiteness of its values – does represent fairly accurately the type of life led by women students in 1920 and the relationships between them. This fact was accepted with malevolent enjoyment by one reviewer, Mr Charles Williams, who more than once ran 'The Dark Tide' to earth with an assiduousness worthy of a nobler cause. In *The Isis* of October 31st, 1923, Mr Williams – whose critical reactions have become, I hope, less adolescent with time – visualized himself 'years hence, when all the remainder copies of this novel had been reduced to ashes in the grates of Bloomsbury parlours, still taking my surviving copy from the bookshelf and . . . chuckling over the unconscious humour of this undiscovered masterpiece . . . It is the greatest indictment of women since "The Rape of the Lock".'

Doubtless Mr Williams and others have since reflected that you cannot take a hundred young women at an emotional age, enclose them within the walls of a modern cloister, deny them normal unsupervised friendships with their masculine contemporaries, and submit them to overwork and competition which, for economic reasons and through limitation of numbers, has always been fiercer among Oxford women than

Oxford men, without producing certain qualities of pettiness, cruelty, hysteria and a tendency to the disproportionate exaggeration of trifles, which seldom exist among women who live in a more natural society.

'It is impossible,' the contemporary *Oxford Magazine* remarked of Chapter III of 'The Dark Tide,' 'to believe that any society would arrange a whole debate on purpose to show one individual member how much they disliked her.' But this, as I have related in 'Testament of Youth,' actually happened; and I myself was the victim. What is more, I am sure I thoroughly deserved it. It was not the fault of my exasperated fellow-students that they did not realize the background of personal history which made me an intolerable companion for adolescents.

Incidentally, because of this episode, it was assumed when 'The Dark Tide' was first published that one of its two 'heroines,' *Virginia Dennison*, was intended for a portrait of myself. If so, she was one of those 'wish-fulfilment' portraits by means of which the young are apt to compensate for their own failures and humiliations. Between the brilliant, priggish Virginia, with her easy First in History and her dogmatic control of difficult situations, and myself with my hallucination-haunted university career and calamitous Second, there was all too grievously little in common.

Where 'The Dark Tide' did, of course, emphatically depart from university experience was in the amorous adventures of its five chief characters. It is hardly necessary to add that *Raymond Sylvester*, the wicked don who subsequently became a 'diplomatist,' and with whom marriage, as Mr H. C. Harwood pertinently remarked in *The Outlook*, resembled 'being run over by a motor-bus,' was a hyperbolic figment of my too-inventive brain. 'When a lecturer,' commented *The Birmingham Post*, 'proposes to one of his pupils at 11 a.m. and to another the same afternoon, we know this is not Oxford.' Quite so. Whether Oxford might be a happier and healthier place if modified versions of such occurrences became less impossible than they were in 1923, is hardly for me to say. Probably not one of its academic inhabitants would think so; but the question is at least arguable.

A further naïveté was subsequently pointed out by Mr Gerald Gould in a review which nevertheless gave me greater hope for my literary future than the hard facts of the time seemed to warrant:

'"The Dark Tide" is a remarkable book, though crude. It starts off with a somewhat lurid picture of Oxford life . . . and the author displays, in the interests of the wicked tutor's subsequent career as a diplomat, an engaging disregard of the distinction between the civil servant who is *in* a government department and the politician who aims at being the temporary head of it. But she has the root of the matter in her. She knows how to communicate sympathy. She has spiritual understanding of character. Some day she may write a good book.'

The chief criticism involved in this paragraph is perhaps a comment on the methods of history tuition at Oxford immediately after the War. No doubt some blind spot in my own mentality accounted for the fact that I had 'done' Modern History without learning anything whatever about the workings of the British constitutional machine; but the further fact that the Final Honours School of 'Modern' History ended comfortably at the year 1878 must also be held partly responsible. I had changed from English, my original subject, to History in order to understand the causes of the War and to discover what means existed for the prevention of such catastrophes, but the present Honours School of 'Modern Greats' had not then been established, and the only help obtainable for my quest had to be derived from a School which not only told me nothing about the Great War, the Treaty of Versailles or the League of Nations, but stopped short before the first Hague Conference and the South African War.

Nevertheless, 'The Dark Tide' still appears a surprisingly melodramatic and immature production for a young woman who had seen four years of War service and three of University training. It stumbled towards a technique which I have since repeated with possibly better results – the relation of an individual story against a larger background of political and social events – but the story was over-emphasized and the background lamentably inaccurate and incomplete. Yet, by the time I began the book, I was well into my twenties; I had passed through a veritable lifetime of annihilating experience; and I was not, I think, exceptionally unintelligent. Why was it that, as *The Queen* so justly pointed out, 'Miss Brittain knows next to nothing of the adult society, with its laws and politics, which she sets out to describe?' The answer, I think, lies in precisely that annihilating experience. The young men and women who grew up to be immediately absorbed in the War developed emotionally at the expense of their intellectual equipment and their *savoir-faire* – except in, quite literally, matters of life and death. As I have endeavoured to explain elsewhere: 'Crowded living and a great rush of events probably do retard development in some ways as much as they hasten it in others; after all, one of the chief factors in mental growth is time to think and leisure to give one's thought some kind of expression. Those of us who got caught up into the War and its emotions before our brains had become mature were rather like Joseph II of Austria – we had to take the second step before we took the first.'

'The Dark Tide' was finished in the late spring of 1922.

Then began the series of vain attempts to place it which seemed interminable, though I have since learnt from contrasting my early struggles with those of other authors that my period in the wilderness was comparatively short. Various eminent individuals, such as Miss Rose Macaulay, Mr J. D. Beresford and the late Mr Robert Leighton, took a benevolent interest in the fate of my story. Their generous assistance could not persuade even one of the first dozen or so publishers whom I tried that my future as a writer was likely to be of any importance to anybody; but by means of such criticism as they valiantly offered me I was enabled to redeem my despised novel from even worse faults than those which still appear. After this process of revision had been perseveringly repeated on several occasions, the book was eventually accepted by Mr Grant Richards on account of certain qualities of 'freshness and vitality' that he perceived in it, and was published, very elegantly bound and printed, in July, 1923.

Several rather surprising consequences followed publication. To begin with, a serious and favourable criticism appeared on the main fiction-review page of the *Times Literary Supplement*. This notice must have been even more astonishing to my publisher than to my hopeful self, since most of the other critics took refuge in the genial charitableness which experienced reviewers are prepared, to their credit, to extend to the work of a new author; or in the obvious opportunities for irony and humour with which the story so lavishly presented them.

In the second place, I was immediately involved in a *contretemps* with, of all newspapers, the *Manchester Guardian*. On p. 157 occurs a sentence, discreetly altered from the original edition, which refers to the reading by 'Mrs Lethbridge' of the *Manchester Sentinel*, and her efforts to induce a harassed reporter to include an account of her daughter's wedding. In the first edition this sentence actually ran as follows: 'Mrs Lethbridge, with the *Manchester Guardian* on her lap, sat gloating over the paragraph on whose account she had bribed an accommodating reporter with champagne.'

How this naïve and monstrous libel on that noble newspaper – of which, incredible as it now seems, I was then only ignorantly and remotely aware – should have escaped so many distinguished and experienced eyes still strikes me as amazing, but the fact remains; and the *Manchester Guardian* very naturally threatened proceedings. Acting on the advice of Mr Grant Richards, and impelled, indeed, to take the same step by sheer panic, I wrote to the Editor frantically explaining that I was a graduate only recently down from Oxford, and had intended nothing libellous. Mr C. P. Scott himself replied, dismissing the whole affair as 'a piece of carelessness,' and with characteristic generosity agreeing to take no further action if a printed slip apologizing for the error be inserted on the appropriate page. Three years later I was accepted by that forgiving newspaper as a constant contributor, and have written for its magazine page for over eight years.

Only a degree less disturbing than the agitation over the *Manchester Guardian* was the attitude adopted towards 'The Dark Tide' by the Oxford authorities themselves. I had ingenuously expected to arouse a measure of critical but benevolent interest in my guileless if highly-coloured production; instead, I encountered acid disapproval and a ban by my own college upon the circulation of the book. The fact that the college authorities of that day took my preposterous story so seriously, instead of ignoring it or regarding it with humour, now appears to me as evidence of that lack of a sense of proportion which academic life so often instils. At the time, however, these unexpected attacks upon my innocent fledgeling reduced me to a condition bordering upon nervous breakdown, and with the overwhelming desperation of inexperienced youth which regards every tragedy as permanent and final, I closed my London flat and sought refuge in the country, convinced that my career as a writer and my reputation as an individual were alike at an end.

But a quite different and even more unforeseen consequence of my book's publication was still to come. I had only been away for a few days when a letter – the first 'fan-mail,' I think, that I ever received – reached me from a reader who had purchased my novel at Blackwell's book-shop in Oxford as soon as it appeared, and wrote to express his deep interest in the story. My correspondent is now a Professor of Politics, a well-known writer on political and economic subjects, and prospective Labour candidate for Sunderland, but he was then a young lecturer holding his first post at the University of Sheffield. We had been at Oxford together as returned war-undergraduates, but though my name was familiar to him through my university journalism, we had never actually met. The following summer, when he returned to England after holding a year's Fellowship at Cornell University in the State of New York, we did meet for the first time. A year later we were married.

I have done, I hope, rather better work than 'The Dark Tide' in the twelve years which have succeeded its appearance, and many hundreds of letters have been written to me about these later publications, but not one has had such momentous personal consequences as that brief note from a then obscure young scholar which reached me in the disturbed summer of 1923. It still seems surprising that a book so immature and so unimportant should have been involved in so many adventures.

Vera Brittain.
October, 1935.

'Life was not the full sea flood, but the dark tide, moaning and desolate, going out in storm and rain.'

'The sea of which he is always dreaming is terrible and cruel as well as august and ennobling. But he is sure of one thing: it is through the struggle with is and such is it that man alone can become Man.'

F. MELIAN STAWELL

Chapter I

Drayton

The poets who love to think of Oxford as a magic city of dreaming spires must have welcomed the aeroplane as an æsthetic mode of transit. The Great Western Railway was not planned to aid the artistic imagination. Its road to Parnassus lies between the local cemetery and the gas-works, which challenge attention before Tom Tower and the spire of St Mary's. But for Daphne Lethbridge, gazing eagerly from the carriage window, the familiar view had never been so full of enchantment, and she clasped her suit-case in an ecstasy as the grey towers emerged from behind the fat, bulging sides of the gas-works. She was glad that she was Daphne Lethbridge, glad that she was twenty-two, glad most of all that the war was over and she was going back to college.

She was thoroughly bored with a war that had brought her neither personal sorrow nor romantic adventures, but had simply come as an unwelcome interruption. She had been conscious of it much in the same way as a duck is conscious of a thunderstorm. Her secure little pool of existence was merely ruffled and disturbed; only from afar had she seen the lightning and heard the fury of the rain.

She was never very clever at finding her luggage, and by the time she emerged from the involved mass of bicycles on the platform all the available taxis had disappeared. As the hansom she was obliged to take rattled under the railway bridge, her year at Drayton College seemed much nearer to her than the two years' motor-driving at Portsmouth which had followed it. It seemed so unbelievable now that, despite academic opposition, she had gone down 'to do war work' at the end of that first year, and had found rest for an uneasy conscience in the transport of naval officers.

Of course it had not been the kind of war work she would have chosen; she was never certain that all those motor drives were really quite necessary. She would greatly have preferred the vivid realities of an army hospital, or the Women's Auxiliary Corps with its raided camps. But Mr and Mrs Lethbridge would not dream of such horrible experiences for their only child. So Daphne had perforce to content herself with the motor-driving, thereby winning the well-fed approbation of Thorbury Park, the Manchester suburb where she lived with her parents.

Well, it was over at last, and she need no longer repress her yearning ambition – that ambition which wanted to learn everything, and get the best degree in History that woman ever had, and then to write things which would make the name of Daphne Lethbridge a household word in English literature.

She felt rather lost a few minutes after the cab had deposited her at Drayton, and moved self-consciously across the little entrance hall, whose windows were darkened by the burnished leaves of the autumn creeper. Her own year had gone down at the end of that summer, and the groups of unfamiliar faces regarded her with the insolent curiosity usually accorded to a new-comer in her first term.

'They think I'm a fresher,' said Daphne to herself indignantly, and she proceeded to read the notices with apparent unconcern. She had scarcely turned her back on the crowd of strangers when her hand was seized and shaken jubilantly by a small round person with a smiling chubby face. Daphne was quite relieved to recognise Julia Tait, a member of her own year who had likewise caught the infectious fever of patriotism, and had gone down at the same time as herself. 'It's really Daphne! How absolutely topping to see you again! Isn't it simply ripping to be back?'

'Splendid!' Daphne agreed; 'but a little strange after doing such different things. One feels rather lost, you know – just to begin with.'

'Yes – one does. I did too – but I was awfully lucky to get let off from the Ministry in time to come back last term and see our year go down. They were dreadfully sick you couldn't manage it too.'

'I tried,' said Daphne, 'but it was no good. June was the best I could do. I envied you tremendously.'

'Never mind, I'll tell you all the news.'

This was no idle boast on the part of Julia, who was privately known among her friends as 'Who's Who.' Her power of acquiring information amounted to genius. There was scarcely a member of Drayton with whom she had not corresponded at one time or another. She was on intimate terms with the whole of the Senior Common Room, and knew the private love affairs of all the junior dons. She continued the conversation volubly.

'I *should* have missed you if you hadn't come back, though the Second Year's an awfully decent crowd. I never expected you to arrive so soon, though. Had lunch?'

'Yes, I had it before I started. I've only come from London to-day. I've been staying with some cousins.'

'Good. You'll have heaps of time to settle in. It'll jolly well take some doing, though, after two years. I'll come and help you – our rooms are quite close.'

Daphne sighed, and looked vaguely up and down the list of rooms on the notice-board. Julia was certainly a little overwhelming just at first; but she was very friendly and kind, and Daphne felt suddenly grateful to her for being there. It would have been so strange to come back to Drayton without a year to belong to, and find that one knew nobody at all. At Portsmouth, with the remembrance of a glowing first-year reputation crowned by Distinction in History Previous, it had seemed so easy to return impressively to Drayton, obtain a brilliant First, and then embark upon a career of uninterrupted triumph. But she felt a little frightened now that she was back among the beloved buildings, which had watched the struggles of so many ambitions, and had seen so many generations pass to whom failure was a more familiar name than success.

'Where are our rooms – Martindale or Wilson?' she inquired, turning from the notice-board to Julia.

'Oh, Martindale, of course. Wilson's crammed with freshers as usual. You've got 105 and I'm 110. I wrote and asked the Bursar to put us close together; I knew she'd do anything for you.'

Daphne started guiltily.

'Goodness, I'd almost forgotten! Of course I must go and see her at once. Look here, Julia, I think I'll get my interviewing done before I start to unpack. Miss Lawson-Scott's sure to expect me to see her before anyone else, and then I suppose I'll have to go to the history tutor some time.'

'Oh, Miss O'Neill! You'll like her all right. She came here the term after we went down. She's a ripping person and quite young – oh, thirtyish or thereabouts, I suppose, but she looks a kid.'

'I'll go and see her before the crush, if I can,' said Daphne.

'I feel all in a muddle about my work. P'r'aps I'll see you in the hall at tea-time.'

'Right-o! If you don't I'll look you up directly after,' and Julia trotted amiably down the passage, leaving Daphne at the foot of the stairs which led to the Principal's office.

Daphne went up and knocked at Miss Lawson-Scott's door rather tentatively, for generations of Drayton students had not learnt to call their Principal 'The Law' without good cause. The white-haired, ruddy-cheeked woman with the gracious manner and the iron will always made Daphne feel incapable of speaking the truth. But she possessed one advantage over most of her fellow-students: she was one of the few who could talk to Miss Lawson-Scott without having to look up.

The greeting, when it came, contained nothing that could terrify her.

'How do you do, Miss Lethbridge? I'm very glad to see you back again after such a long absence. I hope the war work hasn't *quite* put everything out of your head? That's right! I'm sure it will all come back to you as soon as you begin. I haven't forgotten what excellent work you gave us in your first year at Drayton.'

Daphne was spared the trouble of looking for the Bursar by colliding with that lady at the foot of the Principal's stairs. Miss Jenkinson was the one thorn among Daphne's Drayton roses, for, being her godmother, she took a proprietary and somewhat inconvenient interest in her welfare. She was an angular and lugubrious woman, with a remarkable eye for people's little defects, and an invariable habit of stripping the glamour from one's dearest friend in a single sentence.

'Dear me! Careless!' she gasped, almost overthrown by the energetic impact of her god-daughter. 'Dear me! Steady! Steady!'

Then, as Daphne stood murmuring hasty apologies, Miss Jenkinson suddenly changed from irritation to her nearest approach to a smile.

'Why, it's my dear Daphne! I might have known! How very pleasant to see you among us again! Let me look at you, my dear child,' and she lifted Daphne's unwilling face to the light. 'Ah! yes, it tells, it tells – all the strain of that terrible hard work – out in all weathers, too, your mother told me. There's nothing like a strain, is there, for drawing lines on a young face? I hope, my dear, you won't find that the other students seem very childish. I'm afraid you'll be much older than the year you'll have to work with!'

Daphne, who had been so delightedly conscious of her youth in the train, began to feel a dismal sense of age creeping over her, but her thoughts were immediately diverted by Miss Jenkinson into another channel.

'And how's your dear mother? Still enjoying as good health as ever? Not growing any stouter, I hope?'

Long ago, when they were both small children, Daphne's mother and Miss Jenkinson had been at school together. Ill-assorted as they seemed even then, they had never ceased to maintain a regular correspondence, though their subsequent careers had been as different as two women's lives can well be. Daphne's mother, only daughter of Megson's Manchester Emporiums, had early achieved a step upwards in the social scale by marrying Herbert Lethbridge, a young shipbuilder whose modest fortunes received an immediate impetus from the wealth she brought him. Daphne had no recollection of their first home close to the docks. She only remembered Thorbury Park, the fashionable Manchester suburb, and the series of moves through various houses of gradually increasing dimensions till they ended in 'The Gables,' an ample dwelling with a large garden and two tennis courts, which exuded prosperity from every blade of grass.

Nobody, on the other hand, had wanted to marry Miss Jenkinson. In her early days she had been considered 'scientific,' but a Fourth in Zoology at Oxford convinced her that she had mistaken her vocation. She possessed, however, that faculty for clinging to university jobs which is often denied to her more brilliant sisters who achieve Firsts, and her experience in the domestic department of various provincial universities had finally brought her her heart's desire, the Bursarship of Drayton College. When, to the proud satisfaction of Daphne's mother and the secret misgivings of her father, Daphne was found at school to be turning out 'intellectual,' it was to Miss Jenkinson that Mrs Lethbridge, who had never derived any profit from her own education, had written for advice. The result had been that the already willing Daphne was entered for Drayton College at an early age.

After a few minutes' conversation Daphne managed to shake off Miss Jenkinson for the time being – not very cleverly, because Daphne was by no means a tactful person. She left the rueful Bursar still standing at the foot of the stairs, and hurried off down the long corridor to find the history tutor, Miss O'Neill.

She was immediately disconcerted by the slim, dark-haired girl who answered 'Come in!' to her knock. Thirty? Well, perhaps – but all the same— Daphne was always a little disturbed in the presence of youth triumphant. She liked to find achievement middle-aged, and to see authority with grey hair and spectacles. It was always her tendency to overestimate the age of celebrities.

'She must be at least forty,' she would say, looking enviously at 'A new portrait of Miss So-and-so, the talented young authoress of—'; and sometimes to a friend at a concert: 'That girl on the platform must be years older than she looks.'

Daphne longed, of course, for the time to come when she could *really* begin to write, but all the same she was sometimes appalled at the thought of that terrifying plunge into Chapter I of her first novel. The universal middle age of genius spared her the distresses of envy and misgivings about the rapidity of her own progress, and prolonged to a comfortable indefiniteness the pleasant period of promise.

But here before her was youth, holding one of the most important positions at Drayton – youth grave and brilliant, yet shy and humble and astonishingly tolerant, perhaps because of the remote humour that lurked behind those baffling grey eyes. For the gods had been in a delightful mood when they made Patricia O'Neill.

'You're Miss O'Neill, aren't you?' Daphne began uncertainly.

'Yes. And you are Miss—?'

'Lethbridge. I've been away for two years, you know, and I thought perhaps I'd better come and see you early.'

'Miss Lethbridge! Of course I remember. You wrote to me, didn't you?' and Miss O'Neill took up from her desk a slip of paper with names written upon it. 'But I thought,' she said, 'that I'd put you down on the list to come and see me between six and seven.'

'The list?' Daphne looked vague.

'Yes; the list of names on the history notice-board in the hall.'

Daphne flushed crimson.

'I – I'd quite forgotten that one looked on the notice-board for the time,' she stammered. 'I'm so sorry. I'll go away and come back again at six.'

Quite gently Miss O'Neill restrained her.

'It doesn't matter a bit. It's difficult, isn't it, to remember things for two years? Now you're here I'll see you at once. Do sit down, won't you?'

Daphne collapsed into an arm-chair much too low for her. Miserably she drew her knees up to her chin, then decided to stretch them out again.

Miss O'Neill did not notice her; she was rummaging for Daphne's letter in the chaos of papers on her table.

'Let me see – I think you told me that your Early English was weak, didn't you?'

Daphne agreed volubly.

'Yes, very weak. I really never knew very much, and now it seems such a long time since I did anything at all that I feel all in a muddle.'

'I know,' Miss O'Neill quietly stemmed the tide. 'But I'm sure you'll get on all right as soon as you really begin again. Miss Lawson-Scott has told me what good work you did in your first year. Nobody seems to do any Early English at school,' she continued. 'I expect you'll find you know as much as the others. I think, though, that I'd better take you for it myself; I'm taking most of the Second Year, and as you feel weak in the subject I'll try to give you an hour separately. I'm afraid you'll have to share for your Foreign History, though. It was Period 8 you wanted to do, I think?'

'Yes, if that's the most modern one.'

Miss O'Neill abandoned her search for Daphne's letter and consulted another list.

'I am sending you for that to Mr Stephanoff – 5 P.M. on Fridays at Gloucester. He'll see you first at 6 P.M. on Monday.'

Daphne gasped at the unfamiliar name. 'Mr – *who*?'

'Stephanoff,' repeated Miss O'Neill, smiling. 'I believe he's a Pole, but I'm not quite sure; I've never actually met him. But he used to be at Gloucester as an undergraduate, and now he's just come back to be a don after various adventures in journalism and other things. He's supposed to know nearly everything there is to be known about the nineteenth century. He takes very few women, so I was lucky to get him for you and Miss Dennison.'

'Miss Dennison?' queried Daphne.

'Yes. We didn't know she was coming back when I wrote and told you that all the Second Years were fixed up and you might have to coach with someone from another college.'

'Is Miss Dennison a Second Year, then?'

'She will be working with the Second Years,' said Miss O'Neill. 'But she's really very much senior to everybody, and probably some years older than you. She was up for a year at Drayton right at the beginning of the war, and then she went down to do war work, so at least you'll have that in common.'

Daphne looked thoughtful. These Drayton patriots seemed to be accumulating; they rather detracted from the glory of one's personal achievement.

'Do you know what kind of war work she did?' she inquired.

'Oh, nursing of some sort, I believe,' answered Miss O'Neill. 'But I don't know much about it, except that it was mostly foreign service. From what I hear, though, she seems to be quite a brilliant girl. I know she writes, and has published a book, so I'm sure that you'll find her interesting.'

'Oh, I'm sure I shall,' agreed Daphne, with a warmth that she was far from feeling, and proceeded to consult the lecture list with Miss O'Neill.

She felt a little chilled and frustrated as she went up the dark stairs to find her room. Quite definitely, though a little shamefacedly, she disliked the idea of coaching with this Miss Dennison. She had known that she would have to share at least one of her coaching times, but never doubted that it would be with someone to whom she could show – very kindly and generously, of course, but quite unmistakably – her own superiority, both in intellect and experience. And now Fate had sent her the one person to whom she could exhibit neither! Once again she was to be thrown into intimate contact with someone who had crossed in youth the gulf between ambition and attainment – someone who could boast of foreign service and a published book, the two achievements which of all things in the world Daphne most envied! Peering along the dark corridor, she at length discovered her room, gloomy in the autumn twilight, and littered with her luggage. As she knelt down to light a fire in the cold grate, coming back to Drayton did not seem to be such a triumphant business after all.

She had just made the fire go, and opened all her boxes, when Julia bounced in. Julia had changed for dinner, and across the front of her hair she wore a bright-coloured ribbon whose particular shade had no relation whatever to the rest of her clothing.

'Hello! Got the fire to go? What luck! I say, I've discovered another of our year who's coming back.'

'Who?' asked Daphne, wrestling with a recalcitrant drawer.

'Oh, not one of our little lot, but quite a nice person – Cecilia Mayne, English school, you know. She had an op. for 'pendy the vac. after we left, and it went wrong, and she's been away for two years. Hallo, what a 'citing-looking evening dress!'

Daphne regarded the bright blue spangles dubiously.

'Oh, do you think so? It was made by Mother's dressmaker, but I'm not quite sure that there isn't rather too much colour about it.'

'Well, I expect it's a relief after that horrid Women's Legion uniform. You know, Daphne,' Julia edged closer to the boxes, 'I'd made quite certain that you weren't coming back.'

'Why ever not? I always meant to come back.'

'Yes, I know. But it was something in your letters. The others noticed it too; I asked them last term.'

'My dear Julia, whatever do you mean?'

'Well, you know . . . it was that naval officer you wrote so much about; we were all quite sure, really, that you were going to get engaged.'

'Oh, Captain Grant!' Daphne flung some underclothes irritably into a drawer. 'He was simply the officer who used my car more than the others. There wasn't anything of that sort at all.' She flung in more underclothes, more irritably. 'I never had any idea of getting engaged.'

Nor, as Daphne well knew, had anyone else. Julia's insinuations had aroused an old bitterness within her. How ludicrous that her friends should have imagined such a thing! She thought again of all the girls at the depôt who had received letters, who had had invitations to stay, and of the half-dozen or so who had become engaged while she was there. And she wondered, as she had wondered so many times during the past two years, why of all those naval officers whom she had driven, and had tea with, and flirted with, none had ever written to her or come back to see her as they came back to the others. Why was it? She had been much cleverer than most of the girls, and though she was often untidy, and some people thought her remarkable-looking, she knew that she could never really be called plain. The girls at the Manor School at Northport had always said that she was beautiful, and had given her a leading part in most of the school plays. She was rather too big for the heroine, but she had often been the handsome hero, whether the Scarlet Pimpernel, or Romeo, or Hiawatha.

She was not mistaken in thinking that she had suited these parts very well, though the slightly masculine element in her aquiline nose and strongly moulded chin was discredited by the perpetually parted lips and wide-open china-blue eyes full of an eager vitality. Her cheeks were usually pale, but the richness of her colouring was assured by her thick, slightly waving fair hair, not flaxen, but gold with the reddish tinge of ripe corn. Her light brown lashes were long, and curled delicately at the tips.

The strong profile came from some unknown ancestor, but Daphne owed to her mother much of her colouring, and to her father her splendid height. Mrs Lethbridge had fortunately failed to bequeath her florid complexion and short, expansive bulk, so that Daphne possessed a refinement of form and feature to which her mother even in extreme youth had never been able to lay claim. Daphne, regarded by her relations as 'a fine girl,' was broad-shouldered and deep-chested, but many a mannequin at a fashionable dressmaker's would have envied her slim waist and hips. She suffered, however, from a perpetual inability to decide what to do with her long legs and large, clumsy hands. Her splendid physical development disguised a mental immaturity that was almost chaotic, though she only realised the chaos at intervals – just whenever, in fact, she particularly wanted to be dignified and impressive.

'How did you get on with Miss O'Neill?' again began Julia, gathering from Daphne's silence that the last topic had been somewhat unfortunate, not to say unproductive.

'Oh, all right. She's taking me herself for English, but for Foreign I'm to go to Mr Stephanoff at Gloucester, with a Miss Dennison who's come back from nursing or something.'

'Oh, I can tell you *all* about them,' and Julia settled down to enjoy herself.

It was just like Julia, thought Daphne, still rather irritated, to come back last term and find out everything about everybody.

'Miss O'Neill told me about Mr Stephanoff,' she said aloud.

'Yes – he was up at Gloucester last term, giving some lectures before he settled in,' began Julia, nothing daunted. 'You'll have a killing time if you're going to coach with him. He took one or two of our year for revision just before Schools; they said he was awfully bright and bucked them up no end. He's rather queer-looking, too, and has a bit of a foreign accent.'

'How old?' inquired Daphne, hastily putting away her shoes, which always depressed her because they were size eight.

'Oh, youngish middle-age, I suppose. It's difficult to tell; he's rather fat. But he's done all kinds of frightfully thrilling things, and as for Central Europe—'

'Julia,' interrupted Daphne firmly, feeling the need of information about a possible rival more urgent for the moment than that which concerned a tutor, 'what do you know about this Miss Dennison?'

'Oh, a heap, in one way and another. I heard about her from Miss Tavistock, who knows her quite well – used to take her for Latin when she did History Previous. And then I had tea with Miss Lawson-Scott' (Julia always included herself in her stories whenever possible). 'It was the first holiday I'd had from the Ministry after we went down, and The Law was simply full of Virginia Dennison's book, which had just come out. It caused quite a sensation; one or two reviewers found out her real age and made such a fuss because they'd hardly believe a girl could have written it –

said it was the point of view of a cynical woman of forty. I suppose you've read it?'

'No, I've never even heard of it,' admitted Daphne, not quite sure whether to be proud or ashamed of the fact.

Julia looked at her incredulously.

'Well – you *are*! And a Draytonian too! I read it ages ago.'

'What is it – a novel?' asked Daphne.

'No, not exactly. It's more a sort of satire. It's called *Earth's Extremity*, and it's about the attitude of some people in a small country town towards the war. My word! It is merciless too – simply tears those people's insides to pieces. You'll have to sit up, my child, if you're going to coach with Virginia Dennison. The Law thinks no end of her.'

'I think she sounds most unpleasant,' said Daphne, whose apprehensions were increasing, 'and, anyway, I don't suppose she'll remember much history after all these years.'

'I don't know. She did History Previous just about the time when H.P. was started, and they say nobody's ever got such a brilliant Distinction since. But of course she's knocked about a lot since then – France, and the East, and hospital ships, and all sorts of places.'

Daphne made one last effort to discover some loophole for superiority.

'But what's she *like*, Julia?'

'I haven't an idea, really. She must be getting on, though – quite twenty-six or seven. Miss Tavistock says she was very pretty in her first year, but of course that's ages ago. She says she was always reading Dryden, and Swift, and those eighteenth-century satirist Johnnies. I believe she made no end of a splash when she came up. Her father's 'Dennison's China,' you know. Pots of money.'

A sudden burst of laughter from the staircase broke

the thread of Julia's discourse. She dashed to Daphne's door and opened it a little, finding the corridor flooded with light.

'Hallo!' she exclaimed. 'That sounds like the Set arriving!'

'The Set?'

'Yes – that topping Second Year crowd I told you about. That's what they call themselves – it's half joke and half serious.'

She looked down the corridor, but there was no one to be seen, so she closed the door and came back.

'I got to know them all last term – the whole ten of 'em. They're all congregated round this corridor now.'

'Was that your doing too?' Daphne inquired, beginning to think that Julia's managing powers had no limit.

'Yes, more or less; I got round the Bursar. We fixed it all up at the end of last term. They wanted me to join them – they're not a bit in awe of me, little devils, although I'm really a Fourth Year. They want to know you too. I've told them all about you.'

Daphne felt quite sure that she had.

'Look here, I tell you what,' Julia went on, 'suppose I have them in to cocoa to-morrow evening, and ask you, and then you can meet them. No, not to-morrow – let's say Monday; that'll give them all time to arrive. That's really them!' she exclaimed, as a fresh burst of laughter came from the corridor. 'I must go and see them,' and she dashed out of the room.

Beginning-of-term conversation immediately broke out in a spasm just opposite Daphne's door.

'Hallo, Eileen!'

'Why, it's Julia!'

'Hallo, Julia!'

'Hallo, Jane, had a good vac.?'

'Topping, thanks, done no work.'

This went on for a few minutes, and then the door was burst open and Daphne dragged by Julia into the midst of the crowd of strangers. 'Eileen – Gladys – Jane – here's Miss Lethbridge, whom I told you about last term – got back to Drayton at last.'

'How do you do, Miss Lethbridge?'

'I hope you like coming back.'

'It must be very queer after being away all that time.'

Their voices broke on Daphne's bewildered consciousness like waves upon the shore of some distant sea.

'I say,' sang out a voice from the circumference of the circle, 'I've just made some tea. That stuff in Hall was absolute dish-wash. Come and have some, all of you. Do come and have a cup, Miss Lethbridge, won't you?'

'Yes, come along!' exclaimed Julia, seizing her by the arm. So Daphne was dragged away from her half-finished unpacking, and received amidst an uproar of conversation into the genial exclusiveness of the Set.

Chapter II

Virginia

Daphne was always late for everything. She had never been able to get rid of a childish conviction that the hands of the clock would stay where they were until she was ready for them to go on. People who have never realised the grim inexorableness of time often have this feeling.

On the first Monday evening of term Daphne really tried very hard to be ready for her interview with Mr Stephanoff at six o'clock. It would be so dreadful to go to him for the first time in that state of heated perturbation which lateness always produced in one – to say nothing of meeting Virginia Dennison, who had only arrived on Sunday evening, and of whom Daphne, despite many attempts, had as yet been unable to catch even a glimpse.

In spite of all her efforts the clock was striking six as she turned into the Broad, and she had almost to run to reach Gloucester at a reasonable interval after the hour. By the time she arrived outside Mr Stephanoff's door, after many false turnings through the intricacies of Gloucester's corridors, her cheeks were hot and her hair hung over her forehead in little damp wisps.

But the odd-looking man who stood by the fireplace seemed good-humouredly unconscious of her lateness as she gasped her apologies.

'Do not worry, Miss Lethbridge, it does not matter. Miss Dennison and I have been discussing one little spot in Europe that we both know rather too well. Will you not sit down?'

Daphne flopped into an arm-chair too close to the fire for her perspiring discomfort, and scanned Mr Stephanoff as she recovered her breath.

There was no beauty in his square solid form and his pale square face, but he wore his loose jacket and baggy trousers with an air of conscious distinction, and the twinkle in his large round eyes was prepossessing. Alexis Stephanoff had no illusions, but he possessed an enormous sense of humour.

Daphne did not spend much time in observing him. Her attention was immediately diverted to the girl in the chair opposite to her, for Virginia Dennison was one of those individuals of whom other people are always aware, and cannot help being aware, however anxious they may be to appear indifferent. She was small and dark-eyed and pale; beneath her black hat her face wore a brooding air of ironic remoteness. Her slenderness seemed to be exaggerated in her cheeks, which were a little hollow, and her rather wide mouth was hard at the corners. To a casual observer she looked like one who had prematurely worn out her prettiness, but her clothes did not share this disadvantage. Daphne had never learnt how to choose her own garments, but she knew when someone else was really well dressed. Beside that quiet perfection of style she felt like a vulgar barmaid in her Sunday best. She herself wore a blouse of orange crêpe de Chine with a brown velvet coat and skirt, and on her fair hair was a vivid green hat of best quality velours. Altogether she gave the impression of a rather uncontrolled kitchen garden.

She hated Virginia Dennison already for making her feel

so clumsy and so common. There was no reason why she should either, Daphne thought angrily. Her father, after all, was only 'Dennison's China,' and everybody knew it.

Stephanoff interrupted their mutual observation with the practical business of the evening.

'You have both been up at Oxford before, I think. Your tutor, Miss O'Neill, told me in her letter that you have both done war work. You did not have much time for reading while you were working, I am afraid?'

'No, scarcely any,' Daphne answered immediately. 'One got so tired, you know – one never felt inclined for anything at the end of the day but a few magazines.'

'I did not read a great deal of History then,' Virginia admitted. 'Too much was being made. I preferred books of another kind – people like Dryden and Swift and Defoe.'

'Ah – you admire Swift?'

'I do – very much.'

Stephanoff smiled at her; then he sighed and shrugged his shoulders.

'Ah, well, the war was a great interruption. Often that thought used to cross my mind when the Germans were shelling my dug-out. . . . Now when were both of you demobilised?'

'June,' Daphne replied.

'Not until September,' answered Virginia.

'September? That did not give you much time to read for this period you are taking with me.'

'I am afraid not,' said Virginia. 'Only for one or two really necessary things, like De Tocqueville.'

'De Tocqueville – that was good. And you,' he asked, turning to Daphne, 'have you read De Tocqueville?'

'De – what?'

'De Tocqueville – *Ancien Régime*.'

'N-no – I haven't. I'd quite forgotten there was such a book.'

'Well, never mind,' said Stephanoff. 'It is short; you will soon read it. Now tell me, what have you read?' He mentioned two or three indispensable introductions to the French Revolution. 'Have you read any of those?'

'No,' stammered Daphne, 'I'm afraid I haven't. I – I never really had very much time.' She was beginning to be uncomfortably conscious of those tennis teas and garden-parties at Thorbury Park, to which her mother, anxious to display a demobilised daughter, had continually persuaded her to go. She had generally felt unwilling – and yet it had sometimes been quite a relief to abandon the books which two years' vegetation had not made less fatiguing.

Stephanoff turned again to Virginia:

'And have you read any of those books, Miss Dennison?'

'Oh yes; I managed to read all those. And a certain amount of Sorel as well.'

'Splendid! Splendid! You must really have worked very hard to get through all that since September!'

'I didn't particularly. I had nothing else to do,' said Virginia indifferently, stretching out a thin hand towards the fire. Her weary, sophisticated youth would have been pathetic to anyone less hostile than Daphne, whose growing mortification made her long to kick or pinch or prick her – to do anything, in fact, that would disturb that complete composure.

'You adopt a very cynical attitude towards your own industry, Miss Dennison,' remarked Stephanoff.

'Surely an attitude of cynicism is the only possible one to adopt towards anything?' Virginia said this very firmly, seeing immediately that Daphne believed that she meant it. But Stephanoff looked at her with a grave twinkle in his eyes.

'Very likely you are right. I have yet many things to learn.' He pulled up another chair and seated himself between them.

'This period we are doing is a colossal piece of history. Is there any part on which either of you want to specialise?'

Daphne shook her head vaguely, but Virginia replied: 'Yes; I want to specialise on the Eastern question as far as possible.'

Stephanoff looked at her disapprovingly.

'Why ever on the Eastern question? That is tiresome enough when you meet it in your morning paper. The Balkan States are the *enfants terribles* of Europe, and Turkey is the poor relation.'

'But poor relations are so much more amusing than rich ones,' said Virginia. 'They're quite entertaining even when respectable, but if they're disreputable they really add a zest to life. Think how dull Europe would have been in the nineteenth century without a Sick Man!'

Daphne looked indignantly at Virginia; she hated people who tried to be clever; but Stephanoff was smiling again.

'Very well – you shall specialise on him if you wish. But this first time I should like you to do a general essay; that will give me the chance to see what you know. Take the effect of the French Revolution on Europe for the first three years – it is hackneyed, but it will give you a good review of the situation in 1789.'

As he finished speaking he rose and opened the door to indicate that the interview was at an end.

'I like my essays in the day before, if that is possible. If you could let me have them on Thursday night, it would be kind,' he said as they prepared to depart. He piloted them both along the dark, winding corridor, and showed them out into a dimly lighted quad. The clock on the tower was striking a quarter to seven as they left Gloucester gate.

Daphne was in a hurry; she wanted to get back to Drayton in time to change for dinner. She was going that evening to Julia's cocoa-party to meet the Set, and she wanted to impress them properly by wearing her evening dress with the blue spangles. She started to walk quickly, but Virginia maintained quite firmly her own deliberate pace. Away from Stephanoff's large presence, in the dark, gleaming street beneath the frosty October stars, Daphne suddenly felt a little afraid of Virginia Dennison. This fear added to her irritation, and she was conscious of an overwhelming desire to run away. Instead she said: 'What a lot you seem to have read! Mr Stephanoff was quite impressed by it!'

'Well, you see, I gave up most of my time to it after I got home.'

'You were lucky to be able to.' Daphne plunged into unnecessary explanations. 'I really haven't had any time at all ever since I was demobilised. You see, we entertain a great deal at home, and my mother goes out a lot and likes to have me with her. You see, I'm an only child, and naturally the people one knows expect—'

Somehow, in the face of that quiet attention which considered every word, it all sounded so unconvincing. But not for the world would Daphne have acknowledged to Virginia the prolonged struggle between the books and the tennis-parties. She went on hastily: 'Anyhow, I didn't mean to do much work last vac. I think that after war work it's much better for one to have a good rest than to stay indoors stewing over books.'

Virginia's thoughts had gone back to the overcrowded wards in France – France and the shattering spring of 1918.

'Was your war work very hard, then?' she inquired.

'Oh – quite. I was out in my car practically the whole of the day.'

'It must have been a strain on one's nerves, driving the wounded,' said Virginia sympathetically; 'there can't have been anything quite like it. I used to admire the pluck of those ambulance girls in France tremendously. Were you up the line at all?'

'Oh – er – no. I wasn't in France. I was stationed at Portsmouth. And I wasn't an ambulance driver. I – er – used to take the naval officers about.'

'Oh, I see.' Virginia's comment was quite expressionless, but it somehow infuriated Daphne, already maddened by a baffling sense of disadvantage. This dreadful young woman was even worse than her imaginings.

'Can you possibly walk a little quicker?' she asked. 'I want to get back in time to change; I'm going to a big cocoa-party after dinner.'

'Certainly,' said Virginia politely, trying to adjust her little steps to Daphne's stride.

'And what are *you* going to do?' Daphne inquired, with an assumption of heartiness. 'Cocoaing somewhere too, I suppose?'

'Oh no – I'm going to begin to look up for the essay he gave us.'

'What! – you're going to start Mr Stephanoff's essay already?'

'Yes,' Virginia answered. 'He wants it in on Thursday night. That only gives us three days.'

'Oh, well, it doesn't take me three days to do an *essay*.' Daphne's tone was superior.

'Doesn't it? It would take me a good deal longer if I had longer to take – after not writing one for four years.'

'I dare say you *have* got out of it a good bit, after being away such an awful age,' Daphne remarked patronisingly.

'Yes,' said Virginia, 'I have. Haven't you?' she added pleasantly.

'Oh no, not very much really. One's memory keeps quite good, you know, so long as one's well under twenty-five. Besides,' Daphne continued untruthfully, 'I came back here to have a good time, not just to please whoever happened to be coaching me.'

'Did you really? It must be very pleasant to feel so unconcerned about one's work.'

'It is.' Daphne was arguing hotly, and even more with herself than with Virginia. 'It's the only possible way to get on that I can see. You don't get anything out of college life at all if you never enjoy yourself and always go worrying about your work.'

Virginia gave her a glance of maddeningly unruffled amusement.

'I'm sure you're perfectly right,' she said uncontroversially. 'It must be so nice not to worry – really very, very nice.'

Daphne looked at her furiously in the light of Drayton's main entrance. 'Well, I must be getting along to Martindale to change,' she remarked. 'You're in Wilson, aren't you, with all the freshers?'

'Not quite all,' said Virginia; 'Miss Mayne's over there – she's your year, isn't she?'

'Oh yes – but I didn't know her. She was a silly sort of lunatic, always grubbing about with dirty old books which she imagined were First Editions.'

'Some of them are very interesting,' commented Virginia gently. 'I had tea with her this afternoon and she showed them to me. She's got a splendid early edition of *Absalom and Achitophel*.'

'Oh – has she! Well, so long. I'll see you at the coaching on Friday, if not before.'

With a relieved sense of escape, Daphne hurried alone through the shadowy garden. Unconsciously she was biting her lip, and her cheeks were burning. She felt like a feminine

St Peter, who had failed to preserve her self-respect even by denying her cherished god of aspiration.

That evening at Julia's cocoa-party, to which Virginia Dennison was so conveniently uninvited, Daphne proceeded to 'get her own back.' She was, when she considered the matter, genuinely unwilling to speak evil of anyone, but was sometimes excited into so doing by a consensus of opinion agreeably hostile to her own pet aversion. Julia's party was so friendly and so acquiescent; Daphne liked her room, too, with its flowery chintz and pink cushions, though she thought that her own, which had a green chintz and orange cushions, was better. The atmosphere was heavy with the fumes of cocoa and cigarette smoke; crumbs of 'College Creams' and the remains of some over-boiled milk clung to the sticky hearth. Altogether the party was very pleasant, and Daphne felt that she was a great success. Julia had placed an electric lamp behind her, which softened the over-vivid blue of her dress and made a glory of her bright hair. Delicate lights and shadows added becomingly to the vivacity of her strong features. She was entirely in her element with these impressionable children of nineteen and twenty, who were only too ready to welcome two presentable Fourth Years into their rather snobbish little clique. Three of them sat on the hearth-rug at Daphne's feet – Jane Donkin, tow-haired, shrewd, good-humoured, with the managing air of the Senior Student in embryo; Eileen Garnett of the soft voice and genteel manners; Margery Carstairs, plump, with wild auburn hair, and a perpetual attitude of flurry, as though everything was escaping her.

Daphne entertained them all with a description of her interview. Her witticisms spared Stephanoff, whom she had thought rather amusing, though odd. But she had no such inclination to spare Virginia.

'Oh, you've no idea! I could hold her in the palm of my

hand, but she looked at me as though she could see over my head – or through it! She talks as if butter wouldn't melt in her mouth. She's been everywhere. She's read everything. She's met everybody. She's got no use whatever for any of us, with our limited notions. Pretty? Oh, I should think she was *once*, perhaps! Nice clothes – but so perfect-ladyish! And as for that little touch of vulgarity which makes the whole world kin – well!' Daphne threw up her hands to indicate its entire absence.

The Set laughed uproariously. They liked to think themselves a lot of jolly good sorts, and were accustomed to laugh at many things which were not really funny.

Julia's entertainment was by no means the only one to celebrate the beginning of a new college year. At both ends of the wide lawn the babble of voices and outbursts of laughter which came through the open windows proclaimed that many cocoa-parties were in progress. Drayton had not yet attempted to settle down to the work of the Michaelmas term.

Meanwhile, alone in the great dark library, Virginia Dennison was reading about the French Revolution. She had quite forgotten Daphne Lethbridge; forgotten, too, for the first time that day, her strangely different first year at Drayton so long ago. She had even, though only for the time being, forgotten those black years between which obsessed her always. For the moment she thought of nothing but Europe's indifference to the downfall of the Ancien Régime in France.

Chapter III

The Debate

By the time half-term arrived Daphne found that she
required not only three days for Mr Stephanoff's essays,
but the whole week. Miss O'Neill protested in vain at
the superficiality of the productions she received. In her
coachings with Patricia, Daphne had only one witness of
her perplexities, and in spite of the weekly protests she
found that one increasingly sympathetic. But at Stephanoff's
coachings Virginia, whose essays were monotonously excellent, sat and watched Daphne writhe under criticisms which
proclaimed her style laborious, her sentences involved, her
subject matter confused, and her spelling abominable. So
Daphne sandwiched her essays for Miss O'Neill into odd
minutes, and spent the rest of her days in the vain endeavour
to appear less contemptible in the eyes of Stephanoff and
Virginia. Behind locked doors – locked against the Set, who
already used her room as a happy hunting ground and her
store-cupboard as a communal kitchen – she wrestled with
muddled brain and aching fingers to produce order out of
chaos. It was not that she did not understand, nor even that
she could not think; her intelligence had always been keen
enough, and her love of history was genuine. But since she
had returned to Drayton she could never find words for the
expression of her thought; the recalcitrant sentences flung

her overcrowding ideas back upon one another until she did not know with which to deal first. Her task was not lightened by the scalding tears which sometimes fell upon the inky pages and rendered necessary the recopying of another laborious sheet. In these circumstances she was not likely to neglect the unexpected opportunity that arose to persuade Virginia Dennison to make a fool of herself.

In the middle of the usual domestic dancing one Saturday evening, Jane Donkin and Sybil Gregson, a large, sardonic Third Year, with prominent eyes and a crimson countenance, bore down upon Daphne. 'Feel like a committee meeting?' they inquired. 'You know, it's the third debate on Friday.'

The Drayton Debating Society had been reorganised that term with much argument, and had received a new constitution, of which its members were very proud. The society was ardently supported by the Set, who thought it smart to learn how to speak properly from platforms. Sybil Gregson occupied the presidential chair, and Jane Donkin was secretary, a position she really hated, but which invariably led to that of president, where there would be more scope for her shrewd eloquence. To Daphne had fallen the thankless task of treasurer. She possessed that uninspired popularity which is usually accorded to good-natured unselfishness; consequently she was one of those people who in a community are always elected to everything. She attacked each new task with a violent energy which exhausted her out of all proportion to its achievement, but this in itself was impressive.

'All right,' Daphne replied. 'Any idea what the subject's going to be?'

'Jane and I have had a brain-wave,' said Sybil. 'We thought we'd have "that a life of travel is a better education than a life of academic experience," and ask your friend,

Miss Dennison, to propose the motion, seeing how she despises everybody at college.'

The mutual hostility of Daphne and Virginia was already a favourite topic of conversation at Drayton. The Set, who thought it amusing, fanned the flame of prejudice whenever possible.

Daphne giggled jubilantly.

'I can just imagine how she'd get going on that topic,' she remarked.

'That's just it! We thought we'd give her the chance to air her views a little, and then let her have a few of ours in return. Nothing violently personal, you know; only just one or two delicate suggestions which couldn't be mistaken. It would add point to the whole thing if we invited the rest of college.'

Daphne looked a little dubious.

'It wouldn't be a cliquish thing to do, would it?' she suggested.

'Cliquish, indeed!' Sybil Gregson laughed. 'You don't suppose, do you, that your little lot are the only ones who'd like to see Miss Dennison taken down a peg or two? The whole Third Year's just about sick of her; she treats all of us as if we weren't fit to black her stupid little boots.'

'You know, Daphne,' said Jane, 'something's got to be done soon. College can't stand much more of it. If we don't tell her what we think of her, someone else will.'

'Yes, I suppose so,' Daphne agreed. 'So, after all, it'll only be like giving Providence a shove – won't it?'

'Right-o,' said Sybil; 'we'll fix it. We'll find the other speakers when we've got her to do it. You approach her, Daphne; you know her better than we do. She's here to-night somewhere; I saw her a little while ago.'

Daphne, who was beginning to enjoy the conspiracy,

willingly acquiesced. 'All right. I'll do what I can. I'll ask her to dance first.'

She wandered aimlessly round the hall in search of Virginia, and eventually found her standing in one of the entrance doors. She was wearing a black tulle frock with a cerise flower at her waist, and looked like a dark shadow against the light woodwork. Cecilia Mayne, the one person who did not share college's opinion of Virginia, had gone to bed early, and in consequence Virginia had no partner.

'Hallo, all by yourself?' Daphne addressed her genially. 'Come and dance.'

'Thank you, I will,' said Virginia, considerably surprised at the invitation. Daphne, who danced quite well through constant practice at Thorbury Park and Portsmouth, found her as light as thistledown. She realised quite suddenly that Virginia looked pale and fragile, and felt a momentary compunction. Then she saw the amused eyes of the other dancers watching them, and was immediately conscious how garish Virginia's slender black elegance made her own evening dress – which was green this time, with a wide patterned sash of orange and scarlet – and how untidy was her fair hair, in which the hairpins never seemed to stay. Her compunction disappeared at once, and she approached Virginia with the Debating Society's request. Virginia's eyes glowed with sombre anticipation.

'It's a subject on which I feel rather strongly,' she said.

'I know. That's why I asked you. People speak so much better, don't they, when they feel rather strongly about things?'

Virginia fell into the trap immediately, as Daphne knew she would.

'Very well. If the Society really wants me to, I will.'

Virginia, to do her justice, had once had a sense of humour. But years in which the locust has eaten, not so much the flowers in one's own garden as in the gardens of the people one loves best, come rather hard upon this desirable quality. Nor is it easy after month upon month spent in close contact with sorrow and hopeless agony to come out of the ordeal as tolerant towards other people's little egoisms and crazes and complacencies as one went in. So Virginia accepted the invitation of the Debating Society with alacrity, because it seemed to offer her the opportunity for which she had been waiting to tell her daily acquaintances what she thought of their attitude towards the acute problems of existence.

When the evening came she told them without hesitation. She looked annoyingly attractive as she stood on the platform, in her soft pastel-blue frock, and addressed almost the whole of college with bitter equanimity. She was too well-bred to single out individuals, but her whole speech was a stinging indictment of her fellow-students' limitations. Her life abroad in various hospitals was represented as a kaleidoscope of experience – as indeed it was – with which to contrast the narrow monotony of an academic career.

Her listeners were not enjoying themselves, and they made mental notes of her accusations for future use in turning the tables upon her. Daphne Lethbridge in her treasurer's chair was writhing with indignation more than any of them. She had come to the debate hot with shame and fury from a coaching two hours ago with Stephanoff, who had found Virginia's essay more excellent than usual, and had treated Daphne more than ever like an ignorant and ingenuous child. Well, Virginia was asking for it now, and she should have it. By the time the somewhat feeble opposition of the set speakers had come to an end the air was tense with excitement and hostility. In the short silence that followed the throwing open of the debate to the meeting Daphne sprang exuberantly to her feet.

'The proof of the pudding's in the eating,' she cried. 'We can only discover the comparative value of travel and a University career by looking at the kind of person they both produce. Now take the case of the honourable proposer; she regards herself as a person who's travelled, and doesn't think anything of education in comparison. Perhaps it isn't quite fair to repeat what somebody's said in a coaching but still— The other day the honourable proposer, who coaches with me, said that the only possible attitude to take towards life in general was one of cynicism. Well, that doesn't strike me as being a particularly happy attitude to take up; in fact, on the whole, the honourable proposer doesn't strike me as being a very happy person.'

Agreeably conscious of approval from the majority of her audience, Daphne continued fluently, too much excited by the impression she was making to realise fully the insolent cruelty of her words.

'Now, I don't see the object of going in for something that's only going to make one unhappy, and a general cause of depression to the people one associates with. So if the honourable proposer's the result of travel, then for heaven's sake give us a University education instead! In the words of Rosalind in *As You Like It*: "I had rather have a fool to make me merry than experience to make me sad; and to travel for it too!"'

Her speech was greeted with a roar of delighted laughter. She had set the note for the whole evening, and the members of the Debating Society proceeded to lose their manners with their heads. Speaker after speaker, the majority of whom had never lifted a finger to serve anyone of more consequence than themselves, rose and laid claim to all kinds of imaginary war service in what they conceived to be a witty imitation of Virginia's own manner. The guffaws which followed these sallies could be heard by a few solitary essay-writers at the other end of Martindale.

As shaft after shaft pierced her, Virginia sat quietly composed, her brooding ironic eyes looking intently at Daphne. To judge from her expression, she was not listening to the debate at all, but only thinking how badly the magenta evening cloak which Daphne wore in order to look impressive clashed with her hair.

But when the debate was over and the time came for her to sum up, her attention did not appear to have wandered in the least. She passed over the personal attacks without reference, and only drew concisely together the remarkably few arguments which had touched the point of the debate. The voting, as might have been expected, went entirely against her. Standing beside her chair, and supported only by her loyal but uncomfortable seconder, she watched the crowd of her opposers go giggling from the hall.

An hour later, as Miss O'Neill strolled back to her room through the garden after a belated discussion on Hellenic architecture with the classical tutor, she thought she heard a faint sound of sobbing quite close beside her. She stood still, disturbed, and then, quite distinctly, she saw something white move among the trees opposite her window. Instinctive reserve and the dread of interference encouraged her to shut out the unquiet sounds behind the thick window curtains of her firelit room, but feelings of humanity prevailed and she moved softly across the grass. She recognised with amazement the huddled, uncoated figure, and the dark head pressed against the damp tree-trunk. Gently she laid hold of the flimsy blue dress, drained of its colour by the all-pervading blackness.

'Miss Dennison! I'm sorry – but do come in! It's – it's so damp; you'll get a dreadful cold.'

'I don't care. I wish I could,' said a muffled voice bitterly.

Patricia, striving in vain to think of something sensible to say, felt dismally baffled and helpless. The next moment she felt even more so, for the self-possessed apostle of cynicism, who frightened Daphne and Drayton even while they sneered at her, stood sobbing uncontrolledly before Patricia, her pitiful reserves all suddenly shattered.

'I'd forgotten what college girls were like. I never realised they'd arrange a whole debate just on purpose to let me know how much they dislike me. Dislike me – just because of those dreadful, dreadful days in the Retreat which I had to live through somehow. Oh, they were comfortably working here and knew nothing of that – and now they think they can mock me just because I can't be happy and forget the men I loved who died – everything and everybody who saved the country and their wretched little academic careers from complete chaos—'

Her voice was choked in sobs again, and Patricia, realising that she had no choice but to hear these revelations, gently tried once more to draw her away from the tree.

'Listen, Miss Dennison – you can't tell me about it here. It's so cold and damp, and you're all wet. Come in and sit by my fire and have a cigarette – you'll be able to explain better then.'

Damp and tear-stained and untidy, and altogether strangely unlike the trim Miss Dennison who presented herself with cold punctuality every week at Miss O'Neill's door for a coaching, Virginia allowed Patricia to conduct her to her large arm-chair, though she refused the cigarette. In the more practical atmosphere of that comfort she gave Patricia a fairly coherent account of the debate.

'It was Miss Lethbridge of all people who started them off. They wouldn't have dared to go nearly as far as they did if it hadn't been for her. She feels so superior with her two years of flirting with naval officers, which she calls war work. Just because I don't respond when she tries to impress me with her Manchestery style and her highly coloured, expensive clothes, she thinks she's got a right to say anything—'

'Come,' interrupted Miss O'Neill, 'don't be spiteful. That doesn't really help at all, and you know it doesn't. You must have a sense of humour somewhere; can't you apply it to the whole of this absurd affair? You're seeing it all out of proportion – you really are.'

'You're every bit as bad as the rest.' Virginia turned on her fiercely. The floodgates were open now, and the concentrated bitterness of the past few weeks poured through them regardless of etiquette. 'You think because you're my tutor you've a right to say what you like to me, and tell me what I ought to do and ought not. But all the same, if it hadn't been for the war, and I hadn't gone while you just stayed behind and got on, I might be standing in your shoes now, dictating to people. I'm quite old enough.'

'No, Miss Dennison, you wouldn't have been standing in my shoes,' said Patricia quite quietly. 'Just how old are you?'

'I'm twenty-five.'

'You're four years younger than I, then, but all the same, if there hadn't been a war, you'd have been in better shoes than mine by now. I've had the chance, week by week, of observing your mind. And I've read your book, which I had to admire, but didn't really like because it was unnecessarily cruel. You're creative and original and powerful – whereas I am only a scholar through and through, quick at learning and perhaps fairly good at imparting. You'd have been something better by now than an Oxford don – a writer perhaps, or the leader of some new movement. You wouldn't have been satisfied with a tutorship at Drayton. It's a good job, but a limited one.'

Virginia listened, dumbfounded by the humility of that mind whose brilliance she had invariably acknowledged week by week, with a sense of justice which was acute when unobscured by passion.

She received the rebuke in silence and Patricia went on: 'You needn't think, all the same, that because I'm satisfied with this job now, it was the one thing I wanted to do these past few years. But my father was a civil servant with a small income, and my mother's had only his pension since he died. And I've got a small brother and sister whom between us we had to keep at school somehow. How could I have done that on the salary of a nurse or a Government clerk? All the same, I was always longing to be in France. I had another brother – my favourite – out there. I was lucky; he came back; but that didn't make it any easier at the time. The one consolation was that he hadn't any worries, because he knew I could help the family while he was away. Well, what do you suppose would have happened to people like me if the remnants of the University had been scattered to the four winds, and everyone made to do war work, as you'd have liked? What would have become of the older dons, who were too old to be uprooted? It was the women here who kept the nucleus of a University and made it easy for the men who were left, and other people, like you, to come back and take up their work again.'

Still Virginia made no comment, and Miss O'Neill continued: 'Many of the students here were in a similar position to mine. They would have been glad to go, but they had to finish their training quickly and get a settled, permanent job so as to make money for themselves or other people. Perhaps one or two stayed when they needn't have done, but most of them couldn't help it. So don't annoy them because you've done war work, and had an exciting time, and they haven't. They're all the more bitter because most of them are jealous. . . . I'm not trying to detract from anything you've done – or suffered. I don't think lightly of your service and your dangers and your sacrifices. I'm not talking like this because I envy you too. I do, but that's not why. You do understand, don't you?'

Virginia's tired voice answered her almost inaudibly. 'Yes, I do understand.'

She understood. But that did not prevent her the next morning from taking her revenge on at least one of the people who had upset her.

'Come to the Cadena?' said Daphne, after the ten o'clock lecture, with the boisterous good-humour she was beginning to assume when *tête-à-tête* with Virginia.

Virginia, somewhat to her own surprise, accepted the invitation. As they waited for their coffee among the little tables with shiny green tops, she listened wearily to Daphne teasing her about her last essay on Napoleon.

'I'm glad Mr Stephanoff suggested I should read it, because it's really awfully good in some ways, but I do think you take Napoleon much too seriously. But so you do everything, of course – yourself included. What you really want is a lot of brothers to rag you – or some cheery men friends.'

The still smouldering embers required only this match. Virginia turned on Daphne, not fiercely, but with cold, deliberate venom:

'I suppose you judge other people's friends by the standard of your own, who evidently were out to save their skins. You imagine that because people have no men left now they never had them at all. You seem to forget there's been a war, but then I don't suppose you did see much of it in your cushy little job at Portsmouth. I did have friends once, and a brother' – her voice faltered a little – 'and someone I was going to marry, but they died because you and your like had to be saved from the fate you deserved. And because I can't forget, you think you've got the right to call me sad, and sneer at me in front of a crowd of gaping schoolgirls. You think you can use your Debating Society to tell people what you think of them when they make you feel uncomfortable, and you daren't say what you mean to their faces. But you won't get your society to prosper if you're going to make the proposer's chair a stool of repentance. These things simply aren't *done* in decent society; you must just take it from me that they're not, because I don't expect you to see it for yourself.'

Her scorn poured over the quivering Daphne like a stream of cold water.

'Oh, I don't imagine you're really malicious or cruel,' she continued. 'You're not clever enough for that. I only think you're rather silly – and utterly tactless and clumsy. You imagine it's funny to travesty a careless remark of mine, which I never meant to be repeated, for the edification of your particular circle of friends. But people with the advantage of a better upbringing would call it the gross impertinence of someone unspeakably ill-bred.'

Scarlet in the face and speechless, Daphne stared at Virginia, her eyes darkened with an agony of remorseful embarrassment. She crumbled the uneatable cake on her plate with large nervous fingers. The shot about her breeding had gone further than Virginia knew, or had intended. There was a dreadful silence while Virginia imperturbably finished her biscuit. Then she turned to Daphne, who was nearly choking over the remains of her coffee.

'I *must* go. I've got to get Miss O'Neill's essay finished before one o'clock. But don't you hurry. Do stay and finish your coffee. I'll pay the bill as I go out.'

She hummed a little tune to herself as she rode her

bicycle up 'The Corn.' Patricia's understanding last night and Daphne's embarrassment this morning had completely restored her to an amused toleration which was more than half contempt.

After all, Daphne hadn't known. She hadn't understood what she was doing. Her offence had been sheer bad luck, due as usual to tactlessness, the result of ignorance and an excess of misplaced enthusiasm.

Chapter IV

The Eminent Historian

Among her numerous official activities Daphne was secretary of the Drayton Historical Society. From time immemorial the president had been the history tutor, who left all the work to the secretary – which is the way of history tutors. Patricia, however, was different. She was still young enough to be interested in occupations outside her immediate sphere. Under her direction the Historical Society flourished exceedingly, and became the means by which many celebrities were imported into Drayton. But she and Daphne thought that they had done unusually well when, in the Easter term, they obtained the promise of a lecture from Sir Roger Barnett, the great authority on the history of the Ottoman Empire. This achievement was largely due to the instrumentality of Stephanoff, who had once met Sir Roger in the East while roaming about Europe in some nameless capacity.

The evening of Sir Roger's discourse was fixed for a date near the end of the term, and was awaited by Daphne with much excitement and some trepidation. The reason for this was that she, of all others at Drayton, was to come directly under the eminent historian's eye. He, of course, would go in to dinner with the Principal, but according to traditional etiquette Daphne as historical secretary would be taken by the senior tutor to the High Table where the dons had their meals, and would sit on the visitor's left. The whole of Drayton envied her this privilege, for Sir Roger was widely known to be a brilliant personality as well as a very famous historian, and he had had some exciting adventures during the war. To sit on his left for a whole forty-five minutes would be even more exciting than to listen to him discoursing on the future of the Eastern question.

None of them, thought Daphne with triumph, had ever had any idea of electing Virginia to the committee of the Historical Society. All they had done was to ask her to read a paper, which was something that anybody could do. For once she and not Virginia would be in the limelight, and Virginia, who appeared so indifferent to celebrities that she must really care about them very much, would secretly envy her all the time. This was a great satisfaction to Daphne, in whose mind the recollection of Virginia's Christmas report from Stephanoff still rankled, especially when she compared it with her own. So she acquired a new evening frock for the great occasion – violet crêpe de Chine with a wide sash of blue and orange ribbon. She increased this splendour by dressing her hair in an entirely new fashion. It felt a little unsteady, and she was not quite sure that it really suited her, but it was at any rate more up-to-date than the style she usually adopted.

As far as Daphne was concerned, Drayton conformed to its traditional etiquette at the dinner-party before the lecture, and she found herself seated beside the tall thin man with the red face and curly, grizzled hair, who was the guest of the evening. The only hitch in the proceedings was caused by Stephanoff, who, according to previous arrangements, had brought Sir Roger to Drayton. Stephanoff had been detailed off to take to the High Table the treasurer of the Historical Society, an obscure Second Year who was quite unknown to him. When he found himself waiting for dinner in the Junior Common Room, surrounded by tutors and students, he suddenly took fright at the presence of so many strange women. Perceiving Virginia in a far corner, he immediately made a bee-line for her, and insisted on taking her in to dinner in spite of Miss O'Neill's hints, expostulations, and indications of his proper partner. This was a little disappointing for Daphne, who had hoped that Virginia would have no place at the High Table at all. At any rate, she was only wearing the same black evening frock that had distressed Daphne on the Saturday evening before the unfortunate debate. Daphne thought it absurd that anyone with so much money as the daughter of 'Dennison's China' should keep the same evening dress for the whole of two terms.

However, apart from the slight disadvantage of Virginia's presence, the High Table, thought Daphne, was very nicely arranged. She herself occupied one of the most conspicuous positions. Stephanoff and Virginia, being on the right of Miss Lawson-Scott, were quite out of the range of Sir Roger's conversation. On the opposite side of the table sat Patricia O'Neill, who had taken pity on the neglected and offended treasurer. At the far end, beyond the French and English tutors with their partners, Miss Jenkinson sat with Julia Tait beside her. Julia went to the High Table nearly every night with somebody or other. She liked going to the High Table, not only on account of the dons' society, which she always delighted in, but because she got a much better dinner there than down below.

Sir Roger soon turned from Miss Lawson-Scott and addressed a few words to Daphne, who had been introduced to him in the Junior Common Room. Conscious of the envious eyes of college upon her, she did her best to look interesting, but only succeeded in appearing affected. He was talking down to her, she thought with some mortification.

'I understand you have recently been to the meeting of Convocation which granted degrees to women. How very excited you all must have been!'

Daphne tried to convey to him that the likelihood of degrees for women at Oxford was a matter for satisfaction, perhaps, but hardly for excitement or gratification. Women's accomplishments in the University had long been equal, if not superior, to men's; degrees were not a privilege, they were simply what women deserved – their due, their right. She became very animated as she argued on this topic.

And then there was a sudden awful silence at the High. A large bronze hairpin had fallen with a clatter into the eminent historian's soup. In the momentary paralysis that descended upon everybody, Miss Jenkinson was heard to remark, by no means *sotto voce*, to Julia: 'I always felt that if only dear Daphne had come under my care a little earlier I could have helped her so *much* with those little social amenities which are so indispensable to everyone.'

Then the whole of the table started to make conversation at once. Daphne, vividly scarlet and very near to tears, gabbled feverish nonsense about nothing in particular. The only unperturbed person was Sir Roger, who in splendid tranquillity continued to drink his soup until just sufficient was left to cover the offending hairpin.

On the other side of Miss Lawson-Scott sat Stephanoff, with an air of being on his best behaviour which occasionally drove Patricia, who was almost opposite to him, into a spasm of suppressed mirth. In the intervals of his conversation with the Principal, Stephanoff turned to Virginia, and discussed themselves and their mutual acquaintances with that unashamed enjoyment which is usually regarded as the special prerogative of women.

'You know too well that you are brilliant, Miss Dennison, and that makes you a little self-righteous. Now you must not look upon your originality as your own. You must merely regard it as some valuable instrument which you are lucky to have more immediate use of than other people. Self-righteousness is one of the seven deadly sins. So it is to bore people.'

Virginia paused in the act of dividing a potato.

'But am I guilty of *both* those offences?' she inquired.

'No; indeed you are not. You never bore me; that is why I am too indulgent to you. Now your friend, Miss Lethbridge— But no; I am unfair. It is my own fault that she sometimes bores me. I criticise her till I make her too conscientious.'

'Indeed, you are mistaken,' interposed Virginia; 'her head is full of nothing but tea-parties and theatres and getting to know undergraduates. Her essays don't interest her; she just gets them done somehow.'

In one respect, at least, Daphne had been successful. Virginia fully believed that she was an incorrigible if somewhat garish butterfly.

'But after all,' she added, 'you can't expect anything else from a person who drives about for two years with all the naval officers in Portsmouth and then calls it war work.'

Stephanoff was wiser, but he only sighed, knowing that it would be useless to say so.

'You are very hard, Miss Dennison,' was his only remark.

The smile on Virginia's lips suddenly died away.

'Yes,' she said, in a voice from which all the vitality had departed. 'Yes, I *am* hard.'

'Ah,' said Stephanoff, 'that is because you are like me

in one thing; you have not any illusions. But yet even in that you are different. The difference is that you have lost your illusions, whereas I never had any. Your tutor, Miss O'Neill, is like me; she never had any either. Now your friend, Miss Lethbridge, is full of them. She thinks far too kindly of a very wicked world.'

Virginia, with the smile back on her lips, considered him critically. 'If you never had any illusions, what makes you think that it's such a very wicked world?'

Stephanoff looked at her for a moment; then he grinned, and extended a broad, firm hand beneath the tablecloth. 'Miss Dennison, I shake hands with you. You are one up.'

Miss Lawson-Scott turned upon him with unexpected suddenness. 'And what is *your* opinion of the present situation in the Balkans, Mr Stephanoff?'

Stephanoff took a long breath, cleared his mind of Patricia, on whose charming face his thoughts as well as his eyes had been dwelling during the conversation with Virginia, and proceeded to give Miss Lawson-Scott his views on the Balkan situation with such bewildering fluency that she did not venture to speak to him again for quite ten minutes.

When dinner was over and the hall cleared for the meeting, Patricia, in her low, rather husky voice, gave Sir Roger Barnett a very adequate official welcome on behalf of the Senior Common Room. Daphne, as representative of the students, was obliged to second this motion. The hairpin episode had not added to her confidence, and she struggled and fought with her words in desperation. She had not ventured on a public speech since the occasion of her unlucky challenge to Virginia, and the recollection of that last performance seemed to rise up and mock her like some disconcerting Nemesis.

Miss Jenkinson, seated by Virginia, at the back of the room, was not exhilarated by her god-daughter's exhibition, so she took the precaution of diverting her own attention by giving Virginia her whispered impressions of Julia Tait.

'A sweet girl, Miss Tait – a very sweet girl! What a pity it is, though, that she's taken to using that mauve-tinted face powder lately; it always gives me the impression that her nose is blue with cold!'

Vivid and illuminating as Sir Roger's discourse was, both Daphne and Virginia were glad when it was over. Daphne desired only to disappear, and if possible forget the evening's failure in sleep. Virginia was tired, and some of Stephanoff's remarks still caused her uneasiness. As the audience dispersed she linked her arm in that of the dreamy, delicate girl with the pale fluffy hair who had been sitting beside her and Miss Jenkinson.

'Cecilia, Mr Stephanoff says I'm self-righteous. Do you think I am really?'

'Frightfully,' answered Cecilia with intense conviction.

Patricia and Miss Tavistock escorted Sir Roger and Stephanoff to coffee in Patricia's room, where further discourse on the Eastern question provoked a heated argument, in which Stephanoff proved that his contempt for the subject did not arise from lack of information. But when their coffee was finished they tended to separate into couples. Miss Tavistock, discovering that Sir Roger knew as much about Byzantine architecture as about the rest of Byzantium, ministered to his vanity with a series of ecstatic interrogations. Patricia drifted into the opposite corner of the fireplace with Stephanoff, with whom frivolous conversation seemed unavoidable for many minutes together. They had fallen into the habit of sparring vigorously whenever they encountered one another.

'He is a great man,' remarked Stephanoff, indicating Sir Roger, 'but he would be much greater if he were not so complacent. Complacence is the last refuge of an ignoble mind.'

'Mr Stephanoff,' said Patricia, 'you have no reverence for anyone, man or woman.'

Stephanoff gazed at her with a rapt expression on his face.

'Ah, Miss O'Neill, you know very well that that is not true!'

Patricia blushed a little and looked away from him.

'Well, at any rate,' she said, 'you reverence the wrong people for the wrong things. Look how you spoil Miss Dennison! What she really needs to give her a sense of proportion is a thoroughly bad report.'

'That,' protested Stephanoff, 'is just like a woman. You are all so concerned about one another's morals that you lose all sense of justice.'

'But you must see for yourself what an egoist she is. She's got a splendid mind, but it's spoilt by a kind of self-obsession.'

'But I should not remove her opinion of herself by doing injustice to her brains. I should only succeed in giving her a bad opinion of me. All the same,' he admitted, 'I agree with you. Intellectually she is a prig; the only human thing about her is her love of *Gulliver's Travels*. What she needs is someone who will first shake her and then cuddle her. But do not be alarmed; I am not going to try myself.'

Patricia carefully refrained from laughter.

'What good do you suppose it would do if anyone did?' she asked.

'Why, they would shake out some of her self-possession and then cuddle a little humanity into its place.'

'I don't suppose,' said Patricia, 'that she's ever likely to let anyone do either.'

'No matter,' Stephanoff remarked inconsistently, 'I like to coach her better than my men. She is the favourite of all my pupils.'

'I don't think she really deserves that,' protested Patricia. Stephanoff beamed.

'No doubt. I object to people who deserve things.'

Patricia turned to the clock on the mantelpiece to hide the twinkle in her eyes.

'After that, Mr Stephanoff,' she said decisively, 'I really think it's time you went home.'

Stephanoff turned to the couple on the other side of the fireplace. 'Sir Roger,' he said desperately, 'we are dismissed. Miss O'Neill has had enough of us.'

Sir Roger rose, with a smile.

'I am not surprised,' he remarked good-humouredly. 'Miss Tavistock and I have been losing count of the centuries, to say nothing of the hours. I must thank you both, and all your college, for a very pleasant evening. Miss Tavistock, I will send you round those photographs to-morrow if I have time to look them out.'

The usual compliments and farewells were exchanged. Stephanoff took Patricia's hand with a profound bow.

'Ah, Miss O'Neill, I shall not sleep for your reproaches. If you did but know how heavily your lightest word weighs upon my mind!'

'Don't be so absurd,' said Patricia, half laughing and half vexed. But she stood on the draughty doorstep and watched them disappear into the night.

And wide awake in her room in Martindale Daphne Lethbridge was thinking: 'Why do I always spoil everything I do by some stupidity? Why do I make myself ridiculous when I most want to be dignified? Why am I always giving people I hate, like Virginia Dennison, a real reason to despise me?'

It seemed a problem for which no solution could be found.

Chapter V

The Summer Term

The middle of the summer term found Daphne in a happier frame of mind. She was getting to know some of the outside acquaintances of the Set, and though she was usually invited to tea as somebody's friend, and very seldom on her own account, at least she was invited, and the rôle of butterfly began to have a better foundation. But perhaps the chief cause of her content was that she was no longer coaching with Virginia. This term they were working separately at Economic History with the gentle and absent-minded Mr Carey, the Dean of Essex College, who liked, or at least sympathised with, Daphne's essays for him.

But as the term proceeded Daphne began once more to find cause for jealousy in Virginia, whose authorship of *Earth's Extremity* had at last penetrated the self-absorbed consciousness of young literary Oxford. As soon as the annual request for contributions appeared, Daphne began to bombard the defences of *Oxford Poetry*, but entirely without success. She had a certain amount of real literary feeling, though as yet she possessed very little sense of literary restrictions. Even now, however, there was promise in some of her work; nearly every kind of writing seemed easier to her than essays. Her stories, though undisciplined, were usually fresh and original, and there was music in many of her short poems. But she was altogether too lyrical for the editors of *Oxford Poetry*, who were nothing if not modern.

Virginia, on the other hand, was rapidly besieged with attentions from long-haired and bow-tied undergraduates, proudly aware of their reputations in a post-war university. In spite of – perhaps, indeed, because of – her irritating air of cynical detachment, she became the centre of admiration to an exclusive circle whose members produced various undergraduate journals, in which they dissected Politics and Life and Art, and passionately reviewed each other's works. Virginia was continually requested to contribute to these publications, or was asked to review lengthy poems, luridly splashed with adjectives, whose meaning even when extricable was quite unessential, and of whose versification the sole claim to distinction was that it had never been used before, and was never likely to be used again.

As a rule she declined these honours; actually she wrote little, being accustomed to maintain that her work for the History School occupied most of her time. This was somewhat disconcerting for her fellow-immortals, among whom it was correct to despise the subjects they were reading, and to take no more thought for their Finals than the lilies of the field for their raiment.

But Daphne, not having Virginia's assured position, was unable to adopt Virginia's attitude, though it would have added greatly to her peace of mind if she could have done so. Sorrowfully she abandoned the short melodious lyrics which she really enjoyed writing, and laboured with aching brows to produce something entirely modern, such as:

> 'Awake
> In the hideous night
> Wildly I struggle

> With my naked soul.
> My soul is a black bat,
> Forlorn, raging,
> Flung upon the storm . . .'

But the editors of *Oxford Poetry* paid no more attention to these masterpieces than to the others.

Daphne's jealousy would not have diminished had she known that the genius with the longest hair and the largest tie had proposed to Virginia five times within a fortnight. Fortunately gossip did not inform her of the fact, but Cecilia Mayne knew it, and brought upon herself a characteristic tirade during a walk round Port Meadow when she reproached Virginia for her heartless indifference to the one admirer and her charming impartiality to the others.

'You're old enough to know better, Virginia – and certainly to behave better. If you're going to be so unapproachable, you ought to nip their young affections in the bud before they get to this stage. As it is, you do nothing whatever to stop them. You're simply sacrificing them to your insatiable egoism.'

Virginia received her bantering criticism with a totally unexpected fury.

'And what if I am sacrificing them to a certain extent!' she exclaimed, looking fiercely at Cecilia. 'Men as a rule do everything at women's expense from their first day to their last. They come into the world at our expense, and at our expense they're able to do whatever work they please uninterrupted. We keep their homes pleasant for them and provide them with all creature comforts. We satisfy both their loves and their lusts, and at our expense again they have the children they desire. When they're ill we nurse them; they recover at our expense; and when they die, we lay them out and see that they leave the world respectably.

If ever we can get anything out of them, or use them in any way that makes things the least bit more even, it's not only our right to do it, it's a duty we owe to ourselves.'

Cecilia listened with resignation till Virginia paused for breath; then she interrupted decisively:

'All right, all right – don't get excited about it! Really, Virginia, to hear you talk one would think you'd suffered a dreadful injury at the hands of some man or other – and yet you're always telling me that all your best friends were men until the war came.'

'So they were,' said Virginia. 'But all my friends were absolute exceptions to the general run of men.'

'They always are,' thought Cecilia, who had heard this before, but she kept the observation to herself.

'After all,' pursued Virginia, 'even if I *am* an egoist, I don't see why I shouldn't be allowed a little indignation sometimes on behalf of humanity in general.' Then quite suddenly she softened. 'You're an aggravating woman, Cecilia! Don't you think that college's opinion of me is a sufficient antidote to my vanity? You might at least spare me your own private views as well.' And she took Cecilia's arm affectionately, and led her across the grass to watch some angry ducks quarrelling on the edge of a pond.

Just before half term both Daphne and Virginia were asked by Miss O'Neill to decide upon their Special Subjects for the following year. Daphne wavered; but Virginia informed Patricia that she had long ago determined to do 'International Relations.'

'Mr Stephanoff calls it a rotten Special; he says it would give him indigestion, and he couldn't possibly coach anyone on it. But all the same it's the only one that interests me. Do you know of anyone good who takes it?'

Patricia reflected. 'Much the best person on it is Mr Sylvester, at St Giles',' she said, 'but he only gives about an hour a week to women, and he likes to take his people for Political Science first, so that would mean two terms with him. You'd better go to his last four lectures on "The Ethics of Diplomacy" and see how you like him. If you do, I might manage to get him for you by singing your praises at the tutors' meeting.'

'Am I the only person doing this particular Special?' queried Virginia.

'I'm not sure yet,' Patricia replied. 'There may be one or two others. Miss Lethbridge is wavering between that and "Representative Government." I'm sending her to Mr Sylvester's lectures too, because I don't really think "Representative Government" would be at all in her line. I wish she'd do "Dante"; it would give her literary gifts a better chance, but she seems absolutely determined to be modern.'

So Virginia and Daphne met once more over Mr Sylvester's lectures at St Giles' College, where the tall dark man at the desk roused critical interest in Virginia and unqualified admiration in Daphne. His face would have been a great asset to any public career, for it gave his audience an impression of unusual power. But the impression was somewhat misleading; the face expressed no real strength of character, but the fitful, passionate force of obstinacy and self-will. Virginia did not like his hard brown eyes, which were deep-set and rather small, nor did she trust the wide, clean-shaven mouth with its beautifully moulded, sensuous lips. She thought that he looked rather dissipated, but this assumption detracted in no way from her enjoyment of his lectures, which were brilliant and witty, and often sailed extremely near the wind of academic impropriety. She determined that somehow or other she would get him to coach her on 'International Relations,' being unaware that Daphne, who was enthralled by the first lecture on

'The Ethics of Diplomacy,' had formed a similar resolution. Daphne, however, did not allow her to remain in ignorance for long.

'Isn't he a splendid-looking man!' she exclaimed enthusiastically, as she and Virginia elbowed their way through the crowd streaming out of St Giles' chief lecture-room. 'I think his nose and chin are just like Napoleon's.'

'Do you?' said Virginia. '*I* think he's exactly like the Bull of Basan. One can almost imagine his mother feeling for his horns when he was young.'

Daphne looked disgusted; Virginia, she thought, had no respect for anyone's brains but her own. She went rapidly back to Drayton to acquaint Patricia with her decision.

This project in particular, and Sylvester's coachings in general, were discussed the following week at a tea-party given by Patricia to Virginia and Stephanoff. Daphne, returning heated and dishevelled from the river scrum on the last day of Eights, saw all three of them sitting cool and comfortable under the trees outside Patricia's window. Virginia had entirely lost the worn and weary look which had spoilt her attractiveness during the first term at Drayton. The strain of working for an examination was nothing to the strain of caring for the wounded and dying; in the comparative peace of Oxford her delicate face had rounded and her dark eyes grown brighter, till she looked as young as the students who had come up the previous October. Her prettiness as she lay back in Patricia's deck-chair in her mauve linen dress made Daphne's heart quite sore. Virginia, as she knew very well, could afford to neglect the last day of Eights for a tea-party. She had been overwhelmed with invitations to barges, to dances, and to the Carlton Club by literary Oxford. Whereas Daphne herself had had to make the most of three invitations, and had tried to give the impression that she had engagements every day by setting out early to take her own punt down the river.

The three were silent as she passed them to take her bicycle to its shed, but as soon as she had gone Stephanoff took up the thread of conversation again.

'I am surprised that they send you ladies to coach with Sylvester. He has the reputation of a gay devil here, but that is nothing to the one he had in the Intelligence Department in Palestine. I think he found the women there too attractive for his peace of mind.'

Patricia looked intensely shocked.

'Mr Stephanoff, you really mustn't say such things to Miss Dennison.'

'I apologise, Miss O'Neill,' said Stephanoff regretfully. 'I am a foreigner; always I forget your English reserve. But I am indignant on this topic; I have not use for a man who has no private standard of decent behaviour.' He turned once more to Virginia. 'There, again I have said too much. Miss Dennison, you are too sophisticated for a woman student; you make me forget the need for propriety.'

His perturbation amused Virginia immensely.

'I wonder,' she said, 'how much you could teach me about social indiscretions that I did not learn in France! Miss O'Neill knows that quite well; she's only pretending to scold you. Anyway, you needn't fear that Mr Sylvester will corrupt my morals. I'm afraid I haven't much chance of coaching with him alone.'

'I am relieved,' said Stephanoff. 'And with whom do you think you will share your coachings this time?'

'I fear – I fear very, very much,' Virginia said plaintively, 'that it may be Miss Lethbridge again.'

'Ah, that is well,' remarked Stephanoff, without sympathy. 'If Miss Lethbridge goes too, everything will be all right; you will counteract each other.'

An interview with Patricia a few days later proved Virginia's surmise to be correct.

'I am sorry,' she said to Virginia, 'that I have to ask you definitely to coach with Miss Lethbridge again. Mr Sylvester is prepared to give you an hour, but he won't take anyone else unless they can share the coaching with you. Miss Lethbridge seems extremely anxious to have him too, and she can't possibly get him in any other way.'

'Oh, I don't mind her coaching with me if she can't have him unless she does,' said Virginia in rather an off-hand manner.

Patricia looked at her dubiously.

'Of course, Miss Dennison, if you really object—'

'Oh, I don't *object*. Miss Lethbridge doesn't affect me one way or the other, really. Let her coach with me by all means.'

Virginia's tone was distinctly bored.

Patricia bracketed their names on her list; then she turned again to Virginia.

'You know you're rather hard on Miss Lethbridge, in spite of everything – in your own mind, I mean. I admit she's sometimes tactless and clumsy, and I'm sure you find it very irritating often—'

'Oh no,' Virginia interrupted her; 'I really don't think about Miss Lethbridge very much at all now – certainly not enough to be irritated by her.'

'But you should. It isn't good for you to be indifferent to someone whom you're thrown with so continuously. Of course I admit the throwing is partly my fault. It's a pity you have to coach together again, but I'm much sorrier for Miss Lethbridge than I am for you. You know, you've made her a little afraid of you – consequently you always see her at her worst. It's impossible to be unself-conscious with people who make one nervous. You emphasise her worst fault –

which is lack of self-confidence. There's splendid material in Miss Lethbridge, both in her character and her intellect, and if she can be made to believe in herself she'll be a fine person some day. I always look upon yours as a specially penetrating intelligence; I should have thought you'd have seen this for yourself.'

Virginia smiled.

'I'm afraid even my penetration doesn't go quite so far. You see, Miss O'Neill, I'm impertinent enough to think I understand you – just a little. I know you always believe the best of people – how you try to see only the good in them, and forget all the badness and stupidity. Your geese are all swans.' She threw back her head and laughed. 'What a cruelly apt simile to apply to Miss Lethbridge! However, I promise I'll be good at the coachings. I'll try not to frighten her any more, poor thing. I only hope Mr Sylvester will be as amused with us as Mr Stephanoff was. Thank you so much for letting me know.'

She left the room, and Patricia took up the preliminary lecture list, but did not read it. Instead, she gazed abstractedly at the gently rustling beech-tree outside her window. The life of a college tutor, she thought, was rather like that of an actor-manager, who had to supervise the movements of the players while seeing behind the scenes too often for his own tranquillity. She knew with what tact and skill she usually arranged her coachings, but unfortunately she could not determine the likes and dislikes of her students so satisfactorily. Here were Miss Lethbridge and Miss Dennison, each able to supply what the other lacked, yet to all appearances their mutual hostility was fundamental and permanent.

Patricia sighed deeply. Life on its personal side was so often discouraging and disappointing. She had said so only the other day to Mr Stephanoff. He sometimes scolded her, but he never disappointed her like the others. And yet – didn't he? Didn't she always feel she wanted something more from him – something that seemed impossible to get at? Now what exactly was that something more she wanted?

The beech-tree still rustled, but Patricia no longer heard it. Nor did she see the lecture list in her hand; and as for Daphne and Virginia, they were as completely forgotten as next term's coaching scheme.

Chapter VI

The Tea-party

It seemed absurd to be so exuberant about a tea-party. But there it was; Daphne was singing to herself as she came back from the library to get dressed. The mere commonplace business of being alive elated her, although she was tired with working at her essay since first thing in the morning, and it was nearly the end of the autumn term, and the last damp leaves had fallen from the trees in the garden, and thoughts of Schools would intrude themselves now and then. It seemed almost too good to be true that Mr Sylvester should really have asked her and Virginia to tea to meet one or two of the St Giles' undergraduates, with the shadowy wife of some obscure don for chaperon. And the letter had been addressed to her too, and not, for once, to Virginia. Virginia had seemed so indifferent about going, but she had taken good care not to refuse, all the same. . . . Daphne didn't think Mr Sylvester really liked Virginia; he looked at her so critically sometimes, and so intently. As for herself – well, after all, what did it really matter whether he liked her or not? But it was nice of him to send the note to her – very nice.

Her pleasant anticipations were spoilt just a little by the thought of her unfinished essay; in spite of all those hours she hadn't evolved a really satisfactory scheme, and somehow or other the essay had to go in first thing tomorrow morning. Of course it really wasn't altogether her fault; she had had so many interruptions from the Set that morning. Even the exigencies of their last year did not seem to make those ebullient young people take their work seriously, except for Jane, who was now Senior Student, and had to. One after another of them had dropped in before lunch – to borrow jam or coal or sugar, or to bring her a cup of tea, or to tell her rumours about the latest engagement. After lunch she had been obliged in desperation to leave her warm room and carry her books to the library. Well, it only meant that she would have to take her essay with her in her muff, and go to the Camera to do it after the tea-party. Probably when she had had tea with Mr Sylvester she would feel more like writing an essay for him. She ran gaily up the stairs to her room. Her feet were frozen, but her heart was light.

Just outside her door she nearly collided with Marjorie Carstairs, who, without much regard for tune, was humming a classical ditty borrowed by Oxford from Cambridge in the early days of women's colleges:

> 'I don't want to go up to Heaven!
> I don't want to go down below!
> Why ain't there some place in the middle
> For a poor woman student to go?'

Daphne had no great friend at Drayton; she made a virtue of necessity, and advertised the rôle of being all things to all women. But she seemed to get on with Marjorie Carstairs more easily than with any of the others, possibly because of an intermittent lack of dignity which they had in common.

'Hallo, Marjorie,' she said. 'Doing anything special?'

'Nothing vital at the moment,' was the reply. 'I've got an essay to give in to-night, but it'll do if I begin after tea.'

'Lucky dog! I wish I could get my essays done like that! I suppose I mind about them too much. Mr Sylvester's such a splendid coach and so hard to please that one feels one has to. Come in and talk to me while I dress.'

She flung her books and papers in a heap on the table, and took down her new green coat and skirt from the wardrobe. It was very expensive, and Daphne loved it – especially as it would make her appear such a contrast to Virginia. Virginia always seemed so fond of black; it was sheer affectation, Daphne thought, to adopt such a sombre style. And this term she had a new musquash coat; she would be sure to wear it, and it made her look quite thirty – at least it would have made most people.

'You know, Marjorie,' said Daphne, as she began to brush her hair, 'I don't know what's the matter with me these days. It always takes me ages to do my essays, and in my first year I used to get the whole thing written in about three hours.'

Marjorie seated herself on the bed, swinging her feet.

'You worry far too much about the beastly things – that's what it is.'

'I know. But Schools are getting so dreadfully near now. Have *you* begun to get Schools' fever yet? I have it in fits and starts already.'

'That's absurd,' said Marjorie. 'What's it matter about Schools anyway, that's what I say! In a year or two's time nobody'll know whether you got a First or a Fourth.'

Daphne turned the contents of a drawer upside down to find a silk petticoat.

'Oh, Marjorie, if only I could get a First! The Law did tell me they expected one from me – at the end of that first

63

year, you know, when she was trying to persuade me not to go down. And Miss O'Neill said my last essay was on the border-line.'

There was a knock at the door, and Norah Duquesne, an Irish member of the Set, with bobbed hair and a shrill voice, stood on the threshold.

'Oh, Daphne, could you possibly be a saint and lend me some tea? I've got a chaperon tea-party in Martindale J.C.R. Pat's cousin Michael Delaney's coming, and I haven't an ounce of tea anywhere.'

Daphne pointed to her cupboard.

'Take the tin. I'm going out to tea; I shan't want it. What's the time now?'

'Half-past three. They're coming in quarter of an hour.'

'Good heavens!' exclaimed Daphne, 'I've got to be at St Giles' in half-an-hour, and I'm not half dressed yet! What *did* I do with my new silk stockings? Marjorie, do be a saint and see if they've got under the chair! And my brown suède shoes – I know I had them this morning. Oh, here they are!'

Then began the scramble that always ensued when Daphne was going out to tea. She put on one blouse, and then changed it for another. She thought her hair was straight and needed curling; having curled it, she disliked the effect and brushed it all out again. At five minutes to four she crammed her half-finished essay into her muff, thrust in the newly acquired cap and gown after it, and emerged panting from her room.

The tea-party was already in progress when she arrived at St Giles' and was ushered into Sylvester's study by a phlegmatic scout. Virginia was sitting on the chesterfield between two undergraduates, and apparently occupied the entire attention of them both. She was wearing the musquash coat, as Daphne had expected, and a little black velvet hat with gold wings. Another undergraduate was waiting on the don's wife, and Sylvester, talking to everybody in general, was swinging himself round on the music-stool beside his piano. He was one of the few tutors who kept a piano in his rooms; he was very fond of music and played quite well. French and Italian composers especially appealed to him, and formed one of his favourite topics of conversation. He rose to meet Daphne as she entered, muttering embarrassed apologies.

'Well, here you are, Miss Lethbridge! I was beginning to be afraid you weren't going to turn up. Come over here and sit by me.'

He signalled to one of the undergraduates to bring Daphne a cup of tea and some bread and butter. He could never see the point of asking his men to a tea-party if they weren't going to save him the trouble of waiting on his guests himself.

Daphne racked her brains for something suitable to say to him, but could think of nothing. Ordinary subjects of tea-party conversation seemed too trivial and unworthy for such a brilliant man as Mr Sylvester, and yet one could not exactly talk about the same things as one discussed at one's coachings. For once she had him all to herself; here he was so close to her, and yet no appropriate topic would come into her head. She swallowed her tea in a sudden great gulp of embarrassment; it was too hot, and she had to put the cup down suddenly to prevent herself from choking. On the other side of the room Virginia's sallies seemed to cause great amusement to the two under-graduates beside her; their laughter was infectious, and Daphne saw Sylvester's eyes beginning to wander in their direction.

'Do you think the women at Cambridge will get degrees now that we've got them here?' she asked desperately, seizing upon the first hackneyed subject that came into her head to keep him beside her.

'I can't say, I'm sure,' Sylvester replied, 'but I should think they'd be certain to make great efforts to obtain the same privileges.'

'You do think they ought to have them, don't you?'

'I'm afraid I don't really know enough about the ladies at Cambridge to be qualified to express an opinion. I do know, though, that there are one or two women students I have coached here from whom it would have been manifestly unfair to withhold degrees any longer.'

And once again his eyes looked across in Virginia's direction. Daphne put down her empty teacup with an unintentional clatter. Perceiving that the useful undergraduates all appeared to be occupied, Sylvester picked it up.

'Let me give you some more tea, won't you?'

'Oh, thank you,' mumbled Daphne, who had just bitten off a large mouthful of cake.

Sylvester went across to the tea-table, waited while the don's wife filled the cup, and then returned with it to Daphne. Seeing him come back to her, she got up hurriedly to take it, and as she rose her muff dropped off her knee and lay, a huge brown lump, in front of her chair. Entirely forgetful of its contents, she stooped to pick it up by one end, and left her crumpled cap and gown with the essay on top of them in a conspicuous heap in the middle of Sylvester's floor. Her sudden confusion was not lost upon Virginia, nor upon the two undergraduates, who immediately broke into an uncontrollable titter. Daphne heard one of them remark in a low tone to Virginia: 'I *say*, Miss Dennison, do women students generally take their essays with them to tea-parties?' and Virginia's supercilious voice answering: 'Oh no! Only a certain type of woman student!'

Scarlet and miserable, Daphne bent down to pick up the

embarrassing cap and gown, but Sylvester forestalled her, restoring them with the essay to the interior of her muff.

'Never mind, Miss Lethbridge,' he said gallantly. 'You've managed to prove most successfully that frivolities don't interfere with your essays for me.'

Daphne, whose one object when with Virginia was to prove that they did, gained very little consolation from this remark. Nor did Sylvester improve the situation by continuing cheerfully:

'I only wish I could say the same of all the people I coach. These young men of mine ought to take a lesson from you, instead of laughing in that rude way.'

He made one or two more determined efforts to console her, but Daphne, for whom all the enjoyment had gone out of the afternoon, utterly failed to respond to any of them. Finally he relegated her to the tepid society of the don's wife, and went across the room to talk to Virginia. Daphne did not stay very long after the tea was cleared away. Remarking quite superfluously that she was obliged to go to the Camera, she shook hands with Sylvester and departed.

She almost ran the whole way to the Camera, and rushed down the stone stairs to put on her cap and gown in the cloakroom, where she scarcely recognised the crimson face and shining, tear-filled eyes that confronted her in the looking-glass. Angrily she banged her best hat upon a hook, and pulled on her cap, which always made her hair untidy, and usually slipped over one ear before she had worn it for half-an-hour. When she went upstairs with her essay she wandered aimlessly round for some minutes before she discovered an empty desk in the corner of the crowded library. She determined fiercely to put the tea-party out of her mind, and never to think again of Virginia's spitefulness or Sylvester's dreadful commiseration until she had finished her essay. But the air was heavy with emanations from radiators and the warm smell of humanity; she tore up sheet after sheet in the vain effort to think, and had scarcely been there an hour before her mind was wandering irrecoverably.

She wondered how she would face the coaching with Sylvester to-morrow evening – the seventh of those coachings to which she always looked forward with secret apprehension and yet with a strange yearning. She could picture his half-amused look above his pipe when she evolved some new political theory that was to put Bentham or Mill in the shade, and Virginia's rapid glance at him to see if he was laughing. He had such a clumsy way of holding the essay, with its sheets crumpled untidily together, and he always pointed to the offending sentence with the stem of his old brown pipe. He never overwhelmed her with a stream of whole-hearted abuse, like Mr Stephanoff – yet Daphne was not sure if, after all, Stephanoff's method were not the less discouraging. Sylvester, when he had finished criticising the essay, would look at her with a smile, and say: 'I really must congratulate you on the amount of work you put in for this. It's a most praiseworthy effort.'

But to Virginia he would say: 'This is an excellent piece of work. You've really got a splendid brain – it's clear – acute – logical – more like a man's than a woman's. In fact in many ways it reminds me of my own.'

Daphne would almost have given her soul for such a criticism from him. Approbation, she felt, could no further go. But Virginia never seemed at all impressed; she would only say: 'Oh, do you think so?' rather dryly, as if she were not a bit interested. It was really very ungrateful to Mr Sylvester to behave with such indifference; Daphne didn't think it right, either, that Virginia should get so much praise when she had made so little effort. Daphne knew she didn't take half so much trouble over her essays as she did herself; she had once watched her write one in the library at Drayton. She never rewrote any of her sentences, nor even copied out what she had written once, let alone twice. It wasn't fair that she should please Mr Sylvester so easily, when Daphne spent all her days and a great part of her nights wondering how she should do it, and yet never seemed really to succeed. She felt that she would scream if she produced another 'praiseworthy effort' – especially after that dreadful tea-party, and the way that Virginia had annoyed her at the end of the last coaching. Virginia had shivered a little as they went out into the street, but when Daphne asked her if she felt cold she only replied gently: 'Oh no. Not really cold. Only my feet. You see, there was no room for them on the hearthrug when yours and Mr Sylvester's were there.'

Suddenly glancing up at the clock, Daphne saw that it was nearly half-past nine. For over two hours her mind had been wandering; she had only half-an-hour more before the Camera closed, and here was to-morrow's essay barely half finished. She made one frantic effort to apply her mind to the argument, but 'The Metaphysical Basis of Hobbes' *Leviathan*' was no subject for a stale and weary brain, and apart from the fact that she had had no dinner, Daphne was worn out with the heavy atmosphere and the stress of her own emotions. She had only accomplished another two pages when the bell rang for the Camera to close.

She hurried back to Drayton under the dark, starless sky, praying for solitude when she returned in which to finish the essay. Surely the others, if they had been in to seek her and discovered that her room was empty, would realise that she was working, and leave her in peace for once. But when she reached her room she found Julia there, putting coal on the fire and folding up the cover off the bed.

'Hallo, old thing!' Julia greeted her with extreme cheerfulness. 'I thought you were never coming home!'

'I've been frightfully busy,' said Daphne desperately. 'And now I've only done about half an essay that's got to go in to-morrow morning. I simply must finish it.'

Julia scrutinised her intently.

'I really think I shouldn't if I were you,' she remarked solicitously. 'You look simply dead. Leave it to-night and have another shot in the morning. You'll feel much more like it then.'

Daphne threw her hat irritably on the bed.

'I tell you I've got to finish it to-night. I can't possibly do it in the morning; it's got to be given in by nine o'clock.'

Julia was gently, sensibly insistent.

'I know one feels worked up after a long evening at the Camera. But it's better not to do your essay at all than get overtired like this. I shouldn't try to finish it to-night, I shouldn't really; I'm sure it wouldn't be at all wise.'

'Look here, Julia,' Daphne began in despair, but Julia, firm and soothing, interrupted her once more.

'I tell you what, you get undressed and get straight into bed and I'll make you some tea. I've made your fire go nicely; I'll put the kettle on and we'll have some straight away.'

By sheer reiteration Julia forced Daphne into her dressing-gown, and, while she was brushing her hair, fussed around the fire with the kettle, made a great clatter with teacups, and retrieved Daphne's bedroom slippers from underneath the bed. Daphne, who was apt to reduce herself to a state of altruistic exhaustion when any of her friends were ill or in need, grew more and more irritated at the sight of someone else pursuing the same course on her own behalf. She wished desperately that Julia would go; tea or no tea, the essay had to be done, and she was aching with fatigue and bitterness, longing to go to sleep and forget. The last straw came when Julia, having made the tea, took her by the arm and gently propelled her towards the bed.

'Now you get straight into bed and be sensible. I want to be quite sure you're in before I give you your tea.'

Daphne's rage came upon her with the suddenness of a tornado. An emotion her inexperience did not recognise had exhausted her sorely tried temper, and Julia's exasperating kindness was altogether too much for it. Suddenly seizing Julia, Daphne shook her furiously, smacked her astonished face, pushed her violently from the room, and flung her bedroom slippers after her down the passage. Then, locking the door, she threw herself into the chair in front of her untidy table, pulled the ill-fated essay towards her, and burst into uncontrollable sobs.

As Cecilia Mayne and Virginia went back to Wilson that evening after having ten o'clock cocoa with Miss O'Neill, they passed the half-open door of a room which belonged to one of the Set. Inside the room Julia was holding an indignation meeting, and as they went by they heard her saying in outraged tones to her open-mouthed audience: 'I shall never try to help her again, *never*! It was simply *disgusting*! I never thought a grown woman could lose her self-control like that!'

Chapter VII

The Dance

It was the last Saturday before Lent, and Drayton was indulging in its final dissipation for the Easter term. The Drayton Hall, in spite of its daily deposit of coffee, mud and pudding, remained one of the best dancing floors in Oxford, and to-night it was crowded with most of the Drayton students and their friends from the men's colleges. The High was decorated with two green curtains, a row of flowering plants, and several of the dons in their best evening dresses. Miss Lawson-Scott, her white hair piled high, stood at one corner by the curtain, carrying a bunch of carnations. She wore her broad rosy-cheeked smile, and gazed benignly down upon the animated assembly. At the other corner sat Patricia, vainly endeavouring to pacify Stephanoff for turning up unexpectedly in response to an invitation which she had sent him purely as an experiment. He was wearing a dinner-jacket, a white tie, and turned-down trousers, on which account he glowered furiously at anyone whose sudden smile confirmed him in his opinion that he was looking a perfect fool. Miss Jenkinson, clad in black velvet, moved amiably to and fro, and gently gave her opinion of the clothes and appearance of the dancers to anyone who would listen.

'Charming evening dress Miss Dennison has on!' she

remarked to Miss Tavistock. 'But it does make one realise how thin she is, doesn't it? One can hardly help noticing her collar-bones.'

But Virginia, in spite of her collar-bones, knew quite well that in her delphinium-like dress, with its soft blues and mauves, she resembled some fragrant and fragile summer flower. She did not really like dances very much, but they gave her a feeling of satisfaction afterwards, because she was always such a success. Her overcrowded programmes were permanent evidence that the black years had not spoiled her attractions after all. This particular evening, though she would not have admitted it, she was really enjoying herself thoroughly – so much so that she felt quite charitably sympathetic towards Daphne, whose crude yellow dress, which had just missed being gold, made her so unattractively conspicuous. But Daphne herself did not care very greatly that the dress was such a disappointment. If it had not been inconsistent with the rôle of butterfly to miss a Drayton dance, she would not have been there at all. For she had not been able even to ask Mr Sylvester, because college functions bored him, and anyway he did not dance. So the evening became just one of those penances that have sometimes to be endured by all of us who care to sustain a part.

Jane Donkin and Marjorie Carstairs, both temporarily devoid of partners, stood talking in one of the entrances to the Hall under cover of the Taphouse jazz band.

'Do look at Pat at the High with Mr Stephanoff!' exclaimed Marjorie. 'Doesn't she look just comic with him in tow! Look at his trousers too – and his tie!'

'It seems to me,' said Jane slowly, 'that Stephanoff's getting what you might call an admiration for old Pat.'

'Oh, is he? Well, the sooner he keeps his admiration to himself the better. Pat doesn't approve of marriage;

she told me so the other day. She objects to the whole idea.'

'Anyhow,' Jane said, 'she wouldn't be likely to look at him – a fat foreigner – even if he is supposed to be witty.'

Their suspicions would undoubtedly have been allayed if they could have overheard the conversation between the objects of their attention. Neither Stephanoff nor Patricia appeared to have much inclination to drift into the mature dreams of academic passion.

'It is not fair,' Stephanoff protested ferociously, 'that you drag me to this platform to be a laughing-stock for your stupid, giggling students. If I had known I had to sit up here I would not have come at all.'

'I thought you'd like the chance of a little pleasant conversation,' said Patricia serenely, 'and after all your tie doesn't show much.'

Stephanoff looked at her furiously; he opened his lips to speak, but then thought better of it, and said nothing.

'You must admit,' Patricia continued, 'that it's nice to sit up here and watch them all enjoying themselves so innocently.'

Stephanoff exploded. 'I do not care about their enjoyment. It is *my* enjoyment that I think of. And always I look upon dancing as a complete waste of time.'

'I don't agree,' Patricia replied. 'If only I'd had time to learn properly I know I should simply love it. You only dislike it because you can't do it yourself. But of course that's just like a man.'

'I do not!' burst out Stephanoff. 'I mean I do! I think it is a futile exhibition. If they must have exercise, why do they not take it out of doors in a healthy atmosphere? It is mere foolishness, this moving in circles round the inside of a room, when the air is stuffy and the hour is late. No wonder that no women can write essays.'

'But there are just as many men here as there are women.'

'Ah! but men are different – more stamina – better mentality – finer physique—'

'You may have forgotten, Mr Stephanoff,' said Patricia severely, 'that last year you told me you liked coaching Miss Dennison better than any of your pupils.'

'Ah! I may have *liked* it, but that does not mean—'

'But you said it did.'

'She is not here to-night – no?' queried Stephanoff, suddenly abandoning a subject that was leading him out of his depth. 'She does not, I am sure, give way to this stupidity?'

'On the contrary, she's one of the best dancers in the room. Look! She's over in that corner with my cousin, in a rather charming blue dress with a gauzy mauve tunic.'

'I see her,' Stephanoff affirmed, with an indication of returning good humour. 'Young Delaney, like yourself, is fastidious; she is a very pretty girl.' His eyes wandered inquisitively over the motley crowd of dancers. 'And there is Miss Lethbridge! What a strange dress she is wearing! It makes her look exactly like an elongated melon!'

'Who is the girl in the mauve and blue dress?' Daphne's partner was asking her at that moment.

'Oh, that's Miss Dennison – Virginia Dennison.'

'Friend of yours?' inquired the partner.

'Oh no! She coaches with me sometimes; she's a clever girl and quite well off, but she doesn't belong to our Set.'

Daphne and the majority of the Set were accustomed to refer in this lofty manner to Virginia, particularly when they had the uncomfortable feeling that she was quite capable, by herself, of putting the whole twelve of them out of countenance. The chief exception was Julia Tait, who had long ago begun to feel that Virginia knew far too many people in the University to be excluded from her list of intimates. Besides, it was Julia's nature to be everything to everybody; to be identified even with eleven other people was not sufficient for her large demands. Virginia, who was perfectly contented with the companionship of Cecilia Mayne, tolerated Julia much in the same way as she would have tolerated a game of bridge or a gramophone. They knew one another quite well now, though their fundamental differences prevented their connection from being anything more than a mere tea-party acquaintance which would never ripen.

The partner who had made inquiries about Virginia did not ask Daphne for another dance, but two dances later she saw him with Virginia, and once again, the next dance but one after that. Daphne's programme did not contain a single name twice over, and she was bored with a constant succession of partners who were friends of the Set and nearly all strangers to her. Moreover, she was genuinely suffering that evening – suffering from the sudden realisation of something which had been growing in strength the whole of that term, and her thoughts were not conducive to polite ballroom conversation. Suddenly feeling unspeakably weary about half-way through the dance, she resolved to cut the rest of her partners, flung away her hateful untidy programme and, without waiting to find a wrap of any sort, slipped out into the damp and murky night. The water from the sodden grass in the garden soaked into her thin gold shoes, but she did not notice it, and wandered restlessly up and down between the trees. The branches dripped cold rain down the back of her bare neck, but she did not trouble to avoid them.

She knew why that evening's entertainment had seemed so flat and dull, just as she understood at last the fierce secret yearning with which each weekly coaching had inspired her, understood how it was that her essays this term had become so suddenly better, and why she hated Virginia Dennison more than she had ever hated her before. She knew, in short, that she loved Raymond Sylvester, and to her sensitive impoverished soul that knowledge was a fact which might equally mean glory or catastrophe. She had neither Virginia's calculation nor Virginia's worldly wisdom to make her stop to consider whether Sylvester was a fit subject for a girl's first and intensely passionate love. Yet had she possessed that calculation and that worldly wisdom, it could, in her present state of mind, have made but little difference to her attitude towards him. Her difficulty was not whether she did or ought to love. Of the one fact she was only too certain, and the second seemed at that moment to count for nothing whatsoever. The problem which she sought to solve as she paced to and fro in the cold wet garden was not even whether Sylvester loved at all, but which of them he loved.

Daphne had never had a suitor, but she knew all the symptoms of love with the bitter accuracy of the bystander. And, with her mind alert to interpret his every movement, she could scarcely fail to notice how completely Sylvester had altered since the beginning of the Christmas term. His manners, which at first had been worse than indifferent, had become solicitous and almost ingratiating. He almost fell over himself in his efforts to open the door for them before they reached it, both when they arrived and when they departed; he even inquired whether they suffered discomfort from the smoky atmosphere and tightly closed windows of his study. On the other hand, his attitude towards their work for him had undergone a strange transformation; he dealt far more trenchantly with Virginia's essays, and far more considerately with Daphne's. And sometimes in the midst of their coachings he fell into strange moody silences, in which he regarded first one and then the other of them with narrow brooding eyes. On such occasions he appeared to become queerly, elusively remote, and was only with difficulty and much plain speaking on the part of Virginia recalled to the subject that they were discussing. Daphne could see the sudden start he would give when one of Virginia's sharp little questions pierced brutally into his reverie; she could picture the pathetic knitting of the wide brow, the quiver of the beautiful lips, and the resolute setting of the powerful jaw.

She knew that he loved one of them – but which? And yet surely only an ultra-sensitive soul could entertain such doubts; it really seemed inconceivable that he could love Virginia, with her abrupt, inconvenient questions, her inconsiderate criticisms, her extreme liability to argument. She seemed to have none of the graceful gentleness, the soft deference, the subtle admiration, which Mrs Lethbridge had taught Daphne that she must always show to men even when she despised them, because they would never like her unless she did. And yet there was no doubt at all that Virginia had some kind of fascination for men. Daphne could only suppose that she behaved quite differently when she was alone with them; that her rudeness to Sylvester when they were together was only a kind of contemptible showing-off. And one had to admit that she was pretty, and growing prettier as the war years drew farther back into the past; even those dark clothes that she always affected seemed inexplicably to add to her attractiveness.

Could he possibly love Virginia? Oh, why had they to coach together – why must Virginia, like some Old Man of the Sea, be to her a perpetual and unavoidable burden, which interfered with her success, with her work, with her pleasure, and now even with her love? How could there be rest for her torment, when she never saw him alone? 'If only I could have him to myself for just one hour I should know,' whispered Daphne, starting as an extra large raindrop splashed down her back.

Surely God was just, sometimes! He let Virginia get heaps of praise for essays over which she never took any trouble; surely He wouldn't let her win as well the love of a man for whom she obviously cared nothing! Hadn't someone said once that a great love was creative as well as receptive; that love, if it were only strong enough, could produce love in return? If that was true – and surely, surely, it must be true – then Raymond Sylvester could not fail to love Daphne Lethbridge. It wasn't possible that anyone could care as she cared without some return.

Shivering and exalted beneath the trees, Daphne raised her arms to the black, indifferent sky.

'Oh, Whatever you are and Whoever you are, please give him to me! Don't – oh, don't let her have him! She doesn't love him – she wouldn't make him happy! But I would live only to bless his life – to serve him – to do whatever he wished me to do to the very end of my days. For I care so much – so much!'

Choked and sobbing with emotion, she gazed up blindly into the misty heavens – as if she expected the answer to come from them at once.

The next day she was in bed with a bad cold.

Chapter VIII

The Coaching

Daphne stood under the electric light, drinking coffee. From the opposite side of the room Virginia, with the note in her hand, gazed at her abstractedly. The simple evening frock of dark blue velvet – one of Daphne's intermittent experiments in dressmaking – was in striking contrast to her customary attire; in it her figure appeared supple and straight as a young birch-tree. Beneath the light her golden hair shimmered like the halo of an angel. She looked tired, and paler than usual. Her eyes had become dark and soft; the blue shadows beneath them seemed to be reflected from their depths. Virginia, as she gazed at her, was conscious of a growing surprise.

'Why, you're beautiful!' she said to herself almost with a start. Then Marjorie Carstairs moved up to the table to pour out some coffee for herself. Daphne, perceiving her, immediately began to talk excitedly, and the previous impression vanished. She opened her mouth and blinked her eyes; everything she said could be heard from one end of the room to the other, and she gulped continuously at the end of every sentence in the effort to get out her words more quickly than she was able to articulate. Virginia felt her customary faint disgust at the sight of such effusiveness; moreover Daphne's lack of reserve embarrassed as well as repelled her even when she herself was not the victim. Going up to Daphne, she put an abrupt end to the loud conversation.

'I've just had a note from Mr Sylvester, about to-morrow. He says—'

'Oh, is it to put off the coaching?' cried Daphne, with a violent sinking of the heart.

'No, it's not to put it off, but as it's the last coaching he wants us to go separately. He says he can't possibly take us both through out time-papers in an hour. He wants one of us to go at eleven and the other one at five. I don't care which I do.'

'If you really don't mind, I'd rather go at five,' hurriedly said Daphne, who felt that she could not bear Virginia to have the last word with Sylvester. 'I've got a Documents' Lecture at Trinity at eleven, and there isn't another like it before Schools.'

'Very well, then; I'll take the morning time,' and Virginia moved away in the direction of the library. Daphne, with cheeks grown suddenly pale, stared after her. She was to have him to herself; would she know?

Virginia, as she knocked at Sylvester's door the next morning, felt very much relieved to think that for once she would get a really good coaching. At the end of that Easter term she was immersed in 'International Relations,' which she found extremely fascinating, and she resented her chance of doing good papers in Schools being spoilt in the slightest degree by the stupidity of the person with whom she shared her coaching. She did not like Mr Sylvester personally, and if he could not teach her properly she had no use for him whatever, but she felt sure that it was Daphne's futile remarks and extravagant theories which caused him so often to lose the thread of his discourse.

Consequently she was not a little chagrined to find him

even more absent-minded than usual that morning. He did not seem to have read her paper thoroughly, and to the few questions she put to him he gave entirely irrelevant answers.

'Have you had a bad night, Mr Sylvester?' at last she asked abruptly.

'A bad night?' He ruminated over the question, and then came suddenly to himself: 'Yes, I had a very bad night indeed.'

'Oh! Where was it? Taphouse's, or the Carlton Club?'

His sallow cheek flushed dully.

'You're as complimentary as usual, Miss Dennison. As a matter of fact, it was neither. I was alone in my rooms here, thinking very hard about something that's been a great deal in my mind just lately.'

'Well, I think you might have read my paper before you started,' said Virginia.

Sylvester gave the paper back to her with sudden determination.

'Miss Dennison, why do you think I specially arranged to coach you and Miss Lethbridge separately to-day?'

'Well, I'm beginning to wonder. I imagined it was to give us both a better coaching than the one you've just given me.'

'Well, it wasn't. I only meant to give you a nominal coaching, and as for Miss Lethbridge, I don't care a damn whether she has a coaching or not. I wanted to talk to you about something else quite different.'

'That doesn't sound very relevant,' said Virginia.

'Oh, but it is – it is – it must be! It's – it's so relevant that I hardly know how to begin to – to say anything.'

Virginia, who realised now what was coming, looked furtively at the door, but there was no chance of escape. So she sank back wearily into her chair, only hoping that he would get it over quickly.

He suddenly rose, and crossing the hearthrug stood beside her.

She shrank back a little, still saying nothing.

'Miss Dennison!' he burst out in a sudden overwhelming flood of passion, 'you know what I'm going to say – you know what I want, but all this term you've been just the little devil that you are – aggravating, alluring, torturing – driving me nearly mad. And never, never would you let me get hold of you alone – till now. That in itself makes me hope – makes me hope just a little bit more. I love you – Virginia – I can't sleep or work or think for loving you! I want you till I feel mad – mad – mad! But I'm not asking you to share this narrow academic existence – I've had a splendid diplomatic job offered me in a new Ministry, and I want you to come and help me with it in London. I don't want you to give up any of the things you like doing – I only want to find you work to do – work for your splendid gifts – but with me – with me! Virginia – my dear – my beloved – wonderful, wonderful little girl – say you care for me a little – say you'll come to me – marry me!'

Virginia waited for the torrent to subside a little. 'No,' she said very firmly.

Sylvester, white and trembling, looked at her with blazing eyes.

'You don't mean that! You don't, you don't! It's another of your cruel tricks – your maddening wiles – Virginia!'

'It isn't,' said Virginia decisively.

'Why – oh! why are you so cruel?' he cried. 'My dear, why do you speak to me like this?'

'Because I don't love you in the least,' replied Virginia. 'I don't even like you.'

'But you might – you might! I've never seen you alone until to-day – you can't know me well enough to be sure!'

'But I *am* sure. I don't want to be your wife, either here or in London. It isn't a position I should care for at all.'

'Why not?' he inquired, his passion turning to rage at her indifference. 'Thousands of women would be only too glad to be the wife of a diplomatist!'

'That's just it – I'm not like thousands of women, and I don't want to be. I'd much rather be myself; I enjoy being what I'm sure you'd call a superfluous woman.'

'You're absolutely unfeeling and unnatural!' Sylvester burst out suddenly in a fury.

'Thanks,' said Virginia, 'but I don't see it. It seems to me quite reasonable that I'd rather do a great many things than propagate my species. Especially as there's no moral necessity for it now; the number of potential unemployed is far too great as it is.'

He stood baffled and fuming before her, incapable in his discomfiture of any wiser remark than mere vituperation. Virginia disliked him intensely; he looked so large and blustering and uncontrolled.

'Anyway, if I wanted to marry, I wouldn't marry you,' she said. And exasperated into forgetting that one does not say these things in polite society, she went on: 'I met your type only too often in France. I know what sort of a time their wives have when once the glamour wears off. And what I've heard about your diversions in Palestine doesn't correct the impression.'

'What have you heard about my diversions in Palestine?' he demanded furiously. 'And in any case, whatever have they got to do with you?'

'If I married you they would probably have a good deal to do with me. As it is – nothing. I've no use for a man, either as a husband or a friend, who's got a moral standard of behaviour for women, but none for himself. You wouldn't want to marry me if I told you I'd been up to the same sort of tricks in the army as you were – though I'm thankful to say I wasn't.'

'So that's what you think of me, is it!' Sylvester exclaimed. 'That's the sort of reputation I've got? Very well, then, I'm going to live up to it. I'm going to make you kiss me before you go, you little devil! I'll have that much satisfaction at any rate.'

He seized both her hands as he spoke, pulled her out of her chair, and began to draw her towards him. With a tremendous effort she managed to get one of her hands free – the one in which she still held her paper. Summoning all her strength she lifted it above her head, and struck him violently with it in the face. He let her go immediately and staggered back, with eyes watering and one cheek crimson from the blow. For a few moments they glowered at one another. Neither of them apologised.

Virginia was the first to recover.

'I think I'd better go,' she said, taking her muff from the chair. Sylvester picked up from the floor the paper with which she had struck him, and held it out to her with ominous politeness.

'Your time-paper,' he said.

'Thank you, I don't want it now,' replied Virginia.

She opened the door and went down the stairs, taking with her all his hopes for a new future and a cleaner, less self-seeking life. She was much too angry to realise that she herself had provoked his last outburst of passion, by falling into the very mistake for which she had condemned Daphne Lethbridge in their first term. She forgot that in her indignant criticism of his conduct she had been not only intolerably self-righteous, but guilty of an inexcusable breach of good manners – which after all amounts to much the same thing.

She went rapidly back to Drayton, and there fastening

the door of her room she opened her desk and unlocked a little leather case which lay in a corner underneath the pigeon-holes. Out of the case she drew a thin worn envelope, slightly discoloured, and marked in one corner with the red triangle of the Active Service Censor.

It was a very young letter – the letter of a boy just beginning to realise his manhood with all its delights and powers, or of a man whose boyhood was still a very recent recollection.

'I feel I must write to you to-night, although I know it's absurd, because long before you can possibly get this letter I shall be with you. I can hardly believe that in forty-eight hours I shall have you beside me, dear. Just one more night in the trenches and then a dash for the first lorry that comes along, to take me straight to our wedding-day. Somehow I wish it were not my turn to be in the trenches to-night. I don't feel at all warlike; I'm full of affection for the world, and at peace with all mankind. There's a Christmas feeling in the air, and it's very much Christmas outside too – hard dry snow, with the moon shining brilliantly upon it. The road crunches delightfully under your feet as you walk along. I heard Alderson whistling outside; that means it's time for me to go. Just twelve hours more, and then! Good-night, sweetheart.'

Virginia read it twice over with bright dry eyes, although she had known it by heart long ago. Then she folded it carefully and put it back in its case.

'No,' she whispered, 'I couldn't have done it. A first-rate brain, perhaps, but a second-rate mind, and third-rate morals. Not after this – no, not after this. It's good enough for me, the remembrance of you.'

Raymond Sylvester was very busy that afternoon, burying the fragments of his shattered dream beneath the burden of his wrath. He would not admit, even to himself, how much he had been counting on Virginia's co-operation when he accepted the new job. He only cursed himself for letting her see how very badly he needed her. She didn't care; she was cruel and frozen-hearted. It was a matter of indifference to her that she had flung back in his face some of the best and, in spite of his conduct that afternoon, the most chivalrous feelings he had ever had. Very well, then, he wouldn't care either; he would find some way of showing her that he didn't. It mightn't be possible to touch her heart, for she didn't seem to have any heart to touch, but she was as proud as Satan, and it oughtn't to be difficult to humble that lofty pride. Unscrupulously he wished that he were going to be one of her examiners next term. The dead ashes fell unheeded from his pipe on to the carpet as he sat before his neglected fire, meditating absurd revenges.

An academic life had never really suited him; he had always longed for a political career, and the work he had done in the Intelligence Department during the war had prepared him for the opening which at last had come his way. But bright as his prospects really were, they seemed that afternoon to have grown unattractively dim; the uprooting of his Oxford habits, with no Virginia to assist in the transplantation, promised a loneliness utterly uncongenial to his gregarious, dependent nature. Besides, he really needed a wife; he would never have any sort of comfort in London unless he found one. He was sick of hotels and bachelors' rooms and landladies; he wanted a place where everything would be ordered to suit his own convenience, and someone else would see to all the tiresome little arrangements that interfered with the smoothness of his daily existence. Of course, he had not really expected this from Virginia, but in her, for about the first time in his life, he had found someone who had counted for even more than his own comfort. It really did hurt him damnably – that bitter devastating thought of her contempt. He would find some way to pay her out, to get even with her for this – he would, he would, he would!

And then, just about tea-time, the idea suddenly came to him.

When Daphne arrived at five o'clock, the coaching he gave her was very different from the one that Virginia had received. He appeared to have an acute, helpful criticism for every sentence of her paper; so occupied was he in taking her through question after question with business-like promptitude that he never appeared to notice her changing colour and awkward, trembling hands. Just after he had dealt with the last few sentences Daphne, sick at heart, heard Oxford's many clocks begin to strike six. The practical, unsatisfactory coaching had given her power of penetration no opportunity whatever. Utterly weary with the bitterness of disappointment, the consciousness of failure, and the knowledge that this was indeed good-bye to her foolish dreams, Daphne rose to depart. But Sylvester restrained her.

'Miss Lethbridge – just one minute. There's something I want to ask you before you go.'

Trembling, anxious, expectant, Daphne sat down again in the big arm-chair.

Sylvester went on hurriedly, though he had no fears of being refused twice. The acute observation of the egoist left him without doubt of Daphne's answer.

'I'm leaving Oxford after next term. I've got a diplomatic job in the Ministry of Arbitration – a new Ministry which is being formed by the government of every Great Power as a representative department of the League of Nations. That means I shall have to live in London, but I don't want to begin living there in the same sort of way as I've been living here. I want a home, and a wife to make it for me. Miss Lethbridge, I should like you to be that wife. Will you marry me?'

There was complete silence for a moment. Between them on the table Virginia's crumpled paper lay like an indictment. Then, in spite of Sylvester's indifference to Daphne, he looked at her in amazement, for she was transfigured before his eyes. In the sudden overwhelming shock of joy, all her shyness and her awkwardness had disappeared. Her whole being glowed with the intensity of her feeling, which seemed to make her eyes more blue, her hair more golden, and to lend a new beauty to her flushing cheeks and parted tremulous lips.

'Why, the girl's quite lovely!' said Sylvester to himself. 'Why ever didn't I notice it before?' And then he repeated his question: 'Will you marry me, Miss Lethbridge?'

She stood up suddenly, eagerly putting out her hands. Her shining excited eyes were almost on a level with his own.

'Marry you! I should just think I would! Oh, Mr Sylvester, you don't know how I've cared! I know it's only for a few months really, but it seems to be the whole of my life that I've loved you. . . .'

He took both her outstretched hands in his.

'I'm glad, so glad – Daphne. I had to ask you to-day, before you went. I couldn't wait any longer. But you mustn't stay now. I've got a man coming for a coaching in about two minutes. Tell your Principal that we're engaged, and get her to give you permission to come back and see me to-night, after dinner. But first you must let me have just one kiss.'

Rapturous and shivering with passionate intoxication, Daphne gave herself up to his embrace with exultant abandon. Her body was warm and yielding, her lips quivering and soft, and as he pressed his mouth hard upon them until she almost cried with the exquisite pain of it, the fiery desire which Virginia had aroused found a momentary satisfaction. Then, even as he held her, he saw as though in a dream a small provocative figure standing on the threshold of his door, heard the quiet disdainful words which had rejected him, and felt again that violent call upon every latent instinct of humanity that was in him, to prevent himself from seizing her convulsively and crushing her little body against his till he had destroyed every atom of life. Abruptly he let go of Daphne, who, tortured and ecstatic, nearly fell from the suddenness of his movement. In an instant he had pushed her from the room and almost down the stairs. Then in a frenzy he tore Virginia's time-paper to shreds, and hurled the fragments after Daphne's departing footsteps.

Meanwhile Virginia in her room in Wilson had been entertaining Cecilia Mayne over a bright fire and a prolonged extensive tea with a picturesque account of her interview with Sylvester that morning. She had just reduced Cecilia to a condition of delighted remonstrant mirth when a sudden vigorous knock resounded on her door. She had hardly time to reply before Daphne burst in, panting, dishevelled, violently excited.

'Oh, you are here!' she exclaimed. 'I did so hope you would be! I simply *had* to come and tell you at once!'

'My dear woman,' said Virginia, irritated out of her mood of complacent cynicism by this boisterous and alien interruption, 'whatever is the matter with you now?'

'Oh, you can't possibly guess?'

'I'm not good at guessing; it always gives me a headache. Do for goodness sake tell me at once what you've come to say.'

'Well, then, I've just got engaged – engaged to Mr Sylvester!'

'*What*? You're engaged to – *whom*?'

'To Mr Sylvester – to Raymond!'

Virginia's cheeks flushed crimson; then as suddenly the flush died away and left her deathly white.

'Oh – oh, I see. I – I congratulate you. When did it happen?'

'He asked me just now, as soon as the coaching was over. And I've come straight away to tell you. I felt you had a sort of right to know before anyone else.'

'Oh – thank you. I'm glad you let me know.' Virginia could hardly trust herself to speak.

Daphne watched her with scarcely concealed triumph. She had never seen Virginia so upset before. She *had* wanted to attract him, then; she must have cared a little, and meant to make him care in return. She'd thought that she could play with him, take her own time; she never dreamt that someone else could be preferred before her. Well, she'd got what she deserved; it was all her own fault for trying to be clever, and showing off like that.

But Daphne was so supremely happy that she had no thoughts to spare even for her victory over Virginia. Joyously she danced away down the passage, as yet too deeply absorbed in her love to care to proclaim the glorious news to Drayton's excited ears. There was an immense embarrassed silence in the room that she had left. Then Virginia turned fiercely upon Cecilia.

'Cecilia, you must never, never breathe a word of anything I've told you this evening.'

'Really, Virginia!' protested Cecilia, scarcely less perturbed herself. 'I'm not in the habit of spreading round college the things you tell me in confidence.'

'Oh, I know you're not – I hardly know what I'm talking about. But I swear it's all true – what I told you before she came in – every word of it.'

'I know that,' said Cecilia. 'I often suspect you of exaggerating, Virginia, but never of deliberate fabrication.'

'But whatever can it mean? He can't be serious! He must have done it for a bet or something – he's just the sort of man who'd lay a pound note that he'd propose to two women both in the same day.'

Cecilia shook her head.

'No; I don't think so, Virginia. There wasn't anything in Daphne's manner just now that wasn't perfectly genuine. In fact it was so genuine that it was almost insulting.'

'But Daphne's such a fool, she'd believe any man wanted to marry her who only asked her for some infamous practical joke.'

Again Cecilia shook her head.

'She obviously loves him too much to be that kind of fool. There's a sort of sensitive instinct in real love which realises only too soon if it's being made fun of, even if it's blind to other things. And I do believe that hers is real love, even though she has a way of showing it that isn't quite the sort that you and I would choose.'

'But what does he mean then, Cecilia? Is he just trying an emotional experiment, or what? Only one thing's clear to me at present – that he's been guilty of something absolutely criminal, either towards her or me.'

Cecilia got up and poked the fire; then she took a long breath.

'There's one thing you never take into account with people – especially with the weak people – and that's their humanity. Of course, I don't pretend to know as much about love as you do; it's not an accomplishment of mine to bring suitors crawling to my feet. But I've always heard that there's such a thing as catching people on the rebound – or perhaps not even catching them, but just happening to be there when they've rebounded. I think that's probably what Daphne's done, you know. It's incredible the amount of things pique seems to account for, especially in a man, and you don't sound to me to have refused Mr Sylvester in a very ladylike manner. He thinks he's paying you out now – at Daphne's expense.'

Virginia flushed a little, but seemed almost entirely to have recovered.

'Oh, well!' she said, 'they're not worth getting a headache about, anyway. I'm sure they'll suit each other very well, so no doubt they'll be perfectly happy. And two lucky people in the world will be spared from having to marry either of them!'

'Virginia, I've told you before now that your cut-and-dried views about the married state really are deplorable.'

'Why not go on and tell me it's sour grapes.' Virginia stood up, laughing a little bitterly. Then she added rather grimly: 'Now let's make quite sure that the thrilling news spreads as fast as it possibly can.'

She ran down the stairs and walked rapidly across the garden to Martindale, heedless of the protests of Cecilia, who followed vainly in her wake. She went straight to Julia's room and knocked at the door.

'Come in!' sang out the voice from within. 'Enter, and take a pew!'

Virginia entered and stood just inside the door, holding it half open.

'Have you heard the latest?' she inquired languidly.

Julia looked up eagerly from her essay on Lamartine.

'No – what?' she exclaimed.

'Daphne's engaged to Sylvester.'

Julia looked absolutely nonplussed.

'*What?* Daphne! Engaged to Sylvester! My aunt! But, Virginia, I thought you told me that—'

'I was mistaken,' said Virginia wearily.

And sure enough, in half-an-hour, the news was all over Drayton. But Daphne, alone in her room, was temporarily locked away from its queries and congratulations. Humbly she was kneeling before her window with happy tears in her eyes, giving thanks to a Deity in whom she herself only believed remotely, but whom Thorbury Park would not have considered it quite respectable to abandon altogether.

Chapter IX

Eights Week

Sylvester paced up and down behind the barges, chafing. The five-minutes gun for the first race had already gone, but there was no sign of Daphne. It was bad enough that she was coming at all to make her first official appearance on St Giles' barge as his fiancée; he so much hated manipulating teacups in a crowd, and carrying on polite conversation with the self-opinionated wives of the older dons. But it was doubly annoying of her to be late, and make him miss the first race, when he was simply itching to run along the towing-path with the St Giles' undergraduates, as he had always run before at Eights and Toggers.

The engagement had been unexpected; it had caused considerable excitement at Drayton at the end of the previous term, and no small amount of furtive amusement at St Giles'. But surprise is never long-lived at a university, and except in Daphne's immediate circle, criticism and speculation had long come to an end. Nevertheless Sylvester realised that he was bound to Daphne as tightly as his engagement ring bound the large third finger of her left hand. She had hoped that he would take her with him to choose something really original, but he had sent her the conventional half-hoop by registered post. Her worship of him was obvious and unrestrained; it provoked some to laughter, others to envy, and just a few to pity. Sylvester knew very well that all were aware of it, and he was not the man to flout public opinion and court adverse criticism by abandoning a girl who, as everyone realised, would never give him up of her own accord.

Besides, he was not sure that he regretted the impulse to which Virginia's contempt had driven him that afternoon in March. His one fear had been that she would spread round Oxford the story of his previous proposal to her; it would have been just like that heartless kind of girl to upset his arrangements in order to amuse herself and satisfy her vanity. But Virginia had been unexpectedly silent; moreover, she had cut him dead that time they had suddenly met face to face in the middle of a crowd at Carfax. These two facts convinced him that he really had succeeded in paying her out. He was certain that nothing but the fear of condemnation had prevented her from giving him away, while that sudden flush and abrupt turning aside, instead of the cold, ironical bow he was prepared for, could only have arisen from embarrassment and humiliation. Yes; he could congratulate himself on having achieved successfully one object of his engagement to Daphne.

Moreover, the more he thought of it, the surer he became that he really did need a wife. And since it could not be Virginia – and he wouldn't have her now at any price, even if she wanted him, the little fiend – almost any other girl would do quite well. The more devoted and submissive she was, the better for him. Of course in his future position he would require a wife with certain intellectual qualifications to act as hostess to the political friends that he was sure to make at once, but Daphne's intelligence was adequate, and seemed to be improving, while her whole-souled adoration was worth a little chaff behind his back.

Of course, he had quailed a bit the first time he had

encountered Mrs Lethbridge. He had been unable (because unwilling) to postpone the tour in Morocco which he had arranged with the Dean of St Giles for the Easter vacation, so he had not yet visited Thorbury Park. But Daphne's parents had come down to Oxford for the night at the beginning of the summer term on purpose to meet him.

Her father, he decided to his relief, was a negligible quantity, but he had not been prepared for that atmosphere of Emporiums of which Mrs Lethbridge's married life had entirely failed to deprive her. However, he decided after a struggle that the Megson guineas were worth it, though, to do him justice, he had had no certain knowledge of them when he first asked Daphne to become his wife.

As a prospective son-in-law he had been accepted with enthusiasm. Nothing, Mrs Lethbridge privately declared to her husband, could so firmly establish the prestige of the family – that prestige which her gold had somehow failed to give it – as darling Daphne's marriage to an Oxford 'professor.' And as Sylvester was to go to London in September to begin his new work, the very date of the wedding had already been fixed. It was to take place the first week in August, as soon as the result of Daphne's Finals, which would be delayed for an unwonted period owing to the number of History candidates, had been published at the end of July.

Sylvester suddenly started irritably; he had been roused from his preoccupation by a dig in the ribs from the Vice-President of St Giles, a large, jovial gentleman with a broad, grinning face.

'Hallo, Sylvester! Waiting for the fair one?'

The minute gun went off as he spoke.

'I shouldn't miss the race if I were you,' he continued. 'She's sure to be late. These ladies don't come on the barges to see the races; they come to be seen themselves

– as you'll know, old man, when you've been married as long as I have.'

His untimely jocularity made Sylvester feel thoroughly aggrieved; the rôle of ardent, expectant lover was not, he felt, at all appropriate to a St Giles' tutor of several years' standing; it was most inconsiderate of Daphne to put him into such a position. So he returned to the barge with the Vice-President to watch the first race. And just as the last boat was labouring strenuously past the Green Cut, Daphne appeared on the barge, looking a little forlorn and disappointed.

That bright week in May was the first indication of the hot brilliant summer that was to follow. The barges and the banks were aglow with vivid colours; the river like a glittering serpent quivered and shimmered in the warm spring sunshine. Above the heads of Daphne and Sylvester the green and purple flag of St Giles' danced skittishly in the breeze.

Love, young and passionate, must surely thrive on such an afternoon. Yet, although she was so intensely conscious of her extreme good fortune, Daphne was the one jaded and weary object in all that sparkling company. She was conscious of looking her very worst for her first official reception by Sylvester's colleagues. Schools were now only three weeks ahead, and Raymond's wife of all people must be able to boast of a First. Miss O'Neill had assured her in a rash moment that the slender chance of such an attainment was hers. Since then Daphne had determined that she would leave no stone unturned to achieve this glorious consummation; let it cost her what it might, she would not fail her lover. Fortunately the rôle of butterfly might safely be abandoned by one who was engaged, and so soon to be married, so Daphne worked frantically, morning, afternoon, and evening, at night, at her meals, and in her bath. The expostulations of her friends and Patricia's entreaties alike failed to restrain her. Fatigue was nothing to her, who was working for Raymond's sake.

Raymond unfortunately failed in his proper appreciation of her efforts when he saw her arriving on his barge with pale face and straight, untidy hair under a huge, blue-feathered tulle hat, which she had thrown on hurriedly after working up to the last moment before changing her clothes. She wore a heavily-made expensive crêpe de Chine, stamped with a large, bright pattern which struck Sylvester as being singularly lurid and inappropriate for that hot, glittering day. (He had recently caught sight of Virginia, cool and charming in white georgette, talking to Stephanoff beneath the trees which shadowed the path below.) To add to his vexation, Daphne had brought odd gloves, both for the left hand. It wouldn't have mattered, Sylvester thought irritably, if they had both been for the right, which was inky. As it was, she could not decide whether to wear one glove or neither, so that she persisted in putting one on and taking it off again in the midst of being introduced to his colleagues till he could almost have shaken her with exasperation.

'Sit here!' he commanded at last, when the introductions were over, dragging a chair for her to the most secluded corner of the barge. 'Sit here, and for goodness sake don't wander about any more till I've got you some tea.'

'Oh, thank you, Raymond!' Daphne looked up at him with tired, grateful eyes. 'I didn't have any lunch, because I'd planned to finish Fournier before I came, and he took so much longer than I expected. Of course I loved meeting your friends – but I've been simply aching to talk to you and have some tea to wake me up – the heat to-day's made me so thirsty.'

'Oh, don't let's talk shop!' said Sylvester rather crossly. 'I'll get you some tea as soon as I can penetrate this infernal crowd, if only you'll wait there and see that nobody takes my chair.'

The secluded corner happened to be the nearest point to the Gloucester barge, which lay next to St Giles', but Daphne's eyes were too weary and her brain too confused to be conscious of the observation of Stephanoff and Patricia O'Neill.

'Don't you notice how tired she's looking this afternoon?' Patricia, who was one of the few who pitied, was saying to Stephanoff as they leaned over the edge of the barge. 'I've talked and talked till I'm weary of the subject, but nothing I can say seems to make any impression. She simply won't leave off at all.'

Stephanoff, who was taking Daphne for revision coachings on her Foreign Period, sighed with resignation.

'I have noticed it. Once she had many ideas, but they have all committed suicide. Her brain this term is like an overworked sausage machine.'

'It's dreadful. I don't know what to do about it at all,' Patricia mused. 'I thought she was nearly working herself to death when she and Miss Dennison coached with you, but it was nothing to this. She's simply ruining her chances – and I know it's all because of that engagement.'

Stephanoff watched Sylvester scowling as he conveyed two cups of tepid tea with extreme difficulty through the crowd on St Giles' barge; then he turned to Patricia with eyes half rueful and half amused.

'It is a strange affair,' he remarked conclusively.

'It is indeed!' Patricia looked a little distressed. 'You know, I simply can't understand a man like Mr Sylvester becoming engaged to Miss Lethbridge. And it's impossible to get anything about it out of her; she always talks too much to be communicative. Now, if it had been Miss Dennison—'

'He knows well that she would not have him,' said Stephanoff with decision. 'And I think besides that she is too independent for him. A man like that, who is – how shall I say it? – elemental, likes his women to be submissive.'

'I don't know,' Patricia meditated. 'I always thought that the primitive instinct was to want a thing more, the more difficult it was to get.'

Stephanoff looked at her sadly.

'Ah! yes; that is a very primitive instinct indeed!' he said with a hint of bitterness.

Patricia was too much preoccupied to notice his remark.

'It does worry me,' she said. 'I do wish it hadn't happened just now – poor Miss Lethbridge!'

'You shall not be worried. We will change the subject,' said Stephanoff with unexpected determination. 'It is her engagement, not yours, and you shall not take the burdens of the world upon your shoulders. I do not like you to go in for a dozen different Schools, but I *will* not have you engaged to a dozen different men.'

The presence of Daphne and Sylvester was not lost upon Virginia, who was also on the Gloucester barge that afternoon. She had, as she was perfectly aware, been invited to engage the attention of Patricia's cousin, Michael Delaney, and so to leave a free field for Stephanoff. The near approach of Schools did not add to her work to any appreciable extent; unlike Daphne, she had never felt the burden of arrears. Consequently she appeared as pretty and as unruffled as she had been the previous summer. She watched the couple on the next barge for a few moments, and then, turning to Stephanoff, began to quote mockingly:

'O lyric Love, half angel and half bird . . .'

'You *are* a spiteful little thing!' interrupted Patricia. 'Isn't she, Mr Stephanoff? I'm always telling her so. I wish when you coached her you'd taught her a little less history and a little more humanity.'

'Don't scold him, Miss O'Neill,' said Virginia, suddenly grave. 'You know as well as I do that he'd like to have done it if he could, but he found out it wasn't any use.'

'Listen!' Stephanoff broke in. 'There is the one-minute gun. Now let us try once more to watch the race. Always we miss it because we talk so much, and after all it is what we really came for. Is it not, Miss O'Neill?' And he looked at Patricia with pathetic anxiety to be contradicted.

'I suppose so,' said Patricia absently, fixing her eyes on the shining stretch of river beyond the Green Cut.

Stephanoff treated all three of them afterwards to dinner at 'The Randolph' and stalls at the theatre. There they sat in full view of Sylvester and Daphne, who were in the dress circle – a position which Sylvester considered quite good enough for anyone's fiancée. It was only with great difficulty that he had persuaded Daphne to abandon her work for the evening and come out with him. She knew that she could not really spare the time and that the next day would be overwhelming in consequence, but she was too tired and too desirous of Sylvester's society to continue the argument any longer. She had had a few moments after the last race in which to return to Drayton, brush her hair, and change into a cooler dress. Fatigue always suited her when she was not untidy, and the dim light of the theatre intensified a pale, statuesque beauty of which Sylvester might well have been proud.

But Sylvester, despite his insistence on her company, was not thinking of her at all. His mind, like his eyes, was occupied with Virginia, who was seated between Stephanoff and Michael Delaney, apparently conducting a vigorous argument with both of them together in the intervals between the acts. Music, however inferior, always stimulated Sylvester's emotion, and the fatuous jests of *No, Daddy!* did not provide a sufficient antidote. His repressed passion for Virginia was rising fiercely once more, and the performances of the orchestra deprived him of the power to restrain it. Daphne's weary efforts to interest him scarcely penetrated his absorbed consciousness; he had eyes only for the quartet in the stalls.

'Can she be falling in love with that beastly Pole?' he asked himself angrily, watching Stephanoff's almost passionate attention to Virginia's conversation. He could not know that Stephanoff, being also susceptible to music, had been seized with a burning desire to kiss Patricia's cool, indifferent hands, and had turned right away from her to Virginia in a desperate effort to conquer that inconvenient inclination.

It was not till the revue was over and Sylvester was taking Daphne back to Drayton that he became conscious of a temporary compunction. It was, after all, on his account that she had consented to go to the theatre, and crowd work that was overdue into an already strenuous to-morrow, and he suddenly realised that he had barely spoken to her the whole evening. Yielding to this passing gentleness towards her he took her in his arms and kissed her in the dark, empty road outside Drayton. Ethereally pale in the starlight, and too tired to seem exuberant or to be anything but tenderly responsive, Daphne lifted her face quietly and confidently to his. This new attitude of hers called suddenly back into life the emotion that had seized him at the theatre. Barely conscious whether he was holding Daphne or Virginia, he gathered her passionately into his embrace and kissed her again and again and again. And Daphne, consoled for his unaccountable silences, uplifted and triumphant, yielded herself proudly to his desire.

'Are you happy, Daphne?' he asked at length, holding

her a little away from him and looking straight into her ardent blue eyes.

'Happy? Oh, I can't tell you how happy, Raymond! Every night when the others have gone and before I go to bed, I think and think and think how happy I am, and sometimes I can't sleep for thinking how wonderful it is that such joy should come to me of all people – really to me! Nothing ever really spoils it, you know. I often feel stupid and get angry with myself because sometimes I do such silly, awkward things – but it's nearly always because I want to please you that I do them, only I go and make myself ridiculous by trying too hard.'

'You foolish, blessed girl!' he said, kissing her again. Her clinging hands, her loving, gentle submission exactly fitted in with his mood that summer evening. She really appealed to him very much, he thought, when her superfluous energy was gone, and with it that lack of restraint which so often jarred upon his nerves.

He stood in the shadow of the gate holding her in his arms until the clock struck eleven, and she was obliged to go into Drayton, leaving him locked outside. He had found her more adequate than ever before, and decided as he walked away from Drayton that though it was Virginia who had aroused his passion, Daphne at least could satisfy it.

Chapter X

Schools

Daphne had been sick all night. It was just her luck to have one of her bad bilious attacks the very evening before Schools, she lamented, as she got out of bed with a great effort. She was too dazed to perceive the intimate relation of cause and effect between her overworked brain and her underworked digestion. Though the morning was hotter than ever, she shivered as she put on her clothes in the bright June sunlight. Her face was not white, but a vivid shade of yellow, which was in striking contrast to the purple shadows beneath her eyes.

'Fountain pen – chalks – ruler – brush and comb – powder,' repeated Daphne to herself as she struggled along the passage to breakfast. What a dreadful lot of things one had to remember to take down to the Schools! Dizzily she poured out a cup of weak tea, doing her utmost to disregard the sardine-on-toast on the plate of her next-door neighbour.

The round, awestruck eyes of Second and First years regarded her from all sides, but her own friends were too much overcome by Schools fever themselves to minister to her need. For once no one sought to offer her condolences. Too many people had been amazed and a little frightened by the strain to which she had subjected herself throughout the term. Too many people had been kept in agitated wakefulness by her rapid peregrinations during the previous night.

There was a seething crowd outside the Schools when Daphne arrived. As *The Isis* trenchantly remarked, the rush to the fashionable summer resort in the High had already begun. From the door of the Schools to the beginning of Longwall Street women in academic dress struggled among men with mortar-boards and white ties. At the foot of the steps Virginia, a little paler than usual, but otherwise unmoved, was listening with a smile to the admonitions of Stephanoff, who had unexpectedly appeared to wish her good luck. The possibility that he had thought that Patricia might accompany her Schools people did not escape Virginia even at that moment. But Patricia, looking quite as white as Virginia, and feeling almost as sick as Daphne, had bidden her students a tremulous farewell in the entrance hall of Drayton. After all, she was still quite young, and the anticipation of a dozen ordeals had cost her a sleepless night.

Daphne, alone in the midst of the crowd, waited agitatedly for those who were blocking her way to the door to go in. Sylvester, in response to her urgent entreaties, had thankfully absented himself from the scene of action. But Stephanoff, suddenly perceiving the saffron hue of Daphne's complexion, came up to her with a face of genuine concern.

'Miss Lethbridge, I am afraid that you are ill. You are finding this absurd business too trying. Will you not let me fetch you a glass of water?'

'No, thank you – only a slight attack of indigestion yesterday – soon passed off – quite all right now,' murmured Daphne, too much occupied with her efforts not to be sick again to be completely conscious of her own remarks.

Somehow or other she found herself seated at a desk in an immense room full of men and women in Scholars' and Commoners' gowns. On the top of the desk was a paper of printed questions on Early English History, which seemed to convey less and less to her each time she read them over. A girl from St Augusta's occupied the desk immediately in front of her. Another from Queen Caroline's Hall was just behind, but in the next row, two desks ahead, sat Virginia, from whose disturbing presence the alphabet had not sufficiently separated Daphne. Virginia read through the questions once with collected concentration, made a few rapid notes, and began to write almost immediately. Daphne, regarding her, felt that she really was bound to be sick again this time, but with a great effort she conquered her nausea and faintness and remained in her seat. On the wall above her head a great clock ticked – ticked – ticked, ceaselessly marking the flying seconds of her precious three hours. Daphne watched its hands, fascinated. It was the sudden triumphant jerk with which the minute hand flung itself on to ten o'clock that roused her from her spell-bound lethargy. Feverishly she started to make notes, first on one question, then on another. All at once an asterisk challenged her attention. Of course – how foolish of her to forget – starred questions – one always ought to do them first, Miss O'Neill had said so – get it out of the way and write one's best answer afterwards – 'at least one of the questions marked with an asterisk must be attempted' – military campaigns – maps – Daphne read the questions over again, more carefully. Possessions of the House of Godwin – foreign policy of Edward I – campaigns of Crécy and Agincourt – good heavens! None of these were maps she had ever done! It was then that she remembered that she had completely forgotten her chalks. . . .

Virginia soon recovered her normal complexion while

retaining the equanimity that she had never lost, but the end of Schools week found Daphne in such a state of nerve-racked exhaustion that Miss Jenkinson insisted on sending her down before the term had ended.

'Now don't say another word,' she exclaimed, when Daphne feebly protested. 'You won't be fit to be seen at your wedding as it is; I'm sure I don't know whatever your mother will say to me. I haven't seen you with such a pasty face since you had ulceration of the stomach as a child. Now get your packing done quickly and never mind saying long farewells to your friends – you'll be seeing them all again after you're married.'

Daphne was really quite glad to obey these instructions. She never spoke to Virginia after Schools, and had scarcely sufficient energy even to say good-bye to the Set. She listened with impatience to their condolences, their good wishes, and their protestations that they had all done far worse papers than she had, but the benign farewell of Miss Jenkinson caused her even greater irritation.

'Take care of yourself, my dear child, and try not to be sick on the journey. I would have gone with you myself to the station,' she added, with a strange grimace that Daphne supposed was meant to be a wink. 'Only I was sure you would rather be seen off by Somebody Else. My best love to your mother – tell her I am *so* looking forward to the wedding.'

Daphne would very much rather be seen off by somebody else. She drove down to the station leaning heavily against the broad shoulder of Sylvester, who had come reluctantly to the conclusion that it was undoubtedly his duty at least to see her into the train. He was, indeed, thankful to see her into it before the arrival of that outburst of hysterics which his horror of 'scenes' made him anxiously certain was impending. In this, however, he was wrong. Daphne's mind was temporarily a blank, and as she lay back with closed eyes in the corner of the empty railway carriage, she could recall nothing of her papers, nor remember which questions she had answered. She had no idea whether she had done as well as Miss O'Neill had expected, or better, or worse. She only knew that she had covered reams of manuscript, and had been sick but determined throughout that horrible week.

She spent the next two days in bed, tended with exasperating fervour by her voluminous female parent. Her body lay inert as a log, but her mind pursued feverish images of maps, economics, European history, and political science. Nevertheless she recovered her vitality with amazing rapidity, for invitations kept pouring in from untiring owners of tennis courts, while she had her trousseau to get ready in a very short time. The Viva Voce was comfortably distant, and Daphne flung herself with ardour into the preparations for her wedding.

The final arrangements had still to be made for the flat which Sylvester had taken in Victoria Street, and shortly before the Viva he came up from Oxford to spend a week-end at Thorbury Park. It was the first time that he had visited Daphne's home, and when she had shown him the stables, and the garage, and the tennis courts, they walked up and down together among the fragrant roses in the Dutch garden with its high sheltering hedge. But at dinner that evening Daphne's exultant delight evaporated. Her father, somewhat overawed by Sylvester's intellectual reputation, sat subdued and silent at the head of the table, but Mrs Lethbridge was not in the least daunted by what she considered the social necessity of raising the conversation to her future son-in-law's level. So she plunged with animation into a monologue – she called it a 'discussion' – on modern social conditions.

'It's simply appalling, all this talk about unemployment! One feels quite uncomfortable at being seen about in expensive clothes, you know – even in St Anne's Square. I don't know what the country's coming to, I'm sure!'

Daphne hastily broke in with an embarrassed commonplace about the economic results of all wars, but Mrs Lethbridge, paying no heed to this remark, pursued her topic with relentless determination.

'What's the Government doing about it? That's what I want to know. What's the good of Lloyd George being Prime Minister if he's going to let the country down like this? I always said it was a mistake, giving that Government dole to the lower classes after the war – and all just because the politicians were afraid they'd make a revolution after getting such extravagant wages paid them at munitions and things!'

'Oh, do you really think so?' murmured Sylvester politely. Daphne felt acutely miserable. Since Raymond had come in with her from the garden she had grown overwhelmingly conscious of many things that she had never allowed herself to know – conscious that her mother was ignorant and flamboyant, that the house was overcrowded with ostentatious furniture, that there were too many gilt-edged mirrors in the drawing-room. . . .

The honeymoon as well as the flat was discussed during the week-end; and a tour in the north of Italy was finally decided upon. Though to Daphne, who had never travelled, Italy outshone Jerusalem the Golden, she had her doubts as to whether Raymond was completely satisfied with the arrangement. And not without reason. Sylvester was as familiar with Italy as Daphne with the inside of the Examination Schools. Apart from music, his taste was for novelty rather than beauty, and he was in the habit of spending the precious summer vacation in regions which he would have described as 'less tripperish' than the tourist-ridden cities of Italy. The idea that there could be any pleasure in showing for the first time to an enthusiastic and intelligent girl the famous places about which she had so long read and written, simply never occurred to him. He would infinitely have preferred the eastern shores of the Adriatic, with their turbulent, important little races. Montenegro especially called to him, with its wild, rugged earth like a sea suddenly petrified in the midst of a storm. But much as Daphne longed to go to Italy, Mrs Lethbridge was even more determined that she should. Mrs Lethbridge's friends understood Italy. They knew that Rome and Venice and Florence were distinguished places, visited by all the best people. But they were entirely vague about Croats or Jugo-Slavs, or even Montenegrins. They thought of the Balkan peninsula – if ever they thought of it at all – as an uncomfortable and far from respectable place, where nasty little tribes of brigands kept on rebelling, and upsetting afresh an already disturbed Europe, which made the price of food and clothes go up.

Even when the question was settled to her satisfaction, Mrs Lethbridge would not let her dear Raymond go without some further admonitions.

'Now, remember, I don't want you to take Daphne to any of those cheap foreign *pensions*. Wherever you go, do be sure and stay at the best hotels – and it would be just as well to find out first if there's English cooking there. Perhaps you could mention this when you write about rooms. My darling's digestion has always been very delicate, and I know she'll be upset at once if she has to eat that horrid Italian food.'

After three days of such instructions, and of introduction to Lethbridge relations as 'Daphne's professor,' Sylvester was heartily thankful to return to Oxford. As he left the north behind him, he blessed the happy geographical chance that had placed Manchester at a considerable distance from London. He was relieved to remember that the social observances of Thorbury Park were continuous and exacting.

Towards the end of July came the Viva Voce for the women. Daphne, suddenly faced with the prospect in the midst of fittings and the issuing of wedding invitations, realised with a shock that the manifold occupations of the past few weeks had driven almost entirely from her head the laboriously acquired knowledge of two whole years. The temporary return to Oxford conditions disconcerted her. She stuttered and stumbled hopelessly before her examiners, and her half-hour's Viva reduced her to a state of exhaustion and bewilderment almost equal to that which had followed Schools week. She returned to Thorbury Park with the old hopes and apprehensions vividly awake. At the end of the following week the results came out.

Sylvester stood in the hall of the Examination Schools, watching them go up. He read carefully through the long list of names, beginning them with sudden emotion, but ending with an angry sinking of the heart. Then he went out, and for a whole hour paced up and down the High, for Daphne had only achieved a Third. Virginia, scarcely to his surprise in spite of the sudden emotion, was in the First class. Afterwards he learnt that her First had been so certain that the examiners had scarcely troubled to Viva her, but had only smiled, and shaken hands all round. Shaken hands with Virginia Dennison, whose proud intellectual security had caused her to scorn his adoration!

His acute disappointment and the bitter humiliation of his thoughts led him at last to hope that a more intimate knowledge of the results would reassure him as to Daphne's capabilities. Perhaps after all there had been some bad mistake. Candidates at examinations were often confused with one another, and this year there really had been an overwhelming number; any mistake would be quite excusable. Fortified by this idea, Sylvester went to Essex College to seek out Richard Carey, who had coached Virginia and Daphne in Economics. He had been one of the examiners that year, and Sylvester knew him better than any of the others.

He found Carey lounging in his study, in a state of semi-somnolence due to the heat of Oxford in July, several good cigarettes, and the consciousness of excessive labours comfortably behind him. On seeing Sylvester he sprang with a start out of his chair, rubbing his weary eyes sleepily.

Sylvester apologised profusely.

'I hate disturbing you like this now it's all over. But I'm leaving Oxford for good in a few days, and I did want a little private information as to how my people have done.'

'That's all right, Sylvester. I'll give it you with pleasure. Shan't remember it long – glad to let you have it before it all goes. Let me see – you're St Giles', aren't you?'

From a heap of papers on the table he produced two or three lists of names, from which Sylvester picked out the men from St Giles'. Carey gave him a brief account of their achievements, and was beginning to feel that he had fulfilled this duty as completely and conscientiously as anyone could expect of him, when Sylvester, with an assumption of carelessness, said diffidently: 'It was really two of the women I wanted to know about as much as anyone.'

'Oh yes – of course.' Carey, who was usually in the world but not of it, vainly tried to recall some information that he had once received. Vaguely he turned over the list of names. 'Let me see – they were—?'

'Miss Lethbridge and Miss Dennison.'

Carey beamed suddenly as recollection began to dawn upon him. 'Ah – your fiancée – of course – of course! Well, Miss Dennison's work is pretty obvious from the results, I think; no one could get a First this year who wasn't exceptionally good. I can't say too much in praise of her papers – she was lucid – brilliant – original – really a splendid mind. Of course it goes without saying that your other pupil, Miss Lethbridge, is not in the same street. Not bad papers, some of them, in a way. She evidently knew a great deal; she was very informative – in fact, much too informative altogether. I should say she had overworked badly and made herself dull – distinctly dull. But Miss Dennison was a joy to a weary examiner, and I congratulate you heartily on her account – I do indeed!'

Sylvester drew himself up stiffly.

'I think you must be labouring under a misapprehension. It is Miss Lethbridge to whom I am engaged.'

Carey, quite dumbfounded, stared blankly at Sylvester for a moment. Then, hurriedly and over-anxiously, he tried to remedy the blunder he had made.

'Of course Miss Lethbridge wasn't at all bad – she did her best, I'm sure. In fact, some of us discussed giving her a Second; we tried to pull her up in the Viva, but she was too stu— I mean, she was unable to take advantage of the opportunity we gave her. It was altogether very bad luck—'

Sylvester held up his hand to stop the unconvincing explanations. 'Thank you for all the information you have given me. I'm afraid I am obliged to go now – got an appointment to keep. Please don't trouble to tell me any more about Miss Lethbridge; I really quite understand. You surely don't imagine,' he added coldly from the doorway, 'that I should want to marry a woman simply for her brains!'

Carey gazed with perplexity and some dismay at the door as it closed behind Sylvester.

'Funny thing,' he murmured, scratching his head ruminatively with the end of his pen. 'But that's just exactly what I should have imagined Sylvester *would* want!'

Chapter XI

The Wedding

The big marquee on the upper lawn was decorated with magenta festoons. Inside it stood Daphne, gazing at the preposterous draperies with unseeing eyes. Her mother had insisted that she herself on her wedding morning should inspect all the arrangements that had been made, and Daphne was carrying out the letter of this instruction. Lest her attention, so obviously absorbed by other and greater things, should disregard some really vital detail, she was accompanied not only by Mrs Lethbridge, but by several of the large and fulsome cousins who were destined to be her bridesmaids. There were eight of them altogether, and Mrs Lethbridge had decided that not one could be left out, unless of course Daphne really didn't care how much she offended her relations, who had always been so kind to her. Whereupon Daphne was obliged to cease her protests that four bridesmaids were enough for anybody, though she continued to wonder uncomfortably how Raymond would feel when he found that he had to give presents to all the eight.

As they wandered from the marquee to the dining-room, and back from the dining-room to the tables on the tennis court, Mrs Lethbridge kept up that running stream of criticism which she professed to expect from Daphne.

'I'm glad now that we got Gregorys' to do the catering instead of Harrisons'. Of course, I always think you get more for the money at Harrisons', but then Gregorys' things look so much better-class – and we have to think of dear Raymond's relations.'

'Yes, mummie,' said Daphne obediently, her thoughts far away.

'I do hope you like the way Morgans' have done the flowers, dear?'

Daphne acquiesced agreeably.

'Yes, mummie, very much. They're splendid.'

'I was very indignant with Alice Jenkinson just now,' continued Mrs Lethbridge. 'You know how interfering she sometimes is? – well, she actually told me she thought with a garden like ours and three gardeners we ought to have been able to do our decorations ourselves, and it was a dreadful piece of extravagance to go outside for them. As if all smart households didn't employ a good firm on special occasions like this! It's only second-rate people nowadays who decorate their own houses for weddings.'

Daphne, for the excellent reason that she had not been listening, made no reply. Fortunately her mother's monologues seldom required an answer.

'I've ordered the ices from Simpsons'; they're coming at two o'clock. Elizabeth will see to them then. They know quite well they'll get no more orders from me if they fail me at a time like this. Daphne dear, I heard – quite by chance, of course – that there may be one or two reporters at the wedding, not only from the local papers, but possibly one from *The Manchester Sentinel*. If they should stop you and ask you any questions afterwards you'll try not to be too much in the clouds to answer them, won't you, dear?'

'No, mummie – I mean yes,' Daphne replied vaguely. It was her wedding – her wedding – to-day she would be

Raymond's wife. That was the only thing that counted. What did it really matter if all the marquees and the ices and the reporters and the floral decorations went down into the Bottomless Pit that very morning! But Mrs Lethbridge was speaking again.

'I wish you'd run along to the kitchen door, dear, and ask Elizabeth if the champagne has come. Daddy didn't think we'd got enough, so he ordered another two dozen bottles from Prescotts' yesterday.'

Daphne seized with alacrity upon the welcome opportunity of escape. 'All right, mummie. I'll go and ask her at once.'

She went along to the kitchen and on the way met Marjorie Carstairs and Eileen Garnett, the only members of the Set who lived near enough to Manchester to be able to accept the invitation to the wedding. Passing on her errand to them, she fled away to the little copse that joined the privet hedge at the bottom of the garden. Flinging herself down on the dry, burnt grass she gave up her mind to those thoughts which had crowded out her appreciation of festoons and carnations and champagne.

She was to be Raymond's wife – and although Oxford had given him to her, the hectic life at Drayton, with its essays, its tea-parties, its late nights, and its petty rivalries, seemed already very far away. Even the thought of her Third had lost much of its bitterness, though the news of that disaster had come to her only a week ago. For one dreadful night, crushed and hopeless, she had wept bitterly over her failure, fighting once more with the old hatred of Virginia Dennison and her perpetual triumphs, and wondering – oh, worst of all! – whether Raymond would repent of the choice that he had made between his two pupils. And then, in spite of the cruel consciousness of weariness endured and labour spent in vain, the next day had turned all to sunshine. For Raymond had come the whole way from Oxford to console her, and to tell her that to a person of real judgment like himself, the accident of a class in Schools meant nothing whatever. He assured her that really he had always considered the result of examinations to be quite unrepresentative. It was, of course, a good thing for the wife of a coming diplomatist to have an Oxford degree, but as for the class, that didn't matter at all; it conveyed nothing to anybody outside Oxford. People like Miss Dennison, he said, had a kind of hard cleverness which made them successful at examinations, but they were not the sort of women that men wanted to live with. He said this to her several times, as if wanting to make sure that she saw how convinced of it he was. For the first time in her life Daphne felt quite sorry for Virginia. She always seemed to get on so well with men, and doubtless prided herself on the fact. If only she could know what they *really* thought of her!

The brilliant August sunlight streamed through the thick leaves of the little wood, making a golden carpet of the dry grass on which Daphne lay. Lazy shadows flitted across her face. Above her head a blackbird chirped among the boughs. Stretching her long body to its full length, and resting the back of her head upon her folded hands Daphne gazed up into the mosaic of green beech leaves and blue sky. For a few transcendent moments, such as she might never know again, she experienced that rare and glorious liberty of the soul in which all apprehensions are lost, and all regrets forgotten. In spite of its superficial failures, her college career seemed to her to have been on the whole a time of prosperity and triumph; she wondered how ever she could have suffered so acutely from little things which now appeared so trivial and absurd. What, after all, did any of them count beside the supreme love which was the consummation of those two years, that love into which she was about to enter with the joy of every woman who comes to her natural heritage? The Virginia Dennisons of this world might sneer and squabble and win little victories in the feverish narrowness of their exclusive, intellectual circles, but to such as her, even to Daphne Lethbridge, were whispered the great elemental secrets of love and marriage and birth. Her life in its fullness and triumph and hope seemed to her to be like a flood-tide, coming in with radiant sunshine that dispersed each tiny cloud in the summer sky, and sparkled upon the waves in a thousand images of beauty and delight.

She had almost fallen asleep, like a tired, happy child in the midst of a warm day's play, when her mother's strident voice broke in rudely upon her dreaming.

'Daph – ne! Daph – ne! Where are you? Time to come and get dressed!'

Abstractedly she wandered back to the house in response to that summons, and meekly allowed the eight bridesmaids to put upon her her heavy brocade wedding-dress, with its elaborate train and rich tinsel embroideries. The thick veil of old Brussels lace almost covered her soft, fair hair.

'You look just like a tall arum lily!' admiringly said Marjorie Carstairs, who had come to fill a little fuller the already overcrowded room.

'Oh no, Miss Carstairs! She's something far more wonderful than that! She's Helen of Troy going out to welcome Achilles!' exclaimed an enthusiastic bridesmaid, who had a romantic turn of mind, but was rather shaky on the subject of Helen's amours. And, indeed, the pseudo-classical allusion was not inapt. Daphne, in her clinging gold draperies, appeared regal and stately as some queen of old mythology, awaiting her lover proudly in splendid attire. She hurried eagerly to the looking-glass to confirm the opinion of the bridesmaids. Without vanity she saw and realised her own beauty, treasuring it humbly and gratefully as a wedding gift for Raymond. She admitted to herself that they would make an imposing couple – she in her tall, fair comeliness, and he with his big frame and dark, handsome face.

It was difficult even to make a pretence of eating the light and attractive lunch with which an adoring cook tried to tempt her excited appetite. The hour came at last when she was able to drive to church with her quiet, unexacting father, who from twenty-five years with Mrs Lethbridge had learnt to keep his opinions to himself until their correctness was demonstrated by time.

Sylvester was waiting for Daphne with the air of a victim about to be sacrificed on the altar. He had originally intended to ask the Vice-President of St Giles to be his best man, but after his first visit to Thorbury Park he had chosen for that office an unassuming younger brother, who had only just left school, and whose criticisms therefore would not be worth much consideration.

He regarded with intense distaste the overwhelming masses of white flowers in the church; they reminded him of one day the winter before last, when his train was snowed up on its way to the north of Scotland. The scent of the roses and orchids was quite overpowering; he was sure that he would feel faint if Daphne did not come soon – and of course on this occasion she was sure to be later than ever. He was quite surprised when she and her father entered the church almost before time, followed by the eight bridesmaids, who strode up the aisle to the familiar strains of Mendelssohn like an army of young Amazons on the march. They had arranged themselves in pink and magenta couples, and each carried a regular nursery-garden of roses and magenta carnations. A rustle of expectation passed through the large congregation; lorgnettes were raised to eyes; eager necks craned forward. Sylvester began to realise with extreme discomfort that a man was unpleasantly conspicuous at his own wedding.

He listened with lips that curled a little to the clergy-man beginning to hurry apologetically over the Rabelaisian directness of the introduction to the Marriage Service '. . . and therefore is not by any to be enterprised, nor taken in hand, unadvisedly, lightly, or wantonly, to satisfy men's carnal lusts and appetites, like brute beasts that have no understanding . . .'

Sylvester was conscious of Mrs Lethbridge just behind him, sheathed in royal blue satin, very tight and trimmed with sequins. He knew without looking round that she was listening to the naked words with the proper air of slightly indignant deafness. How she would have amused Virginia! But then, of course, she wouldn't have been there if Virginia had been his bride. Virginia would have come to him all in white, filmy, soft, delicate, nothing hard or solid about her. 'Clad all in white, as seems a virgin best.' Whoever was it that had written that absurd line? How Daphne's aggressive gold train caught the sunlight, and seemed to divert it from her face just when he needed her to look her very best!

The organist, anxious to give the Lethbridge sovereigns their full twenty shillings' worth of emotion, began to play *O Perfect Love* much too slowly. Something like a sob arose in Sylvester's throat. O love – Virginia – O perfect love! These foolish, vulgar people – why had they compassed him about with all these cruel reminders! Daphne, noticing his emotion, gratefully pressed his hand.

But the bitterest public ordeal is soon over, and the giving of a ring all too swiftly and irrevocably accomplished. Sylvester recovered from the feeling of intense sickness that had followed this part of the ceremony in his indignation at the outburst of *Lead Us, Heavenly Father, Lead Us*, which was his pet abomination among Hymns Ancient and Modern. And in his desperate effort to get the eight expectant bridesmaids kissed and out of the way before his relations crowded round him, he entirely omitted to bestow the embrace for which she was yearning upon his newly acquired wife.

When the handshaking and congratulations were over, the clergyman who had married Sylvester and Daphne compelled the guests to silence by a complacent discourse on the fruitful theme of 'Daphne, our tall fair flower.' Under cover of this oration Daphne whispered hastily to her husband: 'We're simply bound to get away somehow. Our train goes in three-quarters of an hour.'

'Thank God!' fervently murmured Sylvester, who felt that the eloquent parson had done more than enough for him already. As the reverend gentleman's enthusiasm, heightened by champagne, showed no sign of abating within the next ten minutes, Sylvester insinuated himself into the midst of a crowd of guests and, without waiting to see whether Daphne could do the same, slipped hurriedly out of the room. Daphne followed him, panting in her agitation. The need for haste lent her speed rather than dexterity, and when she reappeared twenty minutes later, in her saxe-blue charmeuse travelling dress, she was very much flushed and not a little dishevelled. Sylvester, who had been pacing the doorstep impatiently for some time, literally bundled her into the waiting Lethbridge motor. They drove away almost before the astonished spectators had time to collect their rice and their old shoes.

'These intellectual people, you know!' remarked Mrs Lethbridge complacently to a Megson sister-in-law; 'they have such queer and original ways of doing things, haven't they?'

Miss Jenkinson sighed.

'I'm sure I hope the dear child will be happy. She's always been so sensitive, hasn't she? – and Mr Sylvester has such a *forceful* personality. Eleven years is a very big difference.'

'What nonsense!' snapped Mrs Lethbridge crossly. 'Daphne has never cared for boys; she needs a man a great deal older than herself. I think dear Raymond is just the ideal husband for her!'

Mrs Lethbridge's respect for Miss Jenkinson's academic position was sometimes more than counterbalanced by irritation at her always unwelcome criticisms. And this afternoon her mournful attitude towards life in general was conspicuously out of place. For if Sylvester had probed the bitter depths of vain regret that day, and Daphne was allowed no time in which to display the new splendours of her travelling dress, if Daphne's father had many thoughts which he knew better than to utter, and the wedding guests were deprived of their rightful and time-honoured jocularity, Mrs Lethbridge at any rate had no fault to find with the great occasion. Her daughter's wedding with an Oxford 'professor' marked the climax of her triumphant career from Megson's Emporiums to 'The Gables.'

The next day Mrs Lethbridge, with *The Manchester Sentinel* in her lap, sat gloating over the paragraph on whose account she had harassed an unhappy reporter for half an hour. She could not know that far away in hot and dusty London a pale girl whom she had never heard of was reading that very paragraph and saying to herself with weary reiteration: 'So it's over! It has happened after all! What have I done, and what's it going to lead to?'

The description of the ceremony, in Mrs Lethbridge's opinion, was glowingly satisfactory, and a complete list of wedding presents was given. But it was the last sentence that really afforded her the greatest pleasure, for it testified to that power of argument which had driven a most eminent and intellectual son-in-law into reluctant acquiescence in her plans. Slowly and triumphantly Mrs Lethbridge read that last sentence aloud: 'Mr and Mrs Raymond Sylvester left by the four-forty-five train for London, *en route* for Paris and Italy.'

Chapter XII

The Honeymoon

He was certainly rather frightening when you were alone with him. Daphne shuddered a little, and yet exulted, at the recollection of that passion which had almost terrified her in Paris. Though she belonged to a sophisticated generation, she had not realised that marriage would be quite like this. But not for the world would she have said so to anybody. Of course it was perfectly all right when you loved someone like she did – only it must be rather dreadful for people who married for some other reason.

She turned to look at Sylvester as he sat in the corner of their *wagon-lit*, reading the Italian paper he had bought at Domodossola, where they had stopped to go through the Customs. The paper was called *Il Giorno*, and Daphne thought how splendid it was that he could understand it so easily. She herself could only make out a line here and there. How stern and powerful his jaw looked as he glanced over the paragraphs in silence! He had not spoken to Daphne for quite half-an-hour. With a sigh she returned to her contemplation of the flat, vine-covered country through which their train was passing on its way to Milan. She had never before been so long a journey and was beginning to get very tired.

But she forgot her weariness when they sat down to dinner at a little table in the warm, lamp-lighted courtyard of the Hôtel Lombardy. Their table stood in the corner of the square, open space; the trams, with their laughing, voluble occupants, passed along the road quite close to them, and through the gaps in the hedge they could see lights in the public gardens beyond. The curling tendrils of a vine climbed up the trellis which hid them from the road; a tall lamp lighted above it threw the delicate, swaying shadows of its leaves across their white tablecloth. The courtyard was very full; musical Southern voices rose gaily on the still summer air.

Daphne's soup had restored her primitive enthusiasm to the point of effervescence. Throwing down her spoon she gazed at Sylvester with wide, excited eyes.

'Oh, Raymond!' she exclaimed, 'isn't this simply glorious! I've never had dinner right out of doors like this before! I *do* love it. And aren't these little lamps adorable? They're just like big fire-flies in the dusk!'

But Sylvester's fatigue was not amenable to soup. Nothing less than a whisky-and-soda would have shaken it. Moreover, he was intensely bored with Milan, where he had been obliged to spend the night quite half-a-dozen times on previous holidays.

'For God's sake, don't talk so loud,' he said irritably. 'The whole place is listening! You needn't let everyone know you've never been abroad before. It makes me look such a fool.'

The excitement died quite suddenly from Daphne's eyes, just as the darkness had already drained the colour from her cheeks. What a stupid, irritating idiot she was, she reflected bitterly, as she choked through the rest of her dinner in silence. How like her to forget that Raymond would be tired with having to look after her as well as himself, and that naturally he couldn't be expected to feel interested in Milan when he had already seen it so often.

Originally Sylvester had intended only to spend the night there.

'It's such a dull towny place,' he grumbled to Daphne before the wedding. 'We might just as well spend our honeymoon in Manchester. It isn't as if the opera would be on; it's just like the Italian season not to begin till September.'

But Daphne pleaded so hard to be taken to see Leonardo da Vinci's *Last Supper* in the Convent of Santa Maria delle Gracie that Sylvester grudgingly consented to put up with the place for just one day.

They went to Santa Maria the next morning. As Daphne stood in the grave refectory, with its white bare walls, her ecstasies were stilled into silence. She did not know why she looked so yearningly at the faded tragic Face with its background of blue hills, or what question she wanted so much to ask of those sad eyes, that had seen into the depths of human disappointment. She only knew that she felt strangely lonely when Sylvester hurried her away from the picture, back to the clattering courtyard of the hotel, where an unusually good lunch restored him to the pleasantest humour she had experienced since their wedding. In spite of the glaring heat which radiated from the dusty walls and pavements, he took her in the afternoon to the top of the famous cathedral, whose delicate austerity dedicated to the Lady of Sorrows the skill and devotion of a thousand anonymous creators.

From Milan they went on to Venice, always the Mecca of those dreams of Daphne's which began so early to find England too narrow, and sought to draw the whole earth into the grasp of her inquiring mind. But all that Daphne remembered of that incomparable city was its mosquitoes. On their account the first stuffy night at the Hôtel Tintoretto gathered itself into a quintessence of torment. With fiendish ingenuity they found their way through the gaps in Daphne's torn mosquito net, at first in single spies, but very soon in battalions. As every traveller knows, a mosquito in the net is worth ten mosquitoes in a room with no net at all. As their psalm-singing intensified round her head, Daphne, with the bed-clothes drawn over her face, lay shuddering in the stifling darkness. She dared not light her candle and chase them out lest she should disturb Sylvester, who lay breathing with peaceful regularity in the other bed beneath a comparatively perfect net.

The next morning, in accordance with the habit she had already formed, Daphne got up early and dressed herself quickly in order to be out of Raymond's way. So he did not perceive the ravages of the mosquitoes until breakfast time, when he regarded her swollen and discoloured countenance with a horror that was not only undisguised but entirely unsympathetic.

'Good Lord, woman!' he exclaimed at length, 'can't you do something to your face?'

'I'm sorry it looks so horrid, Raymond,' murmured Daphne apologetically: 'I'm afraid there must have been a lot of holes in my mosquito net.'

'Well, can't you mend the thing?'

'I'll try,' said Daphne humbly.

She tried, but it was impossible to make much impression on a net which appeared to have been designed to catch shrimps rather than mosquitoes. During the nights which followed, the enemy succeeded in discovering all the ground that had been left undamaged in the first attack. It was not until they had been for a week in Florence that Daphne's complexion showed any signs of returning to its normal condition.

Long before this week was up Sylvester was bored almost to distraction. One might perhaps put up with having seen the place about six times already, but the preparations for the Dante festival really provided the finishing touch. The sight of a Dante medallion made Virginia's Bull of Basan see red. And as for the orchestral performances in the Piazza Signoria! . . .

'This damned place is full of bands!' he growled, as he and Daphne sat eating ices one evening at a café close beside the loggia.

'There do seem to be a good many here just now,' wistfully murmured Daphne, who adored them.

'I never thought there'd be another to-night after that awful jingle last night. As if it wasn't bad enough being in Italy when the opera season isn't on, without being pursued everywhere by these infernal pandemoniums! Their one object seems to be to make one forget there's such a thing as good music in the world. I warn you, you must get your sight-seeing here done quickly. I'm not going to stop much longer in the beastly place. It isn't good for either of us in this heat; the Arno stinks like hell. We ought to get away to the hill towns as soon as ever we can.'

Next day he came to her at lunch-time with a beam of satisfaction on his face.

'Look here, Daphne, you're sure to be in Florence again sooner or later. I vote we cut the rest of the sight-seeing and get along to Siena. I've just had a card from Anderson of St Cuthbert's; he's up there doing some archaeological research on the old walls, and wants me to join him. I'm awfully keen, though I don't know a vast amount about it yet, and we ought to get in some fine expeditions. The old walls are still practically perfect there, you know.'

'Oh yes, do let's go! I don't mind how soon,' acquiesced Daphne, brightening considerably at the thought that Raymond was going to enjoy himself at last, instead of having to be bored in places he knew by heart, because she was so ignorant, and had done so little travelling.

'And, Daphne,' Sylvester continued, 'you know all that stuff your mother talked about going to the best hotels? I really think we could cut it out now, don't you? You must surely be acclimatised by this time, and the Cosmopolitan at Siena's a deadly place. Anderson's at the Pension Piccolomini, and wants me to join him. It's quite a decent place; I've often been there, and we shall get a rest from these damned profiteers for a bit.'

'I'd love a *pension* for a change,' said Daphne truthfully.

She was secretly a little bored herself with the endless routine of large polite meals. So in thankful disregard of Mrs Lethbridge, to the Pension Piccolomini they went.

They left Florence by the afternoon motor-bus, and were driving in darkness long before they reached Siena. So it was not until the next day that Daphne was able to see the wide, smiling country with kindly blue hills that stretched away from beneath their window into the heart of the Apennines. The small dim room, with its uncarpeted stone floor and its one rickety washstand behind a chintz screen, seemed crowded and inconvenient after the luxurious hotels. Daphne found greater difficulty than ever in being unobtrusive when Raymond wanted the whole place to himself. She refrained from reminding him that the *pension* was his own choice when he suggested that they had better take the jug and basin home with their luggage, as she seemed to have such an affection for it. But the meeting with Mr Anderson in the palm-shaded dining-room completely restored his good-humour.

Sylvester presented his wife to the thin middle-aged man

with the walrus moustache, and then proceeded throughout the meal to help the archæologist to forget Daphne's existence.

The next morning Daphne fell in love with Siena as soon as she drew back the shutters, and saw that their *pension* stood at the head of a long valley rich with little fruit trees and vineyards. Quite close to the *pension* was a deep cutting bridged with a high embankment of earth, where a party of Italian archæologists were superintending some investigations which did not take them so far afield as Mr Anderson's expeditions took him. For two days Daphne was content to wander alone through the steep, sunny streets of the little town, straggling unevenly over three hills. Still alone, she inspected every chapel and aisle of the black and white cathedral, mounted to the tower in the Piazza Signoria, and spent a quiet hour in the tiny bell-crowned house among the tanneries where Catherine of Siena once lived.

On the third day she ventured outside the old walls, and walked until she reached a tall white villa with green shutters, which she had seen from the *pension* windows. It was almost hidden by a group of dark cypresses, standing in couples against the purple distance. Vines and figs were ripe in the fields behind it; lizards darted in and out of the crevices in its garden wall. Patient white oxen with quiet eyes and enormous horns laboured along the road which led past it, placidly straining at heavy burdens with wide, powerful shoulders. And the tall house, though it looked so indifferent, seemed to lend purpose to all this mild activity; it was the centre of a rich and peaceful life which flowed on perpetually without interruption or complaint. Daphne had been left to herself now for almost three days, and the complacent atmosphere of the villa irritated her in spite of the interest which had driven her to seek it. By the time she arrived at the *pension* for dinner, her mood was neither uncomplaining nor peaceful. The technical duologue which lasted throughout the meal excluded her so completely that when at last she was alone with Sylvester in their bedroom, she went straight to the point of her discontent without wasting time on any judicious introduction.

'Raymond, next time Mr Anderson takes you on one of his expeditions, can't I go too?'

Sylvester looked almost scandalised at this uninvited suggestion.

'My dear girl, of course you can't! Anderson doesn't want to trail a party round with him. He only takes me because he knows I'm interested.'

'But I should be interested too. And it wouldn't make a party if I just came as well.'

But Sylvester was adamant.

'I couldn't even dream of suggesting it. Anderson wouldn't like to refuse, and his whole day's work would be spoilt simply on your account. We have to scramble up all sorts of awkward places, where we couldn't possibly drag you after us.'

Daphne looked for one dreadful moment as if she might begin to cry, and Sylvester went on hurriedly:

'Surely you can't have seen everything there is to be seen in the town yet? And there are heaps of decent walks when you get outside any of the gates. Why don't you ask one of those artist girls from the *pension* to go with you?'

Daphne, who loathed the artist girls with their drawling complacent voices, replied quite quietly: 'I think I like going alone better than with them. It doesn't matter, if you really think I should interrupt Mr Anderson's work. I'll explore some of those roads through the hills that we can see over the cutting.'

And the next day she went alone through the Porta

Fontebranda, and plunged into the first of a series of 'decent walks' which gradually exhausted her superabundant energy, leaving her pale and wistful and weary. And still they remained at Siena, and still the archæological research went on.

One evening the muttered threat of a coming storm drove Daphne back in haste to the town from the open country beyond. Heavy clouds with edges of sulphur light pressed down upon the silent, waiting hills as she hurried through the walls by the Porta Romana, and found herself confronted with a network of streets that looked entirely unfamiliar. The high crowding houses hid from her eyes all the landmarks that might have guided her, and soon she had completely lost her way. She felt suddenly frightened by her own loneliness in this dark, brooding town with its whispered menace of thunder. She began to long passionately for Sylvester's protection in these mysterious, unfriendly streets, which seemed to change their appearance from time to time on purpose, as if they were playing General Post to provoke her.

And then, just as she was beginning to feel that she could walk no longer, she came quite suddenly upon the familiar quiet square round the cathedral, which stood up vividly in its black and white strangeness against the lowering sky. She was not only tired but very sad that evening, for she was becoming aware that Sylvester, however much he might love her, did not seem to regard her as the ideal companion. The cathedral, like Leonardo's face of the Redeemer, seemed to invite a disillusioned, storm-driven traveller to seek refuge there from one tempest more. Daphne stumbled wearily across the empty square and went into the cathedral to rest.

She sat down on a marble seat at the side of the nave, almost under the dome. The blue ceiling with its gold stars, and the delicate arches decorated like an illuminated manuscript above the windows, were swallowed up in the darkness that gathered beneath the roof. The unnatural gloom shrouded in shadows the cruelty of Niccolo Pisano's pulpit, which rested upon four lions, each eating a lamb. Shafts of copper light, falling from the little windows round the circumference of the dome, gleamed fitfully upon the marble pillars with their zebra-like stripes. The cathedral seemed less a building than a being endued with strange life, like one of the mystical beasts of the Apocalypse. Daphne almost expected to see the pillars move, as if they were the heaving sides of a great supernatural creature. She shrank against the wall from their shadows, which fell across the tessellated pavement. Above the arches the sculptured heads of the Popes seemed to lean over and look down at her, like faces gazing from a balcony. Gregory the Great – Innocent III – Clement VII – Pius IX – their familiar names chased one another vaguely through her mind, lulled into drowsiness by incense and fatigue.

And then, all at once, she realised what they were doing there. Of course – this big place with the striped pillars was the hall of the Examination Schools where she was doing her Finals, and all these Popes were the invigilators. What a crowd of them there seemed to be – but then, of course, there were so many History people this year. She wondered if Alexander VI was really going to see what people were writing about him! How worrying these questions were! She could scarcely remember the answers to any of them, and the more confused she became, the more those black and white stripes on the pillars ran into one another. How cold she was getting! The day seemed more like December than a morning in June.

She woke up with a start, her body chilled and stiff from its long contact with the hard marble wall. One last brave shaft of evening sunlight had pierced the heavy clouds like a shining sword, and now gleamed golden and triumphant upon the frescoed wall behind the altar. The images of the stained-glass window through which it shone were carried to the wall with its mellow radiance, and the dark shadow of a crucifix lay across the painted sky of the fresco. Daphne's weary eyes opened upon the stern symbol of adversity. She had started in terror from her seat before she realised that the cause of her fear was only a ghost of Calvary, long ago imagined by a forgotten artist.

The sunshine faded suddenly away, leaving the cathedral almost in darkness. Daphne went out quickly and hurried back to the *pension*, wondering anxiously whether Sylvester would return in time to escape the storm. She only paused for a moment upon the embankment above the excavations, to look across the cutting at two cypresses whose familiarity gave a sense of companionship to her loneliness. One was short and bushy, and the other tall and slender with a delicate tufted head. Their black silhouettes stood out sharply against the wild sunset.

Sylvester had not yet returned, and Daphne had dinner alone. The storm after all did not break, but passed away in low mutterings of thunder. When dinner was over she felt too tired to join the talkative Americans and genteel middle-aged spinsters who form the typical society of an Italian *pension* in the early autumn. Instead she went up to her room and undressed herself slowly. Then, wrapped in her blue dressing-gown, she sat down before the window to wait for Sylvester. A fitful moon, struggling through angry clouds, turned to gold the long fair hair that lay about her shoulders.

Sylvester came in two hours later, and had dinner with the archæologist. When he went up to his room Daphne was still sitting patiently in front of the window, gazing into the darkness. Sylvester's mood was softened by the pleasant fatigue which follows upon a hard but successful day. The sudden sight of her slender form wrapped in the blue gown, and the gentle radiance of the moonlight upon her hair, quickened his eager senses with an expectant realisation of possession. Before she could turn to greet him her body was crushed in his arms, his lips pressed fiercely upon hers. Half exultant and yet half repelled, she struggled for a moment, overcome by the mysterious terror that had seized her in Paris. Then, swiftly, her reluctance passed. Passion responded to passion, and she yielded – trembling, but triumphant. . . . Such moments were quickly over, but their heritage remained.

Sylvester had tarried so long with Anderson in Siena that the honeymoon was almost at an end. Rome, Perugia and Assisi, which Daphne, who had always loved the stories of St Francis, wanted especially to visit, had to be abandoned to Sylvester's archæological enthusiasm.

A week later they joined the Paris express at Pisa; another two days saw them seated at dinner in the Victoria Street flat, which had been prepared for their arrival. Sylvester, ruminating peacefully over port and a cigar, was full of self-congratulation because the Italian tour had not been as completely devoid of interest as he had expected.

'But next time,' he soliloquised aloud, half to Daphne, but mostly for his own benefit, 'I think we'll go somewhere a bit more exciting – somewhere rather farther from the beaten track, you know. Tripoli, perhaps, or the Balkans; even Greece wouldn't be quite so damn full of Americans. Not that I really want to complain, though. There was one place where I thoroughly enjoyed myself, and that was Siena.'

Daphne, remembering her long solitary days there, looked at Raymond's complacent face intently. But she said nothing.

Chapter XIII

The Flat

'I do think you might tell me whether you like the decorations or not. After all, they're your friends who are coming, not mine.'

Daphne spoke rather fretfully. This Christmas Eve party for a few of Sylvester's colleagues in the Ministry of Arbitration was something of an undertaking. She was tired, and a little apprehensive, for though she had had the wives of Raymond's friends to tea several times, an entertainment on a large scale was new to her experience. Besides, she had just pricked her finger badly with a sprig of holly. It was perfectly absurd that you still couldn't have Christmas without the wretched stuff. Sylvester replied with equal irritation from the other end of the room:

'My dear girl, haven't I told you twenty times that I don't care a curse how you arrange the place, so long as you leave my study alone!'

'It's all very well to say that. You do care. Look how annoyed you were that time Lady Wintermere told you Mrs Archer thought the drawing-room was too full of things.'

'Well, so it was at first. The things were good enough in themselves, but you'd got them all jumbled up together till the room looked as if it was waiting for an auction sale. I

138

couldn't help seeing it when Lady Wintermere pointed it out to me. I don't know why you couldn't see it for yourself before she came; it was a lot of use putting it right after. But I might have known what to expect if only I'd remembered the muddled sort of essays you used to write for me.'

Daphne turned sharply round from the top of the steps, but the door banged upon the answer she had ready. Angrily she wiped away two tears that trickled quite suddenly and unexpectedly down her cheeks. But even before the handkerchief was back in her pocket she began to smile. She could not long forget the Christmas gift she had for Raymond, which would inevitably revive that interest and consideration which ever since the honeymoon had waned so unaccountably. It had been hard to keep back for a whole week the knowledge that she was soon to bestow upon him the greatest gift that any wife can give. But Christmas was so near, and those shy, whispered words which must tell her secret would seem doubly appropriate the very night before the infant Redeemer was born. It didn't matter that Daphne was not quite sure whether she believed that He had really been a Redeemer. At least there was no doubt that He had once been a child, tiny, warm, and lovable, nestling helplessly in His mother's arms. Just as— But no, the very thought must be restrained until that hour after tea which she had chosen because Raymond always spent it smoking peacefully in his study. She must not even let her mind dwell upon the wonderful thing, or she would never have the patience to wait even for a few hours more for that moment which was to make everything right.

And indeed, hard though she had tried to keep herself in ignorance of the fact, Daphne knew well enough that things needed to be made right. And yet it would have puzzled her to define exactly where they were wrong, or to say just when she first realised that her relations with Raymond were not quite what she had expected them to be.

Once she had thought it was that afternoon when she fell asleep in Siena cathedral, but afterwards she told herself that it had been a little unreasonable of her to expect any more of Raymond's society at Siena. It was only natural that his eager mind should be anxious to seize the opportunity of learning from so eminent an archæologist as Mr Anderson. She ought to have known how inconvenient it would have been to take her with them on those expeditions, and it was entirely her own fault that she had not made friends with more people at the *pension*.

No, it wasn't Siena – but then when was it? She thought that perhaps she first began to realise on that afternoon when she made up her mind to show him a few of the things that she had written in the long hours while he was away at the Ministry. She had laboured at those short poems and stories, chiselling away unnecessary words, delicately pointing their sentences, till, in a sudden access of joy and pride in her own work, she had thought that they were ready to show to him. And then, after consenting almost unwillingly to read them through, he had told her brusquely that it was no use wasting her time on work that was never likely to lead to anything. She hadn't the gift of style; surely he had informed her of the fact at Drayton, when he used to correct her essays?

Daphne was too inexperienced to realise that the gift of discovering promise in work not yet mature enough to be excellent is withheld from those who are indifferent to all striving other than their own. But at least he had remembered those coachings, and she roused herself from her crushed sense of humiliation to use them as a diversion from her literary fiasco. She believed even then that she could revive his love by reminding him of its origin, which was still such a precious memory to her that she was incapable of realising that it might not have the same value for him.

'And yet all the time you were learning to love me although I was so stupid,' she said humbly. 'I shall always like thinking about those coachings as long as I live, although I often used to go home and cry because I was sure you despised me. And instead of that . . . Raymond, when did you first know you were beginning to care just a little bit?'

Sylvester, who had several important letters to write, got up from his chair impatiently.

'Really, Daphne, I've got too many things to think of to let my mind dwell perpetually on the past. I'd so many coachings to give those terms I was taking you that I can scarcely remember one hour from another. All I know is, I never thought you could write. I daresay your brain isn't bad, but it's receptive, not creative. If you haven't enough to occupy yourself with, why don't you join the London Library and do some decent reading, instead of wasting your time playing with poems?'

Sick at heart, Daphne took him at his word. The only knowledge that there seemed any point in acquiring was a continuation of the special subject on which Sylvester had coached her and Virginia at Oxford. She thought that the study of Diplomacy and International Law would enable her to follow Raymond's work at the Ministry, and render her a more adequate companion with whom to discuss his daily problems. She did not allow herself to be daunted by Raymond's hitherto complete silence on those topics. So she joined the London Library, and surrounded herself with intimidating volumes on legal subjects; she also became a member of the League of Nations Union, and strewed the dining-room table with its pamphlets.

Fortified by the information which she gradually acquired, she began making attempts to prove to Raymond that she was taking an intelligent interest in his work. Sylvester, who always returned from the Ministry at tea-time, had formed the habit of smoking and reading a novel in the hours between tea and dinner. He looked forward to these hours as affording well-deserved rest to a brain which, during the day, had undoubtedly served the Ministry very well. Daphne, whose married life had not yet improved her capacity for choosing times and seasons with discretion, perpetually selected these occasions in which to display her newly acquired knowledge to her husband. Her elementary questions and remarks on subjects long familiar to him bored him excessively, but his frequent attempts to change the subject or persuade her to leave him alone met with no success whatever. Daphne persisted in her efforts until one evening he was driven to tell her quite plainly what he thought of them.

'I do wish, for Heaven's sake, that you'd drop talking shop to me. You've always done it, right from the time we were first engaged. Anyone with any sense would realise that I need a rest from International Relations by the time I leave the Ministry in the evening. I didn't marry you in order to give you a perpetual series of unpaid coachings.'

Sorrowfully Daphne abandoned these vain attempts to please her husband and demonstrate her own intelligence. He didn't need it, she began to realise bitterly; if he wished to talk on interesting subjects, he found his new friends at the Ministry more adequate than her. But how was she to fill her empty days? The difficult problem remained, and no solution seemed forthcoming. She had of course her part to play as the wife of a rising diplomatist, and entertained the wives and daughters of Sylvester's colleagues at frequent afternoon tea-parties. But these formal entertainments only proved to her how ill endowed she was with the qualities of a hostess. They did not help to turn her acquaintances into friends; she seemed to have lost that capacity for easy friendship which had made her so popular with the Set. One or two members of that exuberant crowd were working in London, but teaching appointments had subdued much of their exuberance, and they seldom had time to come to see Daphne. Her days passed slowly and rather drearily, giving ample scope for bitter thoughts because they failed to show her how to please her husband or to occupy herself.

And then, one bleak morning in December, she realised that the wonderful thing had come to pass. Soon there would be no more dreary days or lonely hours; new tasks would fill her time and a new love irradiate her heart. And, best of all, the glorious news could not fail to re-create her in the preoccupied mind of her still adored husband.

The drawing-room was finished at last; Daphne folded up the steps and put them away. Before the first guest arrived to see the laurel and the holly, Raymond would know.

Raymond did know. He was lying back in the easy-chair, smoking placidly, with his feet on the mantelpiece, when Daphne came in suddenly and laid her head shyly upon his shoulder. But when at last he gathered the purport of her incoherent whisperings he put his feet down suddenly and started up aghast.

'Good Lord! Are you absolutely certain?'

'Certain – oh, so, so certain! I was afraid for a long time, because I couldn't believe that anything so wonderful could really happen to me. But now at last I'm quite sure; there's absolutely no doubt any more.'

He stared in front of him in silence for so long that Daphne touched his arm in perplexity.

'Raymond, aren't you glad? Haven't you anything to say to me?'

'Glad! Well – oh yes, of course I'm glad in a way, but . . .' His real sentiments suddenly got the better of his attempts to propitiate her. 'Of course it's a splendid thing to happen. I quite realise you must feel very excited about it; but all the same it's dashed awkward just now, when I'm beginning to see possibilities of a job which would mean our going abroad – exactly the kind of work I've always wanted, too.'

Daphne let go of his arm.

'Oh, Raymond – and you never even told me! But it doesn't matter a bit – about me, I mean. I should be able to go about with you all the time – almost up to the very end. I should really.'

'Don't talk nonsense,' he said testily. 'I'm talking about real travelling now – not a Cook's tour from one Italian health resort to another. The work I mean would probably be on some sort of Investigation Committee, which might have to go into all kinds of rough places. It mightn't even be in Europe. I couldn't possibly take you with me unless you were perfectly fit – and certainly not saddled with a child.'

Irritably he kicked one of the carpet slippers he was wearing across the hearthrug. When first he accepted the post in the Ministry of Arbitration he had no idea that it might lead to even more congenial work abroad. But now that such an opportunity seemed likely to present itself in the near future, it was damned hard luck to be hindered in any way from taking full advantage of it. The wife who seemed so desirable for London began to appear a very definite incubus. She had never been part of that ideal for a new life which was bound up with Virginia, and she did not even play her part as housekeeper in the unobtrusive fashion he had counted on. She was always wanting to talk to him about what she had been doing, and worrying him with her own trivial ideas. And now she was going to add a child to his responsibilities, as if they weren't troublesome enough already! Savagely he kicked the second carpet slipper after the first.

But Daphne's lips were beginning to quiver ominously. He had wounded her more deeply than ever before, not only in her love for him, but in that new pride of motherhood which throughout the week had raised her to such a height of exaltation. And he talked, too, as if she were somehow to blame – as though the prospect of fatherhood had come about entirely without his co-operation.

Sylvester, perceiving her distress, suddenly realised with agitated disgust that a woman who was going to have a child was more than ever likely to cause one of those scenes of which he lived in constant dread. He forced himself to adopt a gentler tone with her.

'Now, for Heaven's sake, don't cry! It's quite all right really – I'm sure I shall be delighted with the kid once it's got here – it's only a little disconcerting to have to cope with all the upset just now. It's the sort of idea that takes a bit of getting used to. Now don't make yourself miserable – go along and get dressed, do. We shall have half the people here before you're ready to receive them, if you don't look out.'

Daphne left the room and went to her bedroom without another word. Listlessly she fingered the tulle frills of her first black evening dress, which was laid out ready for her on the bed. She had been so delighted with it when she tried it on for the last time two days ago, realising with sudden pleasure that black suited her fair skin and hair far better than any of the startling colours with which she used to experiment. But now its fresh attractiveness seemed all at once to have departed. Indifferently she put it on, leaving half the hooks undone at the back, and went wearily into the drawing-room to await the ring which should announce her first guest.

Chapter XIV

The Meeting in Oxford Street

Daphne was glad that there were some little dresses for children in Marshall & Snelgrove's window that afternoon. She was always sorry that they had given up the big building near Bumpus', where tiny frocks and petticoats and shoes were so attractively displayed. But to-day the corner window was full of miniature garments, daintily fashioned out of muslin and blue ribbons and lace. Daphne gazed at them, fascinated, and dreamed how one day she would dress her baby in these delicate fairy fabrics. The child of her imagining was always a little girl; the other possibility barely entered into her head. She knew quite well that she would never be able to manage a boy; it was not likely that even the possession of a son would improve her capacity for dealing with male creatures.

This imaginary dressing of her prospective daughter had become quite a regular afternoon's occupation. It provided an inducement to go out and yet involved her in no strenuous exertion, for which she became daily less inclined now that May was here and the weather was getting warm. There really was very little to go out for in the afternoons, yet Daphne's instinct, growing more sensitive through continued contact with Sylvester, bade her be absent as often as possible when her husband returned from the Ministry.

She was sadly conscious that her presence at the tea-table every day had grown irksome to Raymond.

She was not one of those fortunate women whose excess of joy and tender anticipation bestows upon their coming motherhood a charm all its own. She always appeared awkward, tired, and untidy, and was therefore a constant source of irritation to Sylvester, who did not regard the prospect of fatherhood as sufficient compensation for this perpetual outrage upon his æsthetic taste.

He was impatient on this account for the child's arrival, though he knew that three months of waiting still remained. No definite mention had yet been made of work which would take him abroad, and he hoped now that the final offer might be postponed until he should be justified in the eyes of the world in leaving Daphne behind.

Daphne imagined that the subject had been dropped for the time being, for he never spoke of it to her. In fact he spoke to her very little at any time, and she realised that he avoided her society out of doors. He had told her so quite definitely a week or two ago, when she asked him to take her to a matinée which she wished very much to see.

'If you want to be taken to things, why on earth can't you choose to go at night? It makes me look so deuced ridiculous being seen about with you in the day-time.'

So they did not go to the matinée. Daphne never asked him to accompany her anywhere again, and more than ever acutely conscious of her own disadvantage, she avoided the society of others. The days seemed drearier than before, and the long, wakeful nights were even worse. Daphne's sad heart yearned inexpressibly for those three months to be over, let them end with whatever sharpness of anguish they might. She knew that when once she held her child in her arms all her loneliness would be forgotten, and the pain and shame and fatigue which she had suffered would vanish away as though it had never been.

Daphne must have gazed into Marshall's window for fully five minutes before she became aware that a girl, whose back was half turned towards her, had been contemplating the evening cloaks for almost as long. The slenderness of form and proudly poised head were very familiar to Daphne, which was odd, because the girl wore a nurse's uniform, and Daphne knew no one in the nursing profession. It was not until the stranger turned towards another part of the window that Daphne caught a glimpse of her pale face, with its small, sharp features, and recognised Virginia Dennison.

Daphne's immediate instinct was to move away as quickly as possible, though the nurse's uniform had aroused her curiosity. Virginia Dennison, who had so often made her look ridiculous, was the last person that she wanted to meet in her present circumstances. Besides, Virginia would be sure to mention Sylvester, and Daphne was seized with a sudden reluctance to discuss her husband with anyone who had known him in the Oxford days. She had never forgotten or forgiven Virginia's remark about the Bull of Basan, and her abrupt, direct criticisms which spared no one's feelings. Virginia would fight on the side of those instincts and desires which, against Daphne's will, made her aware of many things that she would so much prefer not to realise.

But Virginia had seen her start and turn away. She had known for some time that Daphne was standing beside her. Looking first at Daphne and then at the little frocks in the window, she drew her own conclusions without much difficulty. Her first impulse had likewise been to depart, for the contemptuous indifference with which she had regarded Daphne at Oxford, coupled with an uncomfortable consciousness that she and Sylvester had somehow wronged her between them, rendered her as anxious as Daphne to avoid a personal encounter. And then a revived professional instinct suddenly came to reprove her immediate determination. The penetrating eyes that a few stern months had taught to observe with greater toleration saw not so much Daphne Sylvester as a pale, tired woman, who was passing through an ordeal in which all women merited consideration. The drooping, unattractive figure beside her was an image of pathetic endurance which moved Virginia to feelings of genuine sympathy. She felt certain, too, that Daphne needed a rest after standing so long before the window. So she went up to her and touched her arm gently before she could disappear into the crowd.

'You haven't forgotten me, have you, Daphne?'

Daphne turned to face her with resignation.

'Not exactly. You're hardly the sort of person that it's easy to forget.'

Virginia, in spite of her pity, was moved to a smile of cynical amusement.

'Do you really want to forget me so badly that you won't come in to Marshall's and have tea?'

'I – I'm afraid I can't. I really ought to get back home – to Victoria Street, and have tea there,' stammered Daphne, desperately anxious to avoid a long conversation.

But Virginia, having made up her mind, did not intend to be thwarted.

'Why, it's past four o'clock already,' she said. 'You'll be ever so tired before you get back to Victoria Street. I'm sure you'd like a cup of tea now, and I know I would. I can't stay very long in any case. I have to be on duty again at five o'clock.'

Daphne felt too genuinely exhausted to protest any longer, and tea began to seem desirable, even though it had to be shared with Virginia. So they walked through the hat and cloak departments, and sat down at a corner table in the pink and gold tea-room.

The conversation flagged for a few moments, but under the reviving influence of tea Daphne's reluctance slowly disappeared. To her intense relief Virginia made none of the expected inquiries about Sylvester, but confined herself to unembarrassing topics. Daphne, after a few safe platitudes, made a bold attempt to satisfy her own curiosity.

'Whatever are you doing in nurse's uniform?' she inquired.

'Oh, didn't you know that I was at St Damien's? I'm training there – training to be a nurse.'

'*You!*' Daphne looked at Virginia in amazement. 'No, I didn't know. Occasionally I see one or two of the Set – but I've hardly heard anything about Drayton for ages. Have you been there long?'

'Ever since last July. I went there directly after the Viva, so I shall soon be half-way through. It's only a three years' training at St Damien's, you know, and I'm let off one because of my V.A.D. work.'

Daphne listened to her with growing astonishment.

'But, Virginia – *why*?' she asked at length.

Virginia smiled rather bitterly.

'To tell you why would involve a long account of my mental psychology which wouldn't interest you in the least.'

'Wouldn't it? I'm not so sure.'

'Well, you're not going to get it, anyhow.'

Daphne leaned back in her chair, puzzled and perturbed.

'If I hadn't seen you in uniform I shouldn't have believed it. And after that brilliant First of yours – what a waste!'

Virginia smiled again.

'Is it?' she remarked uncontroversially.

There was no hope of getting a solution for the puzzle out of her, that was quite certain. Daphne, completely nonplussed, remained silent for a moment. Then she made a lame attempt to change the conversation.

'It's very hot for May, isn't it? Your work in the wards must make you very tired.'

'It does sometimes,' acknowledged Virginia. 'The weather's always rather trying just now.'

'I know,' said Daphne. 'I find it trying too.'

She was amazed at the sudden sympathy in the melancholy eyes that searched her face intently.

'You must,' Virginia said very gently. 'I expect you find that most things make you rather tired just now.'

Daphne flushed a little.

'Yes,' she answered hurriedly, 'they do. It's having to wait so long – months and months – for something that one's a little frightened of, and wants to get over, and that never seems to come. Of course it'll be more than worth while when it *is* finished – but meanwhile everything makes one feel so lonely and depressed. The nights are so long; it seems as if it's never going to get light, and then when the morning comes it's worse than ever, because—'

She broke off suddenly, astonished at the strong temptation which assailed her to tell this strangely unfamiliar Virginia all her doubts and griefs and fears. She called fiercely upon her memory to remind her of Virginia's past cruelties and cynicisms, and thus assist her will to fight the overwhelming desire to speak. For it was impossible to regard any longer as a rival one who for some inexplicable reason had yielded up of her own accord her manifold advantages. Daphne sought wildly for something new to say – something that would obliterate the impression of suffering and solitude which her last words must certainly have given to Virginia. She felt sure, too, that the quiet, grave scrutiny of those dark eyes opposite her was penetrating into the hidden thoughts at the back of her consciousness which she herself refused even to acknowledge.

'Have you seen Miss O'Neill lately?' she faltered at last.

'Oh yes. I see her quite often,' answered Virginia. 'Sometimes she comes up to town for the day, and I usually meet her then. And occasionally I go down to Oxford for days off, or half days. As it happens, I've got a day off next week – it's the last day of Eights, so I've arranged to spend it with Pat. With any luck I ought to get down the evening before.'

'I had one or two letters from her soon after I was married,' said Daphne. 'But it seems ages now since I heard from her. Is Mr Stephanoff still in the offing, do you know?'

Virginia smiled.

'Well, according to Drayton, he seems more firmly rooted there than ever – but then you know what Drayton's rumours are worth! I get most of them from Sylvia Mayne, Cecilia's sister, who's up at Drayton now. But she's a child with a romantic disposition and a *grande passion* for Pat, so you see the truth's rather hard to come by. And, needless to say, I can glean nothing from Pat herself.'

'She always seemed to enjoy being at Drayton, though she was overworked,' said Daphne. 'It would be a pity if Mr Stephanoff persuaded her to do anything that might make her less happy in the end.'

Once again she met Virginia's intent look, and turned her head away as Virginia said lightly: 'I don't think Mr Stephanoff would make anyone unhappy. And at any rate he owes Pat something. I should think he's had a good many sleepless nights on her account.'

She rose from the table, drawing her blue cloak over her

shoulders. 'I must go now, or I shall never be in hospital by five.'

Daphne felt surprisingly unwilling to let Virginia depart. The conversation had been constrained, and full of platitudes which trembled dangerously on the edge of revelation, yet it had come as a welcome break in Daphne's long loneliness. Virginia seemed to understand how she felt without being told; if it had been anyone else, Daphne would almost have said that she sympathised. And she was endued with a quiet strength and determination which mattered so much more than her sharp abruptness, and seemed to Daphne like a kind of anchor in her tempest of feverish uncertainties and doubts.

'When can I see you again?' she forced herself to ask tentatively. 'Now that we've met it seems a pity not to – and, after all, we're both in London.'

Virginia's first impulse was a decisive refusal. She knew that she must not and would not meet Sylvester, and Daphne's genuine desire for her society – possibly, Virginia thought cynically, for any society other than her husband's – did not at once appear to make the risk worth while. And then, for a second time that afternoon, she repudiated her own instinct. She had not studied Daphne during tea for nothing, and had come to the conclusion that the approach of a physical ordeal was not sufficient reason for her white, strained face and tired, anxious eyes. She could only guess at their possible cause, but she realised that Daphne's need of someone, even perhaps of her, was undoubtedly very great.

'I should like to see you again very much,' she said, after a moment's hesitation. 'But there's one thing I must confess before I can commit myself to anything. I haven't seen your husband since the last time I coached with him, and I'm afraid we didn't part on very good terms. We – had rather a heated argument, and I'm afraid I lost my temper. I don't think he'd really care to meet me again; it might be awkward for us both. So if I come and see you sometimes, could it be when you're alone? But perhaps you'd rather not now?'

'Oh no – I want you to come,' answered Daphne without hesitation. The prospect of having someone who would come and see her 'sometimes' outweighed all other considerations for the time being.

'But surely,' she added, 'it wouldn't matter seeing Raymond now? He couldn't possibly bear you malice just for a coaching – and so long ago too!'

'Oh, very likely not,' said Virginia; 'but I'd rather not chance it if you don't mind.'

Daphne considered for a moment.

'Well, it scarcely concerns Raymond if you're not going to see him, does it? And I would so much like someone to talk to when he's out, especially just now, when I'm inclined to get depressed and think absurd things if I'm alone much. Do you often get off in the afternoon?'

'Yes,' replied Virginia. 'That's the time I have most frequently; the wards are usually fairly quiet until after tea.'

'Well, then, do come and see me in the afternoon whenever you feel inclined. Raymond never gets back from the Ministry till half-past four, and it's often later than that. We could have an early tea before you go back on duty.'

'But isn't that taking you away from Mr Sylvester? I mean, doesn't he generally expect you to have tea with him?'

Daphne flushed and stammered.

'Oh no – that is, I mean it doesn't matter. Of course I often do have it with him – but he quite likes having it alone – you see, he's usually got so much to think of when he comes back from the Ministry . . .'

'I see,' said Virginia, with perfect truth. 'I can't make any absolutely definite arrangement,' she continued, after a moment. 'I don't often know the time I'm going to be off beforehand, but if I do I'll write to you – or telephone. Otherwise I'll chance finding you in.'

'Oh, do,' cried Daphne gratefully. 'Except on Saturdays,' she added. 'If you really don't want to meet Raymond. He always gets back by lunch-time on Saturday.'

Virginia held out her hand.

'Very well,' she said; 'and I do mean it. I will come. It's strange you really want to see me, isn't it?' she remarked, with a laugh, as she turned to depart. 'But then I quite realise how it is. London can be a lonely place, especially when one doesn't feel very well – so lonely that one's glad to see almost anyone.'

Daphne, a little disconcerted by this momentary reappearance of the familiar Virginia, stared after her as she hurried towards Oxford Circus.

She found Sylvester awaiting her in a mood of unwonted benevolence.

'Hallo!' he greeted her, 'how late you are! I made sure I should find you in for tea to-day.'

'I didn't arrange to have it out,' said Daphne. 'But as it happened I met – someone I knew. Did you want me for anything?'

'Oh no; not particularly. I was only going to tell you that as we didn't go to that matinée the other day I've got two tickets for an evening at the Orpheum instead.'

'Oh, Raymond, how lovely!' Daphne exclaimed, quite overwhelmed with gratitude and surprise. 'What are they for, and when is it?'

'Not for a fortnight; the Orpheum's closed at present,' Sylvester replied. 'But it appears that an opera company from Milan has taken it for six weeks from the end of

May. They've been touring the provinces, and been so successful that they're putting in a few weeks in town before going back to Italy. Donaldson, a fellow at the Ministry, says they're splendid; he heard them once at Naples. It was quite by chance I got these tickets through him. He knows the new manager, and had a few to spare. They're for *Carmen*.'

'I shall love that,' enthusiastically said Daphne, whose fondness for bands and barrel-organs had given her a better acquaintance with Bizet and Verdi than with most composers. 'And it's just what you'll like too, isn't it?'

'Yes,' Sylvester agreed. 'To my mind there's nothing to beat an opera with a good swing to it. By the way, who was it you had tea with? Anyone I know?'

Daphne, with an uncomfortable recollection of her conversation with Virginia, hesitated for a moment.

'Well, if you're really interested,' she said at last, 'it was Virginia Dennison.'

She was looking away from him to hide her own embarrassment, so did not see his sudden, violent start.

'Oh!' he managed to comment. 'Did she – did she ask after me?'

'Well – no. I can't say she did. We had tea at Marshall's.'

'What's she doing now?' queried Sylvester, with assumed carelessness.

'You'd never guess. She's training as a nurse at St Damien's Hospital.'

Sylvester looked as incredulously astonished as Daphne herself had been. 'Good Lord! Miss Dennison a *nurse*! Whatever for?'

'That's what I wanted to know. It's amazing, isn't it? But there was no getting the reason out of her. She was as uncommunicative as usual about her own affairs.'

Sylvester half turned away from Daphne to ask the

question which had been troubling him ever since she first mentioned Virginia.

'Did she show any signs of wanting to come here?'

'No; but I asked her if she'd come and see me sometimes just occasionally, when I'm alone.'

'Did *you* ask her to come when you were alone?'

'Well, as a matter of fact she suggested that herself,' Daphne admitted desperately. 'She seemed to think – I mean she said something about your having an argument over her paper or something at her last coaching with you – that is, she'd got an idea you wouldn't want to meet her, though it seems absurd, I know.'

Sylvester got up from his arm-chair, kicking the footstool savagely aside. So she'd still a little sense of shame left, had she? No wonder she couldn't face meeting him, after all she'd let him in for! If it hadn't been for her he'd never have married Daphne and had all these worries and inconveniences interfering with his work. Of course, he might have had the same responsibilities if he'd married Virginia, but she'd never have let them be worries and inconveniences, never. As if anything to do with Virginia could be a worry or an inconvenience! What a grand thing life would have been just now if he could have looked forward to seeing his child in Virginia's arms, instead of . . .

He knocked his pipe sharply against the mantelpiece, spilt half the tobacco on the floor before he lighted it, and then turned nonchalantly to Daphne.

'She was perfectly right,' he remarked, with an air of indifference. 'I'm glad she's got enough sense to know when she's not wanted. Brilliant girl – interesting in a way, I suppose, but she always struck me as being intolerably conceited.'

Daphne's face fell.

'Oh, Raymond! Don't you want me to have her here, then?'

Sylvester struck another match for his pipe, which had gone out again.

'It's entirely a matter of indifference to me whether you do or whether you don't. Have her here as often as you like if it pleases you – but mind, whatever else you do, that you keep her out of my way.'

Chapter XV

Another Eights Week

At Oxford the Summer Eights were nearly over. After the third race on the last day but one the Gloucester barge was practically deserted except for Stephanoff and Patricia O'Neill. Patricia's cousin had gone down at the end of the previous year; nevertheless she was having tea on the Gloucester barge for the fourth time in five days. Throughout the hot, crowded afternoon she had conversed with animation over ices and early strawberries, but now she could think of nothing more to say. Stephanoff, equally silent, regarded her with large round eyes. Neither of them showed the slightest inclination to go.

Stephanoff was the first to break the silence.

'It is cooler now,' he remarked suggestively. 'Would you not like a short walk round the meadows before you go back?'

Patricia scratched the floor meditatively with her scarlet sunshade.

'It would be rather nice,' she agreed.

Except for stray members of the various crews, the meadows were almost empty, but for some time the two dons were as silent as they had been on the barge. Finally Stephanoff said abruptly: 'You do not approve of marriage, do you, Miss O'Neill? For yourself, I mean?'

'No, I don't,' answered Patricia at once. 'I know people think I'm rather absurd about it. Most women would still rather get married, even in these days, when they can have so much better a time if they don't. They want children, I suppose. I admit I like people to amuse me, but I've never wanted to marry anyone. In fact, the thought quite repels me.'

'All the same,' Stephanoff said slowly, 'you are going to marry me, you know.'

Patricia looked up without surprise.

'Indeed!' she remarked languidly. 'It's likely, isn't it, when I advised Miss Dennison not to think of being your secretary that time about a year ago when you said you wanted one! I told her quite rightly that you'd be so exacting and dictatorial. And marrying you would be far worse. It would be like a permanent secretaryship without any of its financial advantages. Besides, you usually despise women, and I object to that.'

'You,' said Stephanoff, with a grave face and a remote twinkle in his eye, 'have taught me to think differently.'

Patricia smiled demurely.

'You know quite well,' she said, 'that nothing will ever teach you to think differently. You'll make reservations and exceptions, perhaps, when it suits you. But your general opinion will always remain the same.'

'Well,' Stephanoff took her up, grinning broadly, 'you must admit that the number of stupid women is simply colossal.'

'So's the number of stupid people altogether,' responded Patricia. 'There are just as many stupid men. And a stupid man's infinitely stupider than a stupid woman.'

'I do not agree!' Stephanoff exclaimed vehemently. 'A stupid woman is one thousand times worse. Now, a stupid man can—'

'Yes, but a stupid woman—'

They wrangled furiously for a few minutes.

'Look here,' said Stephanoff at last, mopping his brow with a purple silk handkerchief, 'you haven't told me you're going to marry me yet.'

'Well, I don't think I'm going to tell you. Why should I? I'm very happy as I am. I don't want to marry. I like Drayton. I like Oxford. I like my work. I don't want to leave them.'

'No, of course not,' broke in Stephanoff. 'But why should you? I do not ask you to do that. You will marry me. I will coach at Gloucester as now I do, and you can coach and lecture, and write your *History of Local Administration under the Protectorate* – if you *must* write it.'

'But I can do that without marrying you,' said Patricia, 'and enjoy it just as much – probably more.'

'Ah, Patricia, but you must marry me. I want you. I love you – I cannot argue about that. Look here, I will make more money for you. I have a brother in Warsaw; he is clever and he has a business, which has not suffered greatly from the misfortunes of my country. I will go to Warsaw for a year and help him to build his business again. Then I will take shares in it and return to Gloucester, and we will get married.'

'But how do you expect me to coach at Drayton for a whole year without any teas with you at Gloucester?'

'There!' Stephanoff exclaimed triumphantly. 'I knew it. You do love me. You will let me kiss you – Patricia?'

Yielding all of a sudden, she lifted her face obediently. The next moment she was completely enveloped in a vast, bear-like embrace. She was rather pale when he let her go and looked a little frightened, yet still amused, still immensely intrigued with her experience.

'We will go and tell them all,' Stephanoff proclaimed

fervently. 'I am too proud to wait. I will tell everyone at once.'

Then his tone altered to one of intense seriousness.

'Patricia, you do mean it? You will not change your mind, my dear?'

'No, Alexis. I shall not change.'

He bent down again and kissed her demure little mouth.

'Patricia, I adore you. I shall always love you. I shall always love your mind . . .'

'Oh, dear!' she sighed, as at last they left the meadows. 'You don't *know* what a dreadful time I shall get at Drayton for this. Unfortunately they know my views on marriage only too well.'

And really, as she complained afterwards, the unmitigated fervour of Stephanoff's ardent, unembarrassed proclamations to everyone he met that evening made it quite impossible for her to go in to dinner at Drayton. As it was, her name was on everyone's tongue; she couldn't possibly have stood their eyes as well.

The news was none the less thrilling because it could hardly be called unexpected. It greeted Virginia on the very doorstep of Drayton when she came down that evening to spend the next day on the river. She hesitated for a moment outside the History tutor's door, choking down some unwonted emotion before she knocked. Then she went in, to find Patricia alone and for once unoccupied, sitting with folded hands and looking intensely out of the window.

Virginia squeezed her fingers hard, but she only said lightly: 'Well, Pat! So I hear you're the latest deserter from the noble army of superfluous women!'

Patricia came to earth and looked at her ruefully.

'It does seem rather a betrayal, doesn't it, after the views I've upheld for so long? You needn't emphasise the fact; I've absolutely no excuse to offer.'

'Except the only one that really matters. You've loved him for ages, Pat – longer than you know, and as for him, he's worshipped you ever since he came to Oxford. I knew it almost as soon as I came back after the war. Of course you're an incurable minx; you've driven the poor man nearly mad with longing and uncertainty. But you're worth it all, and he knows you are, and always will know it. You're lucky; it's a very wonderful thing to be worshipped. I knew what it was like, ages ago.' She laughed rather bitterly at her own emotion. '"I was adored once too," as Sir Andrew Aguecheek would say!'

Patricia regarded her in silence. The mixture of pity and respect with which Virginia always inspired her made speech for the moment impossible. Virginia, throwing a cushion on the floor, sat down at Patricia's feet and went on slowly: 'Pat, why does this one thing make all one's work and all one's achievement seem dust and ashes, however much worth while it really is? I suppose it's the knowledge that you're going to play Mary Queen of Scots to my Elizabeth.' She took her handkerchief out of her pocket and began crumpling it into a ball with restless fingers. 'In a few years' time I expect I shall be saying, like Elizabeth said: "The Queen of Scots has a gallant son, but I am a barren stock" – and all because my lover went down in the war. It's one's future, not one's past, that they really hide – those graves in France.' Then her voice lost its bitterness and became unwontedly tender. 'You'll have dear little dark babies, Pat, as sharp as needles – the very latest intellectual combination. And you won't know which way up to hold the first one – and you'll try to feed it on Ovaltine and water, badly mixed. I know you will. You are a dear, Pat, really.'

Obeying a sudden impulse, she got up and kissed Patricia with unexpected warmth. Then she sat down on the cushion again and abruptly changed the subject.

'Pat, have you heard that Daphne Sylvester's going to have a baby?'

'No, I haven't,' replied Patricia, instantly as ready as ever to put her own affairs aside for someone else's. 'Is she expecting it soon?'

'Fairly – I should think about August.'

'She must be tremendously pleased, isn't she?'

'Well,' Virginia said slowly, 'that's just what I wonder. I'm not quite sure that she is. One of the things I specially wanted to talk to you about was Daphne.'

'Yes?' queried Patricia. She did not appear astonished at Virginia's sudden interest in someone whom she had hitherto despised, nor did she ask her how it had arisen. But Virginia proceeded immediately to enlighten her.

'I always wondered very much how those two would get on. But I was very busy in hospital during the winter, and I never heard anything about them after the wedding, except that they were living in London. And then the other day, quite by chance, I met Daphne in Oxford Street, by Marshall & Snelgrove's. She looked very lonely, and wretchedly tired and ill, so I took her into Marshall's with me to have some tea. She talked a fair amount, and although she obviously didn't intend to say anything in particular, I got a distinct impression that she was unhappy. Of course it may have been simply her health, but all the same I couldn't help feeling there was more in it than that. I don't believe that things are right between them.'

'I'm afraid I shouldn't be very surprised if they were not,' Patricia said slowly. 'I never could understand that marriage; it puzzled me right from the beginning. Daphne seemed the very last person one would expect Mr Sylvester to choose. Now if it had been you—'

'That's just it,' Virginia said quietly. 'It was.'

Patricia looked distinctly perturbed.

'It *was*? Virginia, you must tell me what you mean.'

Virginia put away her handkerchief and turned resolutely to Patricia.

'I will tell you now. I'm only too glad to – for it's been on my conscience ever since it happened. Mr Sylvester arranged that Daphne and I should coach separately with him the day he became engaged to her, ostensibly to give us more time over a paper we'd done for him, but really – or so I imagine – to ask me to marry him.'

'*You*?' Patricia looked more puzzled than ever.

'Yes. I coached with him first, in the morning, and he asked me then. Of course he mayn't have meant it, but I never saw a man look more as if he did. I refused him – rather rudely, I must own. And the next thing I heard, that very evening, was that he was engaged to Daphne. She came in to tell me so, just as I was giving Cecilia Mayne a fancy account of his proposal to me. I hadn't had such a shock since the war ended.'

'But what an extraordinary thing! Whatever could he have meant?'

'God knows. I've wondered ever since – wondered whether he didn't mean what he said to me, or whether the way I refused him made him commit himself with Daphne on some sudden, strong impulse of reaction. If it was my fault, and she's unhappy now, then I suppose I'm more or less responsible. At any rate, I feel responsible. Pat, what *ought* I to have done? I wondered and wondered at the time whether I ought to tell her, and then in the end I did nothing. I tried to get out of it by telling myself that they were admirably suited to one another. But they weren't, and I knew it.'

Patricia, more disturbed than ever, meditated for a few moments.

'I don't really see how you could have interfered,' she said at last. 'It was an extremely difficult position.'

'I didn't see how I could either. But all the same I've felt ever since that I ought to have done, somehow. And since I saw Daphne the other day I've thought so more than ever. You know how I used to despise her; she always seemed so effusive and uncontrolled. But after that tea at Marshall's I began to change my mind. She could obviously have said a great deal, and I think she wanted to, but she was too loyal to let herself go. Either I was wrong about her self-control, or else she's acquired it since she left Oxford.'

Patricia did not remind Virginia that she had always told her she was wrong about Daphne. She only said slowly: 'Well, do you think there's anything we can do for her?'

'Yes.' Virginia spoke almost eagerly.

'She's apparently alone a great deal; she needs people to see her and talk to her and cheer her up as much as ever they can. I've promised that I'll go sometimes when I'm off duty. Will you go too, Pat, if ever you happen to be in town?'

'I will indeed,' Patricia answered. 'I have an appointment in London the week after next, as it happens, and I'll go and see her then. I'll write to-morrow to let her know. But I shall want to see you too; you must let me know when you're off duty. How's the hospital getting on?'

'Oh, much as usual,' Virginia said lightly.

'And you still find you can tolerate it?'

'I still intend to. It's really not so bad, you know; it's very like any other institution full of women. Only instead of Eights or the Union or Napoleon we talk about operations, and lumbar punctures, and empyemas. Our conversation at St Damien's may be limited, but it's very realistic.'

Patricia turned to her impulsively.

'Virginia, give it all up and come back to the other things. We could do with you here badly. We're very short of people to coach on Period 8.'

Virginia shook her head, smiling sadly.

'"Get thee behind me, Satan!" It's no use, Pat, and you know it as well as I do. I've put my hand to the plough and I'm not going to look back. I've done that too often already. This time I mean to go forward, right up to the end.'

Chapter XVI

Carmen

'Much *you* heard of the whole thing!' grumbled Sylvester, as he piloted Daphne through the crowd outside the Orpheum when *Carmen* was over.

Daphne, ready to drop with fatigue, struggled hard to stifle another yawn. 'I'm sorry I've been so awfully dull. I don't know what's the matter with me to-night. I felt half asleep before we ever started.'

'A fine lot of use it is going to extra trouble to take you to anything! Whatever I choose you don't seem to enjoy it—'

'I did enjoy it, really, Raymond – all I heard, I mean.'

He hailed a passing taxi and pushed her into it before he answered:

'All you heard! Yes, you may well say that! You don't know what a fool you made me look when the curtain went up after the second act and everyone could see you were asleep.'

'I do *wish* I hadn't been so tired,' sighed Daphne apologetically. 'It really was a very good company.'

'Very good! I should just think it was, especially that Carmen. I've never heard of Lucia Farretti before, but she must be a personality off the stage as well as on it. I don't suppose you even noticed her, though.'

'Oh, but I did – once or twice. Her face vaguely reminded me of someone I know, but I couldn't think who it was.'

'Couldn't you?' Sylvester leaned away from her and looked out of the window. Under his breath he was unconsciously whistling:

> 'When shall I love you?'
> I do not know.
> Perhaps never, perhaps to-morrow.
> But not to-day, that's certain.'

He knew well enough of whom Lucia Farretti reminded him. He could see her face still in the lamplit darkness outside the taxi window – either her face or that other of which hers so much reminded him, he was not quite sure which. For somewhere inside his brain a voice was speaking quite loudly:

'Virginia – Virginia – if I mayn't see you, at least I can see your image! And isn't your image better than you, after all? It's you vitalised – human – sensuous where you're cold – alluring where you're cynical. I must go and see Carmen again, for she tells me all about you – tells me more of you than you know yourself – Virginia.'

He had almost forgotten that Daphne was with him when he turned round again, still whistling 'Perhaps never, perhaps to-morrow,' and saw her leaning back in the corner. How damned uninteresting she looked, with that drawn, white face and those sleepy, half-closed eyes! He did wish too that at least she'd keep her hair tidy. One long straight wisp was hanging down right over her nose – quite enough to make her squint if only she'd been sufficiently wide awake to see it. Now if she'd got half the spirit of that little Carmen. . . . He pulled up the window with such a clatter that Daphne almost jumped out of her seat.

'Oh, Raymond, how you startled me!' she murmured, pushing back the hair out of her heavy eyes.

'Startled you, indeed! What on earth's the use of my taking you to the theatre if you can't even keep awake till we get home!'

'I'm sorry – but I really did like it,' repeated Daphne, too tired to be anything but meek.

The taxi stopped in Victoria Street and they went up to their flat.

'For God's sake, get undressed and go to bed,' said Sylvester to Daphne, as she hovered round him while he poured out a whisky-and-soda. When she had gone he took a large, leather-bound book from one of the shelves in his room and sat down in his big arm-chair to read it. The book contained a synopsis of famous operas, and Sylvester was studying once more the libretto of *Carmen*.

'Like to go to the Orpheum again to-night?' he inquired of Daphne at the end of the same week. 'They're doing *Madame Butterfly*.'

He did not really see any need to tell her that Lucia Farretti was taking Butterfly's part.

Daphne, who for want of other occupations had now begun to stitch monotonously, looked up at him from her needlework. 'It's very sweet of you to ask me again, Raymond, but I really don't think I will. I seem to get so sleepy in the evenings now; I'm afraid I quite spoilt all your pleasure last time.'

'Very well, don't if you don't want to,' he said, immensely relieved. He added, in a fit of sudden irritation: 'Why on earth can't you sometimes put away that eternal sewing? It's making your eyes so red – quite apart from getting on my nerves.'

'I must do something,' exclaimed Daphne, suddenly petulant.

'Oh, sew if you like then – but don't expect me to stay in in the evening to watch you do it.'

'I don't expect you to do anything of the sort,' Daphne protested plaintively. 'You know how sorry I am I can't be more of a companion to you at present. I'm only too glad you've found something to do that you really enjoy.'

She gave him a similar answer when he asked her to go to *Carmen* again a few days later.

'I can't to-night. Miss O'Neill's in London for the day, and she's promised to come and see me after dinner. I want to see her particularly, as I've heard hardly anything of her for ages, except that she's engaged to Mr Stephanoff at last. But *you* go. I shan't be a bit lonely with Pat here.'

Patricia came about half-an-hour after Sylvester had departed. Much time had passed since her youthful brilliance of achievement had dazzled and humiliated Daphne at Drayton; no sense of rivalry was left now, and consequently no envy nor embarrassment. Daphne's early dreams of a great career seemed to her like chimeras vanishing into the dusk of remembrance. All hopes, all visions, all ambitions had long been absorbed into the one aspiration of winning back her husband's love through her child. It amused her to be reminded of those strenuous coachings, whose anxieties appeared so childish when compared with the experiences of a wife so soon to be a mother. So she was genuinely glad to see Patricia again.

'When are you going to be married?' she inquired, after the conventional congratulations which were all that she could manage, though she had racked her brains intently for something more original to say.

'Oh, not for over a year. Alexis insists on going back to Warsaw to help his brother in business. He says he'll have a settled income after that; he doesn't seem to think that what he makes as a tutor at Gloucester is quite enough to offer me. I'm sure it would have done, though, as a matter of fact, I haven't the slightest idea what it is.'

Daphne looked a little upset.

'But, Miss O'Neill – don't you *mind*?'

'Mind what?'

'Why, his leaving you like that for a year – almost immediately after you've got engaged!'

Patricia laughed.

'But what should I mind? My dear child, do you think I don't trust him? Don't you remember Donne's *Valediction against Mourning*?'

'Donne? Whoever is he?' asked Daphne, puzzled by what seemed to her an irrelevance.

'A delightful person. One of the best of the Elizabethans,' Patricia answered, and began to quote, half tenderly, half in demure amusement:

> 'Dull, sublunary lovers' love,
>   Whose soul is sense, cannot admit
> Of absence, 'cause it doth remove
>   The thing which elemented it.
>
> But we by a love so far refined,
>   That ourselves know not what it is,
> Inter-assured of the mind,
>   Care less eyes, lips, and hands to miss.'

She stopped suddenly, checked by the look of pain on Daphne's face. Just so Daphne had looked at her coachings, she remembered, when it had been necessary to snub her, and she was feeling humiliated. Vividly she recalled Virginia's account of Sylvester's proposal, and her theory that his marriage to Daphne had resulted from an impulse of passionate reaction. Probably Daphne had realised that

173

by now, though, as Patricia knew, she would be the last person to admit it to anyone. Virginia had certainly suggested that Daphne was lonely and unhappy, that things between her and Sylvester were going wrong. Angrily Patricia chid herself for being so absorbed by her love for Stephanoff, which had made her forget that a sorrow's crown of sorrow is not so much remembering happier things as the sight of a joy that one has wept and prayed for in the possession of another. With a rueful glance at Daphne she said lightly: 'What nonsense I'm talking, aren't I! Getting engaged at thirty seems to make one even more self-centred than one would have been at twenty. And I really came to see you, not to talk about myself. . . . Is it to be a girl, Daphne – and shall you send her to Drayton?'

Daphne folded her hands and looked earnestly at Patricia. 'Oh, it must be a girl – it must, it must! I shouldn't know in the least what to do with a boy. But as for sending her to Drayton – I don't know.'

'I shall – if ever I have a daughter,' said Patricia. 'But my wants are quite different from yours. If I must have children – and I suppose I must, though the prospect doesn't attract me at present – I should like them to be sons. Imagine the responsibility of a daughter with Alexis' temperament! Drayton wouldn't be large enough to hold her!'

'Don't you think,' Daphne began slowly, 'that people go to places like Drayton when they're much too inexperienced? I mean it seems to me that you ought to have learnt wisdom before you ever go there, or else you find that you're faced with problems that you've no idea how to solve. And because you can't, you try to make everybody think you can, and consequently find yourself worried by all kinds of people who misunderstand you as much as you misunderstand them.'

Patricia looked at her as intently as Virginia had done.

'You know, you were at Drayton at a very difficult time,' she said, after a moment's reflection. 'For two years after the war Oxford was full of people who were either suffering from reaction, which made them despise work, or from the aftermath of sorrow, which made them despise play. The majority of both men and women were upset by passions and emotions which aren't at all conspicuous at a university in ordinary times. Most students must have found it hard to keep a normal point of view.'

'It wasn't only the problems, but the problematic people,' said Daphne. 'Now take Virginia Dennison. She was a kind of bogey to me all the time I was at Drayton. Whenever I tried to do anything she made it seem as if it wasn't worth while. She never failed in anything she did, and people – especially struggling people – seemed to count so little with her in comparison with her own successes. And yet all the time she can't have thought much of them. Look how little use they can possibly be to her now, in this new life she's chosen. Miss O'Neill, why did she give up everything she was doing so brilliantly and go to that hospital to train as a nurse, which anybody can do?'

A reflection crossed Patricia's mind and she half smiled. 'Once,' she said, 'I made a similar remark to yours, and Virginia challenged it immediately; she said that just what was wrong with the nursing profession was the idea that anybody could nurse, and it was up to people like herself to create the impression that anybody shouldn't. And the first time I wrote to her about it, telling her I thought she must be mad and that she ought to give it up at once, she sent me an answer which made no reference to my letter till quite at the end. And that was only an ambiguous postscript which said something like this: "If sometimes what I'm doing disappoints you, remember I have only one great enemy, and that's my own intellect."

Apart from those two little things I know no more about her sudden resolution to be a nurse than you do. Virginia Dennison interests me tremendously, but I've always found her a puzzle, and I suppose I always shall.'

'What a strange thing to say about her intellect,' meditated Daphne. 'She can't have been as ambitious as I thought, after all.'

'On the other hand,' said Patricia, 'she may have chosen as she has just because she was.'

'But how do you mean?' queried Daphne, mystified.

But Patricia only smiled and made no attempt to explain.

Daphne seemed to be alone for hours after Patricia departed. The sound of Sylvester's key in the door roused her from a doze into which she had involuntarily fallen, and she got up yawning from the sofa to see with surprise that the hands of the clock pointed to one.

'How late you are, Raymond!' she exclaimed as he came in. 'I must have been dozing or something; I never realised it was as much as one o'clock.'

He started violently when he saw her, and sleepy as her eyes were she fancied for a moment that a furtive, half-guilty look passed across his face.

'Good Lord! You up still! Why on earth didn't you go to bed at the proper time?'

'Well, you didn't tell me you were going to be late. I would have gone to bed, only I was expecting you to come in at any minute.'

'How perfectly absurd – as if a man couldn't do something on the spur of the moment just because he hadn't let his wife know it was possible. I – happened to meet a friend at the opera, and we went out to supper afterwards. If ever I'm late again you mustn't dream of sitting up. It makes me feel so damned tied.'

He offered no further explanation of his lateness. There

didn't seem any point in mentioning that it was Lucia Farretti with whom he had had supper, especially as Daphne appeared to have no inclination to question him.

'Of course I'd have gone to bed if only I'd known,' she protested. 'But you've never stayed out after the opera before, so I suppose I just didn't think of it.'

How ridiculous of her to have had that mean, contemptible suspicion! If Patricia hadn't emphasised her trust in Stephanoff so much, the idea would never have entered her head. As she undressed she repeated to herself the phrase Patricia had quoted, 'Inter-assured of the mind.' Why, of course she was!

But only the shadow of death chills more than the first breath of suspicion. Daphne's fears were awake again a fortnight later, when Sylvester went once more to the Orpheum in spite of her entreaties to him to spend the evening with her. He had been several times to the opera since Patricia's visit, and Daphne, who still told herself that his love of Italian music made his neglect of her quite comprehensible, would never have attempted to prevent him from going had she not been feeling unusually ill and apprehensive that night.

All the same she had been rather unreasonable, she told herself, as she lay back in the big arm-chair, hot and thirsty, but too tired to get up and pour out a glass of water for herself. She oughtn't to expect Raymond to stay at home when he wanted to go to the opera, just because she would be obliged to suffer a little for the next few weeks. She was altogether too impatient, she told herself; after all, it was nearly the end of June now, and there were less than two months to wait. Raymond had been quite kind for once too; he actually hadn't seemed annoyed with her when she couldn't help asking him to stay. At least he had promised not to be late this time, as he had been on one or

177

two occasions since that evening when she fell asleep on the sofa.

It might have been some little satisfaction to her to know how heavily that promise was weighing on Sylvester's mind as he listened to Nedda's love duet with Harlequin, and cursed himself for making it when he might have known how irresistible Lucia would be in *Pagliacci*. It was a pity that Daphne could not know, for she obtained no other kind of satisfaction. As the clock crept on to half-past eleven, to twelve, and slowly to one, she paced restlessly up and down the dining-room, half distraught with uneasiness, her growing doubts mingled with lonely fears of her coming travail. Had he met that friend again and gone to supper with him? With *him*? Who was that friend? Did Raymond meet him at the opera? Did he really go to the opera at all, or was it only an excuse to see – whom?

She did not know. Nor could the only voice in the room, that of the solemn ticking clock, tell her that just at the moment that she asked herself those questions, Raymond stood in a little luxurious boudoir she had never seen, holding passionately in his arms a woman she had forgotten – a woman whose face for a few moments had seemed inexplicably familiar, and then vanished out of her overcrowded memory. No wind hurrying through the night brought to her an echo of the fierce burning words on her husband's lips – 'I'm not going till you've promised. God, Lucia – you're Love, you're Life – all that I ache for, body and soul, all that I never get. . . .'

Fatigue at last conquered Daphne's misery, and her shrinking fear of Sylvester's indignation, if he suddenly returned and found her still up, forced her to undress quickly and get into bed. In spite of herself she fell heavily asleep; her body's insistent demands, denied for hours, were too strong even for her apprehensions.

It was three o'clock when Sylvester stood beside her bed, holding a candle above her sleeping face. He cursed her in his heart as she lay there, worn out and weary with the burden of his child, because he felt certain that he would never have betrayed her if she had been different. She had only what she was to thank for his infidelity. He did not curse himself, for he was not one of those who begin to dig up their conscience to see how it is getting on as soon as they have buried it deep in the primitive earth. He sought no way for repentance, for he had no real wish to find one. The forbidden fruit was too sweet.

Chapter XVII

The 'At Home'

Sylvester sat in the office of Lord Wintermere, the Minister of Arbitration. He was excited but a little overwhelmed by the splendid opportunity which had come to him just at the wrong moment. It seemed very hard to have to make up one's mind so quickly. But the beginning of July was already here; the European Commission on the Relation of Disarmament to Economic Conditions in the Far East had to leave in a fortnight, and of course the British Representative was bound to go with them. Lord Wintermere, who, apart from a strong personal liking for Sylvester, had long considered him the most promising of the younger men in the Ministry of Arbitration, continued to persuade him to represent Great Britain on the Commission.

'Of course we've got Johnson – he's a good man and would do the work thoroughly and conscientiously, I know. But it's really you I should like to see as our representative. The job would make your name, too; it's just the kind of experience you ought to have before I can bring your name forward for the Secretaryship to the Ministry.'

Sylvester started.

'The Secretaryship, sir? But surely Morland's not leaving the Ministry, is he?'

'Not just yet – or I shouldn't be sending you away even

for a short time. But his health's breaking up; he told me the other day his heart was worse and he didn't think he could stand the job for more than another year or so. He's been valuable to me – very valuable indeed; I shall be exceedingly sorry to lose him. But I've had you in my mind as his successor for some time now. Of course we ought to find you a seat in the House before we offer you the appointment, but that can wait, that can wait. The first essential is the diplomatic experience; when you have had that we can begin to keep an eye on the by-elections.'

Sylvester got up impulsively.

'It's more than good of you to tell me all this, sir. You don't know how I wish I could accept straight away. I would, if it weren't for just one thing.'

'Well, what's the trouble? We're not asking you to go abroad for ever; the work can't take more than twelve months at most.'

Sylvester hesitated, embarrassed.

'I know. It's nothing to do with the length of time I should have to be away.'

He reflected miserably how damned inopportune things always were for him. In spite of himself he was beginning now to feel Daphne as a weight on his conscience, as well as a thorn in his side. Of course a man couldn't be expected to keep anything so absurdly exacting as his marriage vows when he had to live with someone so inadequate, so irritating to a sensitive temperament. There was some excuse for what he'd done already, but what would people say if they found out that he'd left her at a critical time as well? And then, what a beastly scene she'd make if he even suggested it! People like Daphne made everything so unnecessarily complicated. Now if he'd been dealing with Virginia – but then Virginia would never have been an irritation to his nerves or a burden on his conscience. Or if it had been

Lucia? He could never separate those two in his mind. Lucia's kisses were not quite like Virginia's would have been – nothing ever could be – but they were certainly the next best thing. But Lord Wintermere's questioning glance demanded an explanation.

'It's because of my wife, sir,' Sylvester said at last. 'Unfortunately she's expecting a child – our first, you know – and it doesn't seem quite fair to leave her just now.'

'I see. That's awkward,' Lord Wintermere agreed. 'But surely even in such circumstances Mrs Sylvester wouldn't wish to be a hindrance to your career?'

'No – no – of course not,' Sylvester murmured uncomfortably.

'You're not obliged to decide now, you know,' the Minister added persuasively. 'You need not join the Commissioners in Paris for about ten days, and as far as we're concerned all your arrangements can be made in twelve hours. Talk it over with your wife and let me know what you've decided later. I can give you a week to think about it if you like – though of course, the sooner you make up your mind the better.'

'By the way,' he continued affably, as Sylvester thanked him for the respite, and rose to depart, 'it's really very remiss of me not to have made a point of meeting Mrs Sylvester before this. My wife tells me she's charming, and I am really most anxious to make her acquaintance. We both have a free afternoon to-morrow; would she have any objection, do you think, if we looked her up for tea? In fact Anne could go along and have a talk with her first, and perhaps you'd allow me to accompany you home at half-past four?'

'Certainly, sir. It's most kind – Daphne will be delighted,' fervently answered Sylvester, who knew quite well that she would not, but was determined to lose no opportunity

182

of propitiating Lord Wintermere after his hesitation in accepting the post of Commissioner.

'Good!' Lord Wintermere turned again to his desk. 'I'll tell Anne. Let Mrs Sylvester know we shall look forward to seeing her. And mind you bring me the right answer in a few days' time, Sylvester – in a few days' time.'

Sylvester walked back to Victoria Street, troubled and impatient. He reproached himself bitterly now for the unforeseeing stupidity which had allowed him to marry Daphne on that impulse of fierce indignation with Virginia. Even if he did need a wife he could surely by waiting have found someone much more suitable; Daphne had been nothing but an impediment right from the beginning – she couldn't even keep herself occupied without worrying him, or entertain his friends successfully – though he was determined that whatever happened she should give his chief a suitable reception. And now, just when the great opportunity of his career was presenting itself, he couldn't accept it without having to feel a brute. And, as if things weren't bad enough, the Verdi Company at the Orpheum were giving their last performance to-morrow night, and in a few days' time they would go back to Milan. And after that what of Lucia? What if her contract did come to an end when the company left London – how could he manage to see her again, let alone as often as he wanted? His heart was like lead within him at the thought. Life was altogether too full just now, full of things that were all going wrong together.

He decided as he walked up the few stairs that led to their second-floor flat that he would say nothing to Daphne about the position that had been offered him till after she had met Lord Wintermere. The appointment of the Commission was not yet public knowledge, and he felt sure that if he mentioned the subject to Daphne beforehand, her usual want of tact would lead her to discuss it with Lord Wintermere over the tea-table. She might even get hysterical, damn her, and think she could persuade the Minister to offer the job to someone else. If only she weren't such a limpet, always wanting him to be with her, instead of being a little more ambitious on his behalf! He was so certain that she was not ambitious that it never occurred to him to ask her.

'By the way,' he said, sitting comfortably in his arm-chair while Daphne handed him his tea, 'Lord and Lady Wintermere are coming in to-morrow afternoon.'

'To-morrow!' Daphne looked distressed and a little frightened. 'Oh, Raymond, you did promise me no one else need come here till after baby was born!'

'I can't help it if I did. As a matter of fact it was Wintermere himself who suggested coming here, and you ought to feel jolly well honoured that he wants to meet you – as he says he does.'

'I am – I am,' faltered Daphne, though she thought she might quite well have been spared this honour until the autumn. 'It's only that I wasn't expecting to have to entertain anyone so important, just for the present.'

'I can't help it,' Sylvester repeated irritably. 'It's not my fault he asked to come, and it would have been damned ungracious to refuse when he went out of his way to propose it.'

'Oh, I know. It's all right, really. I don't mind having one or two people to tea, quite quietly.'

'Er – well!' Sylvester handed her his cup for more tea, 'we can't exactly receive a person like Wintermere in the same informal way we'd have someone who doesn't count – one of your college friends, for instance. We must make some sort of an effort to entertain him properly.'

Daphne's heart sank.

'Well, what exactly do you want me to do?' she inquired.

'Oh, nothing much. Just a little "At Home," you know. We can't have anything elaborate at such short notice, but we must get one or two suitable people here to meet Wintermere. I'll ask Irwin and Saunders from the Ministry; I know they're free to-morrow. And you'd better ring up one or two of your lady friends say – Mrs Archer and Miss Dawson.'

'Oh, very well, I will,' said Daphne wearily. The prospect of a visit from Lord Wintermere would once have excited her tremendously, but now she could feel nothing but self-consciousness and apprehension. Nevertheless she realised, far better than Sylvester knew, how much depended on the continuation of Lord Wintermere's favour. So the next morning she made a real effort to prepare adequately for her guests, whose total Sylvester's suggestions had raised to ten.

She had just overheated herself thoroughly by making scones, and was in the midst of cutting sandwiches, while her maid put out the best china, when Virginia Dennison appeared unexpectedly.

Virginia had been to Victoria Street several times since Daphne had met her in front of Marshall's, and the two were drifting into a strange friendship which scrupulously avoided all intimate and disturbing topics. Virginia generally chose the afternoon for her visits, and Daphne was surprised to see her as early as eleven.

'Hallo! Whatever are all these preparations?' inquired Virginia, who had followed the maid into the kitchen.

'I'm having a little "At Home" this afternoon,' Daphne explained. 'Lord and Lady Wintermere are coming to tea, and Raymond didn't think we could have anyone so important without getting in one or two people to meet them.'

Virginia's face betrayed no little concern as she looked

Daphne up and down. Daphne's cheeks were certainly rather flushed, but she had deep rings round her eyes, and the hands that cut the sandwiches were trembling. She really didn't look fit to undertake an 'At Home,' Virginia thought.

'What bad luck having to bother with them just now!' she said at length, thinking how like Sylvester it was to expect Daphne to entertain his friends whether she wanted to or not. 'Couldn't Mr Sylvester have waited till your troubles were over?'

'It wasn't Raymond's fault at all,' Daphne answered immediately and a little indignantly. 'Lord Wintermere told him he wanted to come, and Raymond couldn't very well refuse, could he? It just can't be helped, and I don't mind really; it's only a bit of an effort.'

Virginia made no further comment. She thought regretfully that she had little right to criticise a situation which was largely of her making.

'I expect you're surprised to see me at this time of day,' she said, 'but I couldn't have my usual afternoon because I'm going on leave to-morrow.'

'Going on leave!' Daphne exclaimed, aghast. 'Oh, Virginia, how long are you going for?'

'Only for three weeks,' Virginia replied. 'I didn't expect a holiday yet, but if I don't take it now it means that another nurse can't have hers when the man she's engaged to comes home from abroad. As it is, though, I shall still be back in good time – for you, I mean, of course.'

Daphne looked immensely relieved.

'Oh, that's all right. I hate having to do without seeing you now, even for three weeks, but that doesn't matter so much. I mean, you don't know how I've come to depend on your being in London when—'

'I do know.' Virginia's answer was full of understanding.

She had asked and been told nothing more than she had learnt from Daphne on the day that they met in Oxford Street. But her own observation had since taught her all that she needed to know of Daphne's loneliness, and of the terror which increased as August approached, though she tried to control it with a courage that surprised Virginia. It was her own doing, Virginia told herself bitterly, that Daphne had need of such courage, and she would be glad to make whatever amends she could.

'What time do you go to-morrow?' Daphne asked. 'Can't you possibly come and say good-bye first?'

'Yes, I think I can. In fact, I meant to ask you if you'd like me to. But I don't get off till two, and to-morrow's Saturday. Your husband comes home from the Ministry early, doesn't he?'

'Yes, but he's arranged to play tennis at Hendon to-morrow afternoon. So do come and see me before you go. As it happens I've promised to let my maid go out directly after lunch to see a friend in hospital, so I'd better give you the spare latchkey. I've got into such a habit of falling asleep lately while I'm lying down, and I mightn't hear you knock.'

She opened a drawer in the kitchen table and handed Virginia the spare key in a case.

'Ethel often uses it – but she can quite well do without it to-morrow.'

'Thanks very much,' said Virginia, pocketing the key. 'My train doesn't go till after six, so if you're asleep I'll come straight in without disturbing you. Au revoir.'

She let herself out of the front door, and Daphne, who had finished the sandwiches, went to help her maid to get ready the best silver tray.

By the time that her first guests arrived that afternoon her nervousness and the morning's preparations had reduced her to a state of complete physical exhaustion. She was only too thankful that Lady Wintermere, a tall, spare woman with the weather-beaten face, loud voice and hearty manner common to so many who 'take up' social work, appeared to have eyes for no one but Mrs Archer, who arrived at the same time. Daphne judged from their conversation that they had spent the morning at an overheated committee meeting, whose problems they continued to thrash out while she made the tea.

'Really, I think it was disgraceful the way Mrs Macdonald went on about that five pounds ten! One feels quite humiliated, you know, at having to associate with a person—'

Their voices seemed to come to Daphne from very far away. But she did not care how long they went on; she was grateful for the respite that their argument afforded.

The respite ended as soon as Sylvester entered with the Minister of Arbitration. Daphne's drawing-room was not small, but the Minister seemed to fill it entirely with his large, genial presence and smooth, pink face, that made her think of all the advertisements of Pears' Soap that she had ever seen. Apparently he wished to atone for his former neglect by never leaving her side. If only she could think of something sensible to say in answer to his 'Well, Mrs Sylvester, this is indeed a pleasure – a pleasure I've been looking forward to for some time. Remiss of me not to have come before – very remiss indeed. But we Arbitration people are so busy nowadays. . . .' After all, she felt quite thankful that he seemed so unlikely to stop talking. Her tired brain absolutely refused to work.

The remainder of the ten guests drifted in soon after Sylvester had arrived with Lord Wintermere. How hot and stuffy the room felt when they were all in it! And what ages it took to give them all their tea. July really wasn't a suitable month for an 'At Home.'

When the maid had handed round the tea-cups and every-one was supplied with something to eat, Daphne found herself standing on the hearthrug with Lord Wintermere. He was still talking affably about the weather – the flat – her drawing-room – the Ministry – and fortunately appeared quite able to continue without requiring an answer. Daphne felt helplessly that she was not doing justice to Raymond. She must really try to make herself more interesting to Lord Wintermere – but she did wish that she could sit down first. She looked anxiously round, but all the chairs in the room were occupied. Raymond was quite near to her, sitting in the big arm-chair, but he was so busy talking to Mrs Archer that he never saw her look of desperate appeal.

What was Lord Wintermere saying? Oh yes – 'The other day I met one of the Japanese delegates from the last Assembly of the League of Nations, and he told me—'

What exactly was it that the Japanese delegate had told Lord Wintermere? That teacups in Japan were being made so much bigger now than they used to be before the war – no, surely that couldn't be it? All the same her tea-cup *was* a very big one. In fact it was not only big, but was rapidly growing bigger. Daphne watched it, fascinated, while the rest of the room behind it seemed to grow quite vague and unimportant. Lord Wintermere's voice was coming to her now from an immense distance. Desperately she tried to hear what he was saying. 'But the view taken in China on the subject of artillery—'

It seemed absurd to talk about a view when hers was almost blotted out by the teacup, which was getting enor-mous, colossal, altogether too heavy for her to hold. . . . It was not a cup at all, but a huge abyss full of tea, yawning wide at her feet, ready to receive her when she could stand no longer on the quaking floor. . . . And she must fall – she couldn't keep her balance any more with everything about her rocking like a ship at sea. . . . She clutched out wildly to save herself, but there was nothing to hold except the hot, slippery sides of the cup. Frantically struggling, she toppled headlong into it. The tea rose up all round her, enveloping her in warm, black waves.

The tea's real destination had been the beautiful white spats and polished patent-leather boots of the Minister of Arbitration, whose embarrassed arms had perforce received Daphne in her sudden descent towards the hearthrug. The drawing-room which she had arranged so carefully that morning instantly became a scene of solicitous confusion. Someone rang the bell violently. Two or three women went out after Daphne as Lord Wintermere, assisted by the maid, carried her along the passage to her bedroom. The strained silence which followed was broken by the raucous whispering of Lady Wintermere.

'Of course – poor young thing – of course! Such an undertaking for her just *now*!' she commented in a loud undertone. 'I know just how she must have felt – we've all had our little troubles, haven't we?' she added, turning to her next-door neighbour, an irreproachable spinster of mature years with a post on the Board of Education.

'I beg your pardon. I'm afraid I don't altogether understand you,' replied the spinster rather distantly, sitting up stiffly in her chair.

Sylvester, who had followed Daphne with inward rage in his heart, now returned to the drawing-room, assuming with difficulty the expected attitude of polite concern.

'Oh, quite all right now, thank you. A hot day, you know – just a little fainting attack. I'm only so sorry that you—'

'Not at all – not at all – poor thing, we're so concerned – ought not to have come . . . Yes, we're going at once now, of course – thank you so much. . . .'

The female chorus answered him in a vague buzz. The male element had already grouped itself round the doorway in huddled embarrassment. Sylvester, a strained smile distorting his countenance, stood fuming on the threshold and watched them go down the stairs. Then he returned to the drawing-room, and bade the alarmed servant straighten up the room and stop exciting herself about nothing. When she had gone he stood staring out of the window with tight lips and angry, clenched hands.

At last he made up his mind to go in to Daphne, who lay weak and apologetic behind the down-drawn blinds of her bedroom. 'Are you feeling any better?' he asked abruptly, and then cursed under his breath as he stumbled over the foot of the bed-post in the dimness, violently shaking the bed, and Daphne with it. Daphne, every nerve on edge, burst immediately into sobs.

'Oh, Raymond! I can't tell you how sorry I am! I'd no idea I was going to do anything like that, or I'd have made an excuse and gone out of the room – I would indeed! Whatever will Lord Wintermere think of me! Making you look so silly too. Oh, I shall never forgive myself – I shan't really. . . .'

'Don't talk such absurd nonsense,' Sylvester broke in abruptly. 'What's done's done – it's no use going on about it now. For God's sake, stop crying, or you'll only make yourself worse.'

'I'm all right now – really I am. I shall be quite well again to-morrow,' sobbed Daphne, but Sylvester, too thoroughly exasperated to remain with her any longer, went out of the shadowed room, closing the door sharply upon her words. Feeling his sense of humiliation absolutely unendurable, he helped himself to a strong whisky-and-soda. Under its welcome stimulus he suddenly remembered that Lucia Farretti was singing that evening in the last performance of *Carmen*.

This ghastly business with Daphne had actually put it right out of his head, and now he supposed he really oughtn't to leave her. Things had come to a pretty pass when a man was left to deal with these women's matters!

He went along the passage to Daphne's room and stood outside, looking irresolutely at the door. But the faint sound of a smothered sob from within decided him. Seizing his hat, he strode down the stairs and out into the street.

Daphne, listening apprehensively in the semi-darkness, heard the brief stir of his departure. Then, bitterly ashamed, she buried her head in the pillow and cried herself into an exhausted sleep.

Chapter XVIII

The Dark Tide

That morning at the Ministry had been simply damnable – there was no other word for it. Sylvester shook off his solicitous friends with difficulty, and strode angrily back to lunch. He had not spoken to Daphne before he left home; she had been asleep when he got up, and then had had her breakfast in bed. But not for a single instant had he been allowed to forget her. As if it wasn't bad enough that she had let him down like that yesterday afternoon, without his having to be bombarded all morning with embarrassing inquiries about her health! He might have known she'd upset him somehow or other, just when he already had so many worries that he didn't know what to do. He was no nearer a decision about the Commission, for of course it had been impossible yesterday to speak to her about anything, and it would be worse than ever to attempt to make her see reason when she was in this worked-up state. And then, last night, it had been absolutely hopeless trying to get anything out of Lucia. She simply would not tell him what she was going to do, though he had practically gone down on his knees before her. He felt he'd almost have gone out of his mind if he weren't seeing her to-night. And, thank God, he had that game of tennis with Villers this afternoon – it would get him away from Daphne and the flat at any rate. And it might clear his brain a bit – help to put him in a better frame of mind. Anyhow, he couldn't possibly feel much worse about things than he did at present.

His temper was not improved by the cold, brief lunch which Daphne had arranged, because she had given her maid permission to go out early to visit a sick friend in a hospital on the outskirts of London. Her white, mournful face on the other side of the table made him feel more irritable than ever, and throughout the meal he maintained a sullen silence. But when the table was cleared and the maid had departed he said petulantly:

'That girl's always going out! This flat seems to be run entirely for her benefit. You think far more about her comfort than you do about mine.'

'One's got to be considerate with only one servant,' apologised Daphne. 'I can't expect her to stop indoors all day. Besides, she wouldn't stay if I did.'

'Why on earth don't you keep two then? Your income's capable of expanding, if mine isn't. Your people would give you the extra in a minute.'

Daphne looked at him with reproachful eyes.

'Oh, Raymond! You know how I hate asking them for money! Besides, I don't know where we could put another if we had one – especially as we've got to have a nurse so soon.'

Sylvester threw himself into the arm-chair to smoke a pipe before he went out.

'Oh, all right! I suppose it's no earthly use arguing with anyone so infernally obstinate as you are. And, anyhow, I've got more than enough to think about without being bothered with these beastly domestic details.'

Daphne sat down in the chair on the other side of the hearthrug and watched him as he smoked. His face wore its now familiar expression of lowering discontent, and after a few moments' silence she felt that she could bear it no longer. He had never even come in that morning to ask her how she was before he went to the Ministry. It was dreadful to think that he hadn't forgiven her yet for being so stupid yesterday afternoon! She *must* make him say that he forgave her before he went out to tennis. She couldn't wait for a whole afternoon and evening, after all the humiliation she had suffered since yesterday on his account.

She crossed the hearthrug and, kneeling down beside his chair, began to caress his hand.

'Raymond – I know I'm an absolute fool – I ought to have realised my own limitations better. I ought to have told you I wasn't feeling well before those people came, but I really did think I could get through all right. After all I *was* doing my best to please you, and I can't bear your displeasure – I simply can't bear it any longer. Won't you just say you forgive me before you go out?'

Sylvester pushed away her hand as if it had been a tiresome insect.

'Look here, Daphne, I simply can't start listening to explanations now. It's time I went to get changed—'

He tried to rise from the arm-chair, but Daphne restrained him with clinging, tremulous hands.

'Oh, but, Raymond, you don't know how awful it's been all morning wondering what you'd say when you came in! I can't let you go off for the whole afternoon without a word – you must say something – something—'

Thoroughly irritated by the hysterical note in her voice, he shook her off and said roughly: 'For God's sake, don't begin to make a scene! Isn't it bad enough that you made a thorough mess of things yesterday, without going on snivelling about it afterwards? It makes me absolutely sick.'

Daphne sank back on her knees, deeply wounded by this contemptuous rejection of her apology. She needed all her control for her growing hysteria, and as she fought with herself, the temper that Drayton used to know but Sylvester had never yet experienced began to rise in spite of her desire to propitiate him.

'If you'd any consideration for me you wouldn't talk like that!' she protested plaintively. 'Anyone with a scrap of feeling would have been sorry for me, but you never showed me the slightest bit of sympathy – you went off last night and left me all alone. I really was feeling ill yesterday, and I only tried to keep up because of you. And, after all, it's your child—'

'I wish to heaven it wasn't!' broke in Sylvester, suddenly enraged by her unwonted complaints. 'I never wanted the beastly kid from the beginning. You've made me feel a fool often enough without that, and ever since you knew the kid was coming it's been nothing but an excuse for letting me down over and over again! Every time I want to create a good impression with anybody you somehow go and make me look ridiculous. You began directly after we were married – making a laughing-stock of me at those hotels with your childish remarks about everything. I meant the woman I married to help my career socially. It's the least thing you could have tried to do – and instead of that you've done your best to ruin it at every turn with your damned clumsiness and want of tact.'

Daphne, her last faint hopes of reconciliation absolutely shattered by his rage, broke into loud sobs.

'How can you talk like that when you know I've always done my best to help you?' she gasped, as the tears streamed down her cheeks. 'I've tried and tried to please you ever since we were married, and you've done nothing but trample on everything I ever tried to do! I wanted to write – I wanted to understand your work – I've tried to entertain your friends when I simply hated having them, because I felt ill and knew I was looking my worst. And after all that you tell me I've done my best to ruin you! If you really cared for me you couldn't say such things!'

'Care for you!' broke in Sylvester, roused by her tears to a fresh outburst of wrath. 'Care for you! That's just it! I never really did. You've bored me stiff right from the beginning, ever since before we were married! Any woman with a scrap of penetration would have seen I didn't care long ago, and have left me alone.'

He stopped, for Daphne had gone absolutely white, and was staring at him with her mouth open and her eyes starting out of her head. Then she stood up, holding on to the mantelpiece as though she would fall if she let it go.

'Never – loved – me!' she gasped out slowly. 'Raymond – oh, Raymond – you don't mean that! What about those coachings, when you said—'

Her voice failed and he interrupted her coldly:

'I mean it. I never loved you. I didn't intend to tell you now, but you've made me do it. It's all your own fault.'

Suddenly losing her control completely she flushed scarlet all over her face and neck, and broke forth, her words rising into a shriek at the end: 'Take that back – you must take it back! You don't know what you're saying! You just want to hurt me – you're cruel – cruel – cruel!'

Her violent hysteria drove Sylvester to a point of fury beyond all realisation but the sudden certainty that there was only one solution for his problems. Quite unable to bear the scene any longer, he sprang out of his chair and shouted at her: 'Stop that noise, damn you! You'll have all the people in from the other flats! I tell you I mean it – and what's more, I've finished with you! I married you to help and understand me, and you've done neither! You've hindered me at every turn as well as boring me beyond endurance! I can't stand it any longer, and I'm not going to – because I've found someone who does help and who does understand. I don't want you any more and I do want her – and I'm going to her, too – going for good . . .'

Daphne, almost beside herself, seized his arm and clung to him as he made a movement towards the door.

'Raymond, stay – oh, stay! Forgive me – I'm ashamed – I didn't mean to behave like that! At least stay with me now; don't leave me – please don't leave me; wait until our child comes. You can't go away just now – you can't, you can't . . .'

Sylvester tried furiously to free himself from her grasp.

'Damn you, let go! . . . I can and will. I've done with you, I tell you! Go back to your Manchester relations if you must snivel to someone. They've got money enough to support you and half-a-dozen kids. I don't want you – and I'm going.'

He moved swiftly towards the door, but she threw herself frantically in front of him. Quite past speech, she stood facing him, barring his passage, with the door handle in her hand. It was then that the last remnant of self-control forsook him. With a furious oath he seized her by the shoulders and flung her out of his way. Regardless of consequences, he rushed into the hall, seized his stick, and went out, banging the front door behind him. Daphne, taken unawares by the sudden roughness of his clutch, swayed for a second, staggering backwards in the vain effort to regain her balance. Then she crashed down against the fender, striking her head and her left side as she fell. . . .

The next sound that she was conscious of was the furious buzzing of a fly against the window-pane. Buzz – buzz – it was struggling violently in the effort to escape. The sound came nearer – nearer – grew louder – louder. Then at last she realised that the buzzing was not at the window at all, but in her own head.

She opened her eyes upon the still, sunlit room. She knew then that she was lying on her back beside the fireplace, and made a tremendous effort to sit up. But as soon as she moved the floor and the ceiling began to roll about, gathering themselves together to push her over if she tried to stand. How queer and stiff she felt, and what was the matter with her face? Something hot and sticky was trickling down her neck, but somehow she could not manage to put up her hand to wipe it away. What had been happening? Could she really recollect some dreadful quarrel that had arisen between her and Raymond. Or was that only something she had dreamed while she had been sleeping in this queer position on the floor?

And then, as she strove confusedly to remember, a terrible pain, such as she had never felt before, smote through her body like a sword. Its sudden agony roused her dulled senses to consciousness, and even while she cried aloud in the effort to bear it, the horror of that last scene with Raymond came back upon her in full force. She went over it in her fevered mind, word by word, moment by moment. But long before her memory had reached the end the pain, fierce and insistent, gripped her violently again.

And in that instant she realised that her hour had come – come with a horror of dreadful darkness such as she had never pictured even in her worst imaginings. Frantically she shrieked aloud: 'Raymond – Raymond – Raymond!' But no sound answered her, beyond the distant rattle of a motor-bus, and the drowsy murmur of summer wind in a back street. Then she caught sight of the bell at the corner of the mantelpiece above her head. She struggled and twisted herself against the fender in the effort to reach it, till the floor once more gathered itself up in a heap to strike her face, and the terrible new pain descended upon her, threatening to swamp her in hot, stifling blackness.

199

And even as she discovered that she could not reach the bell, she remembered that the maid was out and would not be back for hours.

After she had realised that she was alone she lay quite still, gripping the hearthrug with her hands in the effort to think and endure.

This, then, was the end of all her striving! The end, because everything had gone. Raymond had gone and so had his love for her; he had made her realise it at last. And because all along she had understood him better than she had allowed herself to admit, she knew that he would not come back. She knew that he was not of those who, having once committed themselves, turn again with courage to face the consequences of their act.

Yes, he was gone; and very soon she would be gone too. The crisis was coming swiftly – swiftly – and there was no one to help her. But what did it really matter, now that Raymond's love for her was dead?

Dead! Had it ever lived? Beckoning images from the past crowded upon her, dreadful in their new enlightenment. Those walks at Oxford when he had so often snubbed her – that day in Eights Week when he had seemed almost ashamed of her, after all the efforts she had made to get her work done and go on his barge. And then his silence at the theatre afterwards – his preoccupation with something that he did not condescend to explain, although he kissed her good-night afterwards at the gate .... (Oh, if only this pain need not go on too long! If only it would get over quickly she might bear it, but if not ...)

She remembered how he had come to Thorbury Park before the wedding, and with what barely concealed impatience he had endured those introductions to her relations. And he had been so curt and dictatorial about the flat, hardly seeming to care whether she approved of his arrangements or not – though she always did approve, of course. Why of course? Why had it been a kind of tacit understanding that he was conferring a favour upon her by marrying her? Could he really have taken up that attitude if he had loved her?

He had not loved her. He could never have really cared, he who was brilliant and impatient, while she was so stupid and clumsy, so irritating and flamboyant. She knew it now, though her memory had travelled onward to her wedding morning, when she lay on her back in the wood, and gazed up into a mosaic of green leaves and golden light. Life had seemed so glad then, and so gay, like the full tide of a summer sea, coming in with sunshine and blue skies. But she had been quite wrong. Life was not the full sea flood, but a dark tide, moaning and desolate, going out in storm and rain. And as it ebbed its black waves engulfed her, drew her with them, and carried her out to sea – a sea of indescribable agony. . . .

Her pain-stabbed recollection had passed on now to her honeymoon. Mosquitoes . . . the Dante festival . . . archaeology . . . cypresses . . . a black and white cathedral in a square on the top of a hill. . . . How queerly those Popes were looking down at her – rows and rows of heads peering over a balcony. No – it was not a balcony after all; the recollection of a picture in the *Divine Comedy* she had used at school suddenly made her realise where they were. They were in Purgatory, of course, looking over one of the walls that went round the mountain – though it seemed strange that people like some of the Popes she had read about at college should go even to Purgatory. Still, she supposed that they had got there somehow, for they were far, far above her, miles and miles away. She herself must surely be down in the lowest depths of Hell;

no other place could hold those sullen, flickering fires, that desperate, unspeakable pain . . .

The hot afternoon sunlight, filtering in through half-drawn blinds, lay about the chairs and the floor in strange shapes and patterns. Light and darkness growing into frescoes . . . Calvary . . . the sorrows of Mary . . . the burden of the Saviour. . . . As Daphne struggled in anguish with her failing consciousness, she thought that she saw once more the shadow of a Cross on the wall of the cathedral at Siena. . . .

An hour later Virginia came in and found her there. There was no time then to ask any questions.

Chapter XIX

Wreckage on the Shore

Virginia sat in Daphne's room, reading *The Tale of a Tub* and thinking at the same time. She knew Swift so well that this was quite easy – as easy as carrying on a conversation with an old friend in the midst of absorbing reflections.

Her face bore the traces of some tremendous strain and stress, but there was a sense of repose in her quiet attitude which told of victory at the close of a long struggle. For to-day Daphne, who had been sleeping so peacefully through the afternoon, was out of danger for the first time for three weeks. Virginia, who during those weeks had scarcely left her side, remembered them as she might have remembered a nightmare upon waking. Her leave from hospital ought to have ended that day, but she had obtained another week's extension. She had had to give up part of her Christmas leave in order to get it, but she did not think it worth while to mention this to Daphne.

She had made up her mind to stay in London with Daphne when first she had found her, moaning and with bloodstained face, half-conscious upon the floor. She had only a confused recollection of the rapid horror of events which followed that discovery – the single-handed struggle with one so helpless and agonised, who could only moan in the less intense intervals of suffering that Raymond had deserted her, but no one, no one must know – the desperate telephoning – the frantic, hurried preparations. And then had come the birth of Daphne's son, who now lay beside her, sometimes whining pitifully – the tiny, deformed child, crippled by Daphne's fall, who would have been so much better dead, but had been born, most unhappily, alive. She thought of Daphne's dangerous operation so soon after his birth, the hushed hours of anxiety, the strained, sleepless vigils which she had shared with the other nurse, the fierce fight with death on behalf of one who had lost all interest in the contest.

And in the midst of it all had come that note from Sylvester, posted at Folkestone, which she had kept from Daphne until yesterday. Virginia clenched her hands again in remembrance of the helpless, bitter anger which his words had roused in her.

'I am leaving for Paris to-day. I do not intend ever to see you again. I have accepted a post in the Far East which will keep me abroad for an indefinite period, so it will be quite useless for you to make any attempt to communicate with me.'

The brief message seemed none the less cruel because Sylvester was ignorant of Daphne's danger. He must have known that his treatment of her could not have been without serious effect, but he had not cared; he had not troubled to find out. With supreme indifference he had abandoned Daphne to her fate – and all because she, Virginia Dennison, had once behaved towards him intolerably. Not even the felicities of Swift could drive away the bitter recollection.

And then had come the overwhelming descent of Mrs Lethbridge, followed by her quiet, sorrow-stricken husband. Three weeks of tears, protests, and lamentations, ending with acquiescence ('because of the disgrace') in Daphne's weak pleading for silence concerning Raymond's behaviour. That silence, Virginia reflected, had not been difficult to keep. Dr Mackintosh was a taciturn Scot who asked no inconvenient questions, while Sylvester's departure for Japan was a public event that surprised no one. Most of his acquaintances thought it was hard on him to have to leave his wife just before such a critical time – or was it just after? They really weren't quite sure. A few, perhaps, thought it rather harder on his wife. But none of them concerned themselves very much. Mrs Lethbridge and Virginia were troubled by nothing more than a few polite inquiries, and after a short time even these ceased. The wives and daughters of Sylvester's colleagues in the Ministry had come to Victoria Street chiefly to see Sylvester. They had never been very much interested in Daphne. As a hostess she was unsuccessful and somewhat embarrassing, and their occasional calls upon her had been of a purely formal nature. London is the easiest of places in which to retire from the world. Sylvester's long absence and Daphne's delicate health were soon to release her altogether from the attentions of his political acquaintances.

Virginia put down *The Tale of a Tub* and turned towards the bed, for Daphne had sighed deeply and begun to stir. The last three weeks had dimmed the gold of her hair, brought hollows to her colourless cheeks, and drawn round her mouth deep lines of pain that no time would ever efface. But her sleepy blue eyes met Virginia's with a faint smile. Virginia, casting off the burden of her thoughts, smiled at her in return.

'How do you feel after that long sleep?' she inquired.

Daphne pushed back her hair with a thin, weak hand.

'Better – much better than I've felt at all yet,' she replied. 'Do you know, I really believe I've improved quite a lot since my people went yesterday! Of course they've been so kind to me and so sorry – and yet somehow or other they've been on my nerves a little ever since I came round from the operation and found them there. I can't help thinking that all the time they're feeling I've let them down – especially mother.'

Daphne's impression had not been wrong. Mrs Lethbridge, in spite of herself, had tempered her intense and genuine anxiety with other and more wordly considerations. She behaved towards Daphne with that peculiar embarrassment common to the unimaginative individual in the presence of one whose phase of life has been a failure – an embarrassment which arises partly from the realisation of human helplessness, and partly from uncertainty whether to feel compassionate or exasperated.

'Poor, dear Daphne! It's terrible for her, terrible,' was her mother's instinctive thought. 'And yet, surely there must have been some way of preventing such a disgraceful catastrophe! I should have thought that a daughter of mine would have managed better than this . . .'

Daphne, too, was not quite the Daphne whom she had consistently displayed to Thorbury Park from her cradle to her wedding. Like all those who return to earth after their first meeting face to face with death, Daphne seemed a little apart from those who surrounded her, for she had experienced something about which they had only dreamed and shuddered.

Virginia alone understood the change, for she had faced death vicariously more than once. She knew that there was nothing but physical service to be done for Daphne, nothing to be said, not even very much to be thought. Daphne had to face facts now about which it was useless to argue, or regret, or lament. She could only accept them, and then make of life, with her acceptance as part of it, the best business that she could.

'Virginia,' Daphne began again after a few moments'

silence, 'I've been thinking about him a good deal since you showed me that letter yesterday.'

'I wish I hadn't had it to show to you, Daphne. But I didn't feel I ought to keep it from you any longer.'

'I had to see it,' Daphne said slowly. 'It's a good thing I did, because, you see, I'd been wondering so often, when you thought I was asleep, whether he really meant everything he said. I knew he meant he'd never loved me; I couldn't doubt that any more when I'd thought it out, that time before you came. Only I sometimes felt he might come back, for fear of what people would say. But now he's gone away, I know for certain he can't – at any rate, not yet. And people won't say anything either; they'll think he's left me just because of his work. I don't believe he made that up about going to the Far East. He was thinking of work abroad as long ago as last Christmas.'

'Oh, it's quite genuine! Mr Sylvester's generally very wise in his own interests, though he has occasional bad lapses,' Virginia said bitterly. 'His appointment was in *The Times* a fortnight ago.'

Daphne looked at her sorrowfully.

'How you hate him, Virginia! But I don't think I hate him, even now – at least not always. It's only when I think of Jack' – she locked her fingers tightly together as she looked at the cradle beside her. 'Virginia, when I think of him I want Raymond to pay with an eternity of pain for the wrong he made me do him, for the years he'll have to suffer through no fault of his own. But just sometimes, when I forget Jack for a few moments, then I want Raymond to come back to me on almost any terms, even though I'm sure from what he said that he's got someone else now, someone who means more to him than I ever could.'

Her earnest, questioning eyes met Virginia's as she continued. 'There's one thing I've wanted to ask you ever since it all happened. He said that afternoon that I'd bored him right from the beginning – he said it two or three times, so I can't help feeling he really meant it. Virginia, did *you* realise that I bored him – long ago, I mean, at our coachings, when it all first started? And if I did, can you possibly imagine why he ever wanted to marry me?'

Virginia got up from the chair beside Daphne's bed, and going across to the window stood with her back to the room. Then she answered Daphne abruptly. 'Yes – I know. And I've got to tell you. I don't want to, but I've known for days now that I must. And I suppose you might as well have it soon as late.'

Daphne clasped her hands tightly under the bed-clothes.

'Is there something more to come, then – something I still haven't heard?'

'Yes. I don't know how much it'll hurt you, because I find it hard to believe you can still care anything for a brute like that. I suppose I've no right to call him names, though, because all through those coachings he was in love with me, and when he asked me to marry him the morning of the day he asked you, I behaved abominably, and expressed opinions I'd no business to express.'

She went on determinedly, in spite of a smothered exclamation from Daphne.

'I don't know why he proposed to you; I can only imagine in the light of subsequent events that he did it to pay me out. I don't think you'd have believed me if I'd told you at the time, but I ought to have given you the chance. I didn't, because I despised you so much. I thought that what happened to you didn't particularly matter. I wish I could make you realise how much more I've since despised myself.'

There was a long silence. Virginia stood looking out of the window, till at last Daphne's voice came to her faintly across the room.

'I see. I'm glad you told me. I understand everything so much better now.'

And then, after another long interval, she spoke again: 'Virginia, was this why you gave up your holiday to stay here and nurse me?'

'I suppose so,' Virginia replied, without looking round. 'I couldn't do much less than try to mend what had been broken because of me, could I? But it wasn't only that. I was so pleased you wanted me to be in London when you were lonely and unhappy. It seemed so strange that you should, after the way I always treated you at Drayton. Most of the opportunities I miss never come to me again, and I didn't even realise I'd missed one till we had tea at Marshall's. You see, I was so busy despising you at Drayton; I never could forget the speech you made about me at that absurd debate. I was always thinking of ridiculous ways to pay you out, but I'm glad I didn't know how I was going to do it in the end.'

She watched a motor-bus turn the corner from Westminster and pass below the window before she heard Daphne speak again.

'Virginia! Come back and sit here again.'

And as Virginia obeyed she continued: 'It's difficult to realise what you've told me all at once, but somehow I don't really feel as if I minded very much. Perhaps I shall mind more when I've thought about it, but never too much to go on wanting you to come here. So many things have happened lately that whatever caused them in the beginning seems too long ago to count. Besides, they haven't really happened because of you. If only I'd been different it wouldn't have mattered that Raymond first came to me like that. If it had been you, you'd have made him care just the same.'

When she had finished speaking she lay so still, staring out of the window into the gathering twilight, that Virginia began to think she was falling asleep again. But at last she said, more to herself than to Virginia: 'I wonder what I ought to do next – about him, I mean?'

'Need you think about it at all yet?' Virginia asked her. 'There's time enough for that when you're better. At present you've got as much as you can do to get well. It will be hard work after an operation as serious as yours. And anyhow, you can't very easily do anything while Mr Sylvester is abroad.'

'I suppose I can't.' Daphne sank back against her pillows with a sigh. 'I find it difficult to think about the future at all yet; perhaps that's why I so often feel I ought to. I can't really believe there's ever going to be a future; it's only the past that seems real.'

The problem of Daphne's future occupied Virginia for some time after she went to bed that night. She came quickly to the conclusion that Sylvester's return and a new beginning were neither possible nor desirable, but the anomalous position of a deserted wife was almost as bad. The only solution of the problem was for Daphne to divorce Sylvester, despite the sufferings which the proceedings would undoubtedly cause her. Freedom from such a husband, thought Virginia, whose hostility towards Sylvester was still too great for her to understand Daphne's complex feelings concerning him, would be cheap even at the price of further pain. But Daphne would not be fit for many months for the strain of such an undertaking; moreover, Sylvester was abroad, and this, Virginia vaguely felt, would probably complicate matters. She was still meditating upon the steps that Daphne ought to take in order to obtain a divorce when she fell asleep.

She mentioned the subject next day to Patricia O'Neill, who frequently called to inquire about Daphne, and sometimes saw her for a few minutes. Patricia was spending the first part of the Oxford vacation at her club in town, in order to see as much as possible of Stephanoff, who was also in London, ostensibly occupied with business arrangements made necessary by his departure for Warsaw.

Patricia agreed with Virginia that Sylvester was unlikely ever to come back to Daphne.

'And of course she ought to divorce him if she can,' she said. 'But I shall be very much surprised if we don't find her extremely unwilling to do it.'

'Unwilling – after the way he's treated her? Oh, she couldn't, Pat! It's the only thing to do.'

'Perhaps you think so. All the same you wait and see if I'm not right. You know Daphne better than you did, but I'm not sure yet if you know her as well as I do. She'll have scruples and reluctances when it comes to the point. She'll talk of forgiving him, of letting him have the chance to make reparation. She may even think it'll still be possible to put the past aside and begin again. It won't be, but nothing will induce her to take action till she's certain. She'll put his happiness before her pride, even now.'

'There's another thing, Pat. Supposing she does ultimately decide to divorce him, has she sufficient grounds for doing it as things stand? Legal grounds, I mean, of course.'

'That's important,' said Patricia, 'because the whole proceeding will be a great ordeal for her, and she mustn't involve herself in it unless the issue's reasonably certain. I suppose she could quite well bring in a charge of cruelty, but as the law stands now it's no use without misconduct.'

'I'm pretty certain of his unfaithfulness, and so's Daphne,' Virginia remarked. 'But we can't prove anything about it, unless something turns up unexpectedly. If only we could, she'd have both charges to bring against him, and that's the safest thing possible.'

Patricia looked meditatively at Virginia.

'But has she no idea at all who the woman is?'

'None whatever. And I don't see how we can find out till Sylvester comes back from the East. *The Times* said his appointment was for a year.'

'And even after that,' added Patricia, 'he may get something else to do and stay abroad.'

'I suppose so. Well, anyway, Daphne won't be fit for much for at least six months. If he does come back when his job's done we may be able to discover something then, but at present it's all so indefinite.'

'Hasn't anyone the slightest idea what he did when he left Daphne?' inquired Patricia.

'Absolutely none,' Virginia replied. 'Of course, the Ministry might know something of his doings, but if we asked them the whole story's bound to come out, and Daphne's implored me all along to prevent that if possible. And what's more, I don't think it's to spare herself at all. I believe she's got some ridiculous idea of shielding him from adverse criticism – though of course she can't keep *that* up when she starts divorce proceedings. Wait a minute!' she exclaimed suddenly. 'There's that letter. I believe it did come from some hotel.'

'Do you mean the note he sent her before he crossed for Paris?'

'Yes. She gave it back to me after I showed it to her, because she said she couldn't bear to keep it, but she wouldn't let me destroy it. I'll get it and look.'

She returned in a few minutes with the letter in her hand. 'Look, Pat, it's written from the Clarence Hotel, Folkestone. It came the day after Daphne's operation, and I was so worried and so busy that I never noticed the address.'

Patricia looked at the letter.

'Tuesday, July 10th, and 9 A.M. on the postmark. He must obviously have been in a hurry to get away from London, but I suppose he had a few arrangements to make and the week-end held him up so that he couldn't leave town till Monday evening. From the time the letter's posted it looks as if he'd spent the night at this hotel. I wonder why he did that? He was quite accustomed to travelling – he'd have thought nothing of crossing by the night-boat.'

'But,' interrupted Virginia rather excitedly, 'suppose he had someone with him who didn't care for night travelling—'

'Yes,' admitted Patricia, 'it's a possibility, though rather a thin one, I'm afraid. Still, if he did spend the night there, and he wasn't alone, there may be some sort of evidence at the hotel. Their names would probably be in the register – or someone might remember them.'

'Would it mean employing a detective to find out?' inquired Virginia.

'That's undesirable at present, and as it happens it isn't necessary. You know Alexis starts for Warsaw next week, and I've arranged to go down to Folkestone with him and see him off by the afternoon boat. After he's gone I can quite well find the Clarence Hotel and see if there's any information to be gleaned. I'd do anything to help Daphne to get rid of Mr Sylvester, though I don't think she'll be particularly grateful to me for doing it.'

'That sounds an excellent plan,' Virginia said eagerly. 'But are you quite sure Mr Stephanoff's going from Folkestone?'

'Quite sure. He told me he might never feel inclined to come back to England if his last impression of it was Dover!'

Virginia smiled appreciatively. Then she said: 'But, Pat, you won't want to go worrying about hotel registers just after you've said good-bye to Mr Stephanoff.'

A shadow crossed Patricia's face, but she answered lightly: 'Oh yes! I shall. A little amateur detective work will divert my mind and be good for me. I'll go to the hotel and have tea; it'll be rather amusing altogether. I can get an evening train back to town and come here and tell you if I've had any luck. He goes on Tuesday, so your leave won't quite be over.'

She was as good as her word. Late on the following Tuesday evening she called at the Victoria Street flat to see Virginia. She was very pale and there were dark shadows beneath her eyes, but she did not mention Stephanoff. She only said abruptly: 'The unexpected's happened. I've got the evidence we wanted.'

'Tell me, Pat!' Virginia exclaimed excitedly.

'I went to the Clarence Hotel,' responded Patricia. 'After tea I put on my most serious air and interviewed the manager. He showed me the hotel register and there I found the names, 'Mr and Mrs Sylvester,' in Mr Sylvester's handwriting. I remembered it from the notes I'd had from him at Oxford, about coachings. Then I asked to see the chamber-maid who looked after their room, and by a little judicious tipping I got her to admit that she remembered seeing them together.'

'And who was the woman?' Virginia asked eagerly.

'I couldn't find that out at all. The maid didn't think she'd ever heard her speak; she only remembered that she was small and dark and very well dressed.'

'But it's enough, what you've found out. I wonder if Mr Sylvester will ever discover that you've been on his track.'

Patricia smiled a little in spite of her weariness.

'I think it's the last thing he'd expect of a Drayton tutor. Oxford dons don't generally go looking into hotel registers with a view to possible divorce cases. Besides, I don't think they're likely to talk at the hotel. The manager seemed very scared at the idea of being associated with a possible scandal; I had to assure him I had other evidence, and only wanted to make certain. He was very kind and sympathetic; I'm almost sure he took me for the wronged wife.'

'A rôle you'll never fill, Pat, though you live to be a hundred. Did Mr Stephanoff go off all right?'

And then Virginia repented of her question, because for the first time since she had known Patricia she saw her look as if she were going to cry. But Patricia pulled herself together and getting up from her chair answered abruptly: 'Oh yes, quite all right, thank you. He says he's coming back a millionaire, but *I* don't believe he'll be any richer than when he started. Don't trouble to come to the door; I'll see myself out. Good-night.'

Chapter XX

The Last Possibility

'But this is good,' said Patricia eagerly, handing back to Daphne the manuscript of a short story. 'Where was the queer villa with the green shutters?'

'I saw it in the country outside Siena nearly two years ago,' Daphne replied, 'but I've never forgotten it. I used to go for long walks by myself, because Raymond went off every day with a friend on archæological expeditions. I could see the villa from our *pension* windows and felt I must walk to it, but when I found it, it infuriated me. It looked so serene and indifferent, and I was feeling so lonely and so worried, even then. But it interested me in spite of that, and I always meant to write its story one day.'

'But why did you hesitate so long before showing me the story? Don't you realise yourself how good it is?'

Daphne pulled a rose from the fragrant bush that hung over the garden seat, and pressed its soft petals against her cheek before she answered: 'I don't know. You see, I made up my mind soon after I was married that I should never be any good at writing, and that all the ideas I'd had for years about being an author were just vain delusions – due simply to ignorance and self-satisfaction.'

'Was that *his* doing?' inquired Patricia.

Daphne hesitated, but finally replied reluctantly: 'Yes,

it was. I began writing things again soon after we came back from Italy, and I worried him with them when he felt too busy – and I suppose too indifferent – to want to be bothered with me and my affairs. He thought them so bad that he'd scarcely the patience to read them through. Then he told me I should never do any good work because I had no style, and I'd much better do some decent reading instead of playing about with poems and stories. I took him at his word and tried to learn about his work at the Ministry. But even that wasn't any good. I suppose really that nothing would have been any good.'

'It's a crime to neglect promise just because it isn't quite achievement,' Patricia said indignantly. 'Mr Sylvester was just as capable of seeing the possibilities of raw material as anyone else, if he took the trouble. But it was like him not to bother about work that was still immature. This story of the villa is not achievement, but it's nearer achievement than anything of yours I've seen yet. I wish you'd begin to work on something big, like a novel. Your days wouldn't seem empty any more then. You see, when everything else is gone, there's always work. I don't think anyone ever realises how much work can mean until the other things *are* gone.'

Daphne did not answer her at once; instead she gazed dreamily across the wide fields to the horizon, where the green hump of Ditchling Beacon reared itself up against the vivid June sky.

'I know – I know,' she said at last. 'It's the only thing no one else can take away from you whatever happens, isn't it? That's what I felt all the time I was getting better, and because I realised then that Raymond had never really been interested in me, I began to hope that perhaps his criticism didn't count as much as I thought it did when he made it. I've had the plot of a novel in my head for a long time, but until I came down here I never felt capable of such a sustained effort as writing one will mean – especially the first one. But if you really think it's any use I'll begin soon. If I can write anywhere I ought to be able to write down here.'

Nearly a year had passed since Patricia had said good-bye to Stephanoff at Folkestone. The Oxford summer vacation had come round again, and she had promised to spend the first half of it with Daphne in Sussex. In August Stephanoff was to return from Warsaw and their wedding had been arranged for September.

'In September,' he wrote to her from Warsaw, 'I shall endow you, not, it is true, with any great superfluity of worldly goods, but with all the prospects that might be mine were I to remain in this environment. For you alone will I return to Oxford, for I feel that as a tutor I am thrown away. Had I but discovered my exceptional capacity for business when I was twenty I should by now have been a Rothschild. But what matter? I should not then have met you, and been saved from the early complacence of prosperous middle age.'

Daphne's recovery had been long and slow. When the dangerous stage of her illness had passed, each new effort to rebuild her world made her realise the more how completely it had been shattered. The struggle became a fight against despair as well as against physical weakness.

Not until the spring was she able to leave London. Then she took a cottage in Sussex, and moved there for the summer with her child and his nurse. Jack, who already exhibited the querulous precocity of delicate children, was beginning to lisp words, but there was little probability that he would ever be anything but a cripple. Because of him Daphne would never be able to put the past behind her; he was a living regret, the embodiment of her failure. Her disappointment that he was not a girl had been swallowed up in the bitter waters that passed over her at the time of his birth. And there was no hope now that he would ever be the mischievous, active little boy whose upbringing she had dreaded. She would gladly have given the little that she still possessed of joy if only he could have been; if only she, and not he, might pay in full for the terrible error which she and Raymond had made. As it was, Jack would be more dependent on her care than any daughter. Round this frail human creature her world must be re-created; she must spend the rest of her days in striving to atone to him for the injury which had incapacitated him through no fault of his own.

Daphne was still Sylvester's nominal wife, though she had had no news of him since the letter written from Folkestone. Stray items of information concerning the Far Eastern Commission found their way into the papers from time to time; she supposed that Sylvester was one of the Commissioners, though his individual work was never mentioned. In spite of his silence she had made no attempt to free herself from him. She had long ago been told of the final proof of his misconduct, but, as Patricia had predicted, she received the suggestions of her friends regarding divorce with unrelenting obstinacy. She never wavered in her determination to take no steps till Sylvester returned from abroad, however long she might have to wait. She also refused to give up the flat in Victoria Street and go home to her people. If Raymond ever came back to London, she said, he must know where to find her.

'But, Daphne,' Virginia had protested one day, 'you surely can't mean to persuade him to come back? It would be an absolutely impossible situation – and all the more so if you really still care for him.'

'I wonder whether it would,' meditated Daphne, unwilling to commit herself to a definite admission.

'I'm never going to ask him to return to me,' she added, for Virginia's satisfaction. 'But all the same I'm not going to take away from him the chance to do it if he comes back at the end of his year abroad.'

She was not to be moved to any decision other than this, and after a brief and tearful struggle, even Mrs Lethbridge had perforce to agree. She declared herself deeply wounded by Daphne's steady refusal to go home, but she was secretly relieved that her daughter did not return to exhibit her humiliation to the place that she had quitted in triumph. Daphne would, of course, have to divorce Raymond in the end, but it would be so much more convenient if she need not do it from Thorbury Park.

So Daphne kept the flat in Sylvester's name, but when April came she took the advice of Dr Mackintosh, and left London to complete her recovery in the sweet Sussex spring. In London too she left the memories of the girl whose unrestrained enthusiasms and untimely caresses had driven an exasperated husband to desperation. She was always quiet now, slow both to appreciate and to complain. But the perpetual expectation in her eyes had not vanished. It had only changed in character. Her expression now was never startled or excited, but grave and intent, as though she were always watching and waiting for something that was bound to come in the end.

And come it did, shattering like a thunderbolt the fragrant peace of Ditchling Common in early summer. One morning, when Patricia had been with Daphne barely a fortnight, she came down to find her pale and trembling, reading a paragraph in *The Times*, with wide, troubled eyes. Patricia, looking over her shoulder, read the paragraph too.

'Mr Raymond Sylvester, the well-known diplomatist, has consented to become Liberal Constitutional candidate in the Ellswich by-election, rendered necessary by the recent death of Sir Francis Walker. Mr Sylvester has lately returned to England from the Far East, where he has been working during the past year on the Commission dealing with the Relation of Disarmament to Economic Conditions.'

Daphne flung the paper down on the table and sprang suddenly to her feet.

'Pat – do you see? He's in England! I must go back to London at once.'

Patricia laid a restraining hand upon her arm, for she was shivering uncontrollably.

'Why, Daphne?' she asked. 'Why should you upset your arrangements because of him? If he really wants to see you he can come down to Sussex.'

'Oh, but don't you see he may go along to Victoria Street, just on an impulse, and if he finds I'm not there he may never trouble to look for me again! Why, he may even have been already—'

'Daphne,' Patricia entreated, 'why don't you get rid of him? You'll have no peace until you do, because you'll always be wondering if he's coming back to you. And you wouldn't be happy if he did. No one could blame you for divorcing him when once they knew the story; you've got more than enough cause. And it oughtn't to be difficult. If this new Divorce Bill gets through you won't even need as good a reason as you have.'

'I know, Pat – but I can't! I can't stop him coming back if he wants to,' Daphne said wildly. 'And if he does come – if he is sorry – then I must be there to receive him.'

Patricia made no further effort to restrain her; she only looked at her sadly as she left her breakfast untouched and hurried out of the room, repeating: 'I must go back to London to-day.'

And back to London she went.

Chapter XXI

The Last Protest

It was the Minister of Arbitration who had brought Daphne's peace to an end. He had not forgotten to watch the by-elections on behalf of the most promising of his subordinates, and the long illness of Sir Francis Walker, the Liberal Constitutional Member for Ellswich, seemed to offer an unusually good opportunity. His death was not likely to occur for a few weeks, which would give Sylvester time to return from his mission. Lord Wintermere knew that the Far Eastern Commission had almost completed its work, so that he felt perfectly justified in sending the cable which Sylvester had received in Japan at the end of April: 'Return as soon as possible. Impending by-election Ellswich. Unusual opportunity.'

Events took place very much as Lord Wintermere had hoped. Sir Francis Walker died shortly before Sylvester landed in England after his six weeks' voyage, and the Liberal Constitutional Association at Ellswich was glad to have a rising diplomatist suggested to them as their candidate. The letter inviting Sylvester to stand for them was sent to him on the day that he returned to London.

'It's a Heaven-sent opportunity for you, Sylvester,' Lord Wintermere informed him benignly, as he stood once more in the Minister's office. 'You've only one opponent, who

222

calls himself a Conservative Independent, and he's not at all the kind of man to suit a Midland cathedral town like Ellswich.'

'Why, sir? What's wrong with him?' Sylvester inquired eagerly.

'It would be easier to tell you what isn't wrong with him,' was the reply. 'I understand from the Liberal Constitutional Association at Ellswich that he is a man of notorious character, who has recently divorced his wife in circumstances that do him no credit – no credit at all. It should not be difficult to turn this information to your advantage,' he continued, without perceiving Sylvester's involuntary start. 'In fact, it suggests to me an excellent basis for your campaign – the very best possible at the present time. You must use "Anti-Divorce" as your electioneering cry. I can answer for it that it will be popular in Ellswich, and you will be doing a service to me at the same time.'

Sylvester looked perplexed and troubled.

'I don't think I quite understand. Why should Anti-Divorce be such a good basis? It seems very personal.'

'Not at all, Sylvester, not at all,' the Minister took him up sharply. 'Only personal by coincidence, not for any other reason. If your opponent has chosen to disgrace himself by dragging his name through the mud of the Divorce Courts, that is his affair. The feeling against divorce happens to be very strong in certain parts of the country just at present, and it is likely to be particularly so in a cathedral town like Ellswich.'

'But why, sir?'

'Of course,' Lord Wintermere suddenly reflected, 'I was forgetting that you have had very little opportunity of seeing the newspapers during the past few weeks. You probably have not realised that there is considerable agitation in the country against the new Bill for the reform of the Divorce laws?'

'No,' replied Sylvester, 'I haven't. I only gathered that such a Bill has passed its second reading.'

'Unfortunately that is so. But we hope even yet to save the family life of England, that family life which I think I may safely call its most precious possession. A disgraceful Bill, Sylvester, disgraceful! I am glad to say it has fallen to my lot to lead the opposition to it.'

'*You*, sir?'

'Yes, indeed – and why not?' exclaimed Lord Wintermere, growing more excited than Sylvester had ever seen him. 'It may be my principal business in life to act as arbiter between the nations, but I cannot make that an excuse for standing aside when the laws of God are set at naught in my own country! Divorce is an evil thing, Sylvester – the ruin of our homes, the worm that gnaws at the heart of our society. No doubt you have not thought deeply on the subject; it is easy to neglect when you have a young and – er – charming wife. My own dear wife, I am thankful to say, is at one with me in this matter. Like me, she has seen the lives of men and women wrecked by this crime against the sanctity of marriage, and unions that might have been sacred dissolved for a disgraceful whim, simply because dissolution is easy. And now some of the agnostics, the so-called progressives, want to make it easier still – want to undermine the strength of England by destroying her morality, by staining more deeply that social purity which ought to be the fairest jewel in her crown! My opponents may laugh at me, they may call me old-fashioned, but in so far as this Ministry is concerned, I will not choose my servants from among those whom this evil thing has touched!'

The agitation which Sylvester could no longer conceal suddenly checked Lord Wintermere's flow of eloquence.

'Forgive me for this vehemence, Sylvester; doubtless it seems to you inopportune. But it is not really so. I assure you that many people feel as I do, especially in the cathedral towns. But if you can make use of the opposition to this Bill in your electioneering campaign, you will not only find it a valuable basis, but you will also be furthering the cause I have so deeply at heart.'

'I will try to make use of it,' faltered Sylvester, newly agitated by the host of perplexities and inconvenient memories which his absence from England had enabled him to put aside for a year.

'That's right.' Lord Wintermere laid his hand on Sylvester's shoulder. 'Get Ellswich to elect you and the Secretaryship's yours as soon as Morland resigns – which may happen at any time now. After that your road's clear before you. It is my hope that one day, before very long, you may be Minister of Arbitration.'

Sylvester started again.

'But surely, sir, you're not thinking of retiring?'

'Not yet, Sylvester, not yet. But I've had a long career – long and often arduous; the war was a heavy trial to a lover of peace – a very heavy trial. I shan't be sorry when the time comes to let go the reins. And there's no one I should like to see in my place better than you. I can think of nobody better fitted to fill it. You're young yet, but you've served us very well, and with your splendid capacities you will serve us still better in the future.'

'Thank you, sir,' was all that Sylvester could say, but as Lord Wintermere held out his hand he murmured incoherently: 'I only hope I shall never disappoint your expectations.'

'I'm sure of that – quite sure,' said the Minister, heartily gripping Sylvester's hand. 'Good luck to you, my boy. Go in and win.'

Sylvester went heavily down the steps of the Ministry, challenged at every turn by the unwelcome images of the past. He might have known that there would be a catch in that by-election somewhere! It was just his damned luck that things had turned out so inopportune again. His complete indifference to Daphne's proceedings in his absence had changed to a lively apprehension. Apart from the by-election, which was the primary consideration at present, he was seriously perturbed by the incongruity of his Minister's views with his own circumstances. In occasional discussions at the Ministry on social questions Sylvester had been secretly amused by some of Lord Wintermere's ideas, which, for a progressive Minister, were surprisingly old-fashioned. But the question of divorce had never arisen between them, and Sylvester had been unaware of his chief's strong prejudices on the subject.

But Sylvester was one of the many who find the contemplation of contingencies other than those that they desire too uncomfortable to be persisted in. Anti-Divorce, he told himself as he walked along Whitehall, was too good a basis for his campaign to be rejected merely on account of a few personal apprehensions, which after all were probably quite baseless.

Daphne's long silence reassured, though it puzzled, him. He knew that he had told her that any attempt to communicate with him would be useless, but he did not really expect her to refrain from trying to reach him; she must have realised that she could send him letters through the Ministry if she wished. Lord Wintermere's obvious ignorance of the circumstances under which he had left her surprised him too; he had expected their relations to be public knowledge by the time that he returned to England. Evidently those common Manchester relations of hers had made her hush the whole thing up to avoid a scandal, at any rate until he came home and something definite could be done.

But what definite thing could be done? He did not believe

that Daphne, even if she wished, had sufficient grounds to institute divorce proceedings against him. His memory of his last few days in England was vague, but he did not think that she would find it easy to furnish herself with proof of his misconduct. She could know nothing of his relations with Lucia abroad, and he was sure that neither she nor anyone with whom he was acquainted had seen him with Lucia in England. Apart from his angry words in the final scene with Daphne, he had made no statement of his unfaithfulness, though he was aware that she must have suspected it. Besides, Lucia's letters to him had always been sent to the Ministry, never to the flat, and in any case he had destroyed them all long ago. He had only a hazy recollection of the note written to Daphne before he crossed, and none at all of when and where he had sent it off. Everything had been so infernally hurried and confused those last two days, but he felt sure that he had given no information in it with regard to Lucia, and it never occurred to him that the letter could contain anything else which would incriminate him.

On the ground of misconduct he therefore felt fairly safe, and he was as yet unaware of those consequences of his quarrel with Daphne which rendered possible a charge of cruelty against him.

He certainly did not intend to see Daphne again if he could help it. It was not likely, he argued, that an interview with her would improve his position. It would probably only make things a good deal worse, and, anyhow, there would be another of those beastly scenes. As if the last one wasn't enough to make a man avoid them as long as he lived! Of course he realised that his return to England would probably rouse her into some sort of action; it was even possible that she might try to see him herself. But though he must be prepared for tears, reproaches, and possible prayers to him to return to her, he need not really expect anything definite enough to cause him anxiety. And even if she had had sufficient cause to institute proceedings against him, that blatant Lethbridge respectability, which must have kept her mouth shut so far, would probably restrain her from courting the publicity of the Divorce Court. With any other manifestation he could easily temporise until he had tided over the present emergency, and afterwards he would doubtless be able to persuade Daphne to agree to a separation. He could thus avoid that particular kind of scandal which would deprive him of Lord Wintermere's favour, and with it his best hopes of a political career.

In any case, he said to himself, as he hailed a taxi to take him to Euston for the Ellswich train, the electoral campaign was real and immediate, while Daphne's proceedings were hypothetical and improbable. The struggle before him would be quite sufficient to occupy his whole attention, and he determined to put his inconvenient wife out of his mind for the time being.

That inconvenient wife, alone with her baby in the Victoria Street flat, waited day after day, but no word came. One evening, when she had been back in London for about a week, Virginia, who had just finished her training at St Damien's, came in to persuade her to hesitate no longer.

'If he wanted to see you he'd have come before now. You don't know how long he may have been in England before you saw that paragraph in the paper. And you're never likely to get him back unless he comes of his own accord.'

'I shouldn't try unless I saw he wanted to come,' Daphne said slowly.

'And if he wanted to come you'd have heard by this time,' said Virginia. 'Mr Sylvester's never very long in making up his mind what he wants and what he doesn't.'

'I know. But it's hard to part with the last hope of things coming right – especially when it's all I've had to live for for a whole year.'

Virginia redoubled her persuasions.

'That's all the more reason for you to divorce him as soon as ever you can; you'll never find anything else worth living for as long as you go on thinking he may still come back. You don't know how glad I should be to feel that you'd lost that delusion before I go abroad.'

Daphne started.

'Abroad! Are you going abroad too?'

'Yes. You know that the Health Section of the League of Nations has just reorganised the anti-typhus campaign in Russia because of that new outbreak which started in the spring? Well, the Ministry of Arbitration has demanded a unit from St Damien's, and the other day our matron asked for volunteers. I said I'd go, and so did one or two of the others, and we've all been taken.'

'Virginia, why didn't you tell me this before?' faltered Daphne, so much overcome by the shock of these tidings that even Sylvester was forgotten for the moment.

'I should have had to tell you soon in any case,' Virginia replied, 'because we're under orders to go almost any day now. But I didn't think I'd spoil your time in Sussex by worrying you with my affairs till I had to. However, now that you've spoilt it for yourself, or rather Mr Sylvester has, there doesn't seem any point in not telling you. And if it helps you to make up your mind about him before I go, so much the better for both of us.'

But Daphne was hardly listening to her.

'It's just my luck!' she exclaimed bitterly. 'All the people I care for either go abroad and leave me, or else live happily ever after with someone else – like Pat's going to.'

'And it's so aggravating of people to do that, isn't it?'

commented Virginia. 'Do you know, I heard the other day that even Julia Tait got married to a doctor at the first place where she went to teach, and is now the jubilant possessor of twins!'

'Oh, don't laugh, Virginia! I don't feel as if I could now, after what you've just told me, not even about Julia. You've made yourself indispensable to me, and now you're going away just when I want you most! Why couldn't you let me go on hating you as I used to? I should once have been so glad to think that you were out of my way for good, but now I can't bear the idea of your wasting your splendid gifts in fighting a plague which people with half your intelligence could fight just as well. I've never been able to understand what made you go to St Damien's, but I did hope that when the two years were over you'd write again, or at least take up some kind of international work. I always thought you might do that when I saw how tremendously interested you were in your Special at Oxford.'

'But that's just what I'm going to do,' said Virginia. 'There's nothing so international as sickness and suffering. When I'm nursing people I work and think in an international way, but when I'm writing or lecturing I'm only wondering what will be the international opinion of Virginia Dennison!'

She turned to Daphne, suddenly aflame.

'Oh, don't you see? Don't you understand why I went to St Damien's? Haven't you realised that I'm one of those unhappy people whose own gifts are their worst temptations? Intellectual success goes to my head like cheap champagne. I had to give up all chance of ever achieving it before I could do anything worth doing, anything that wasn't simply a glorification of myself!'

Daphne looked at her in surprise at her sudden outburst.

But she had long ceased to be annoyed by Virginia's incorrigible egoism, which could not even renounce without emphasising the dramatic side of its renunciation.

'How did I ever manage to think you a cynic?' she said at last. 'You're no more a cynic than I am; you're a fanatic!'

'Call it what you like, Daphne; you know it's quite true, what I've said. At least you knew it well enough at Drayton. That hard, effective cleverness of mine – what was it worth? Did it help the world to bear its intolerable burdens? Did it even help me to endure my own unhappiness any better? Success for me was like a sudden flame that shone to me against the sky from a tree-top. And I climbed for it and I climbed, and when at last I held it in my hand I found that it was only a dead leaf. You've often seen them like that at Boars' Hill, glowing red in the autumn.'

'But, Virginia, are you never going to write anything any more?'

Virginia meditated for a moment before she answered: 'Perhaps I may again, some day. But life where I am going is an uncertain thing. And even if I do, it won't be like anything I have ever meant to write up till now. It will be something which is new to me – something which must first be lived.'

'I don't see how you can learn anything from living among the kind of people nurses generally are,' Daphne protested. 'I can't think how anyone like you can bear the prospect of being with them always.'

Virginia smiled.

'I wonder why you have such a contempt for the nursing profession? One of the inscriptions on the wall of St Thomas' Chapel, which a sister who trained there once took me to see, pointed out, greatly to my satisfaction, that nursing was "a high and holy calling."'

'But do you really think it is, Virginia?'

'No; but I think it could be.'

Daphne leaned forward eagerly.

'If you must nurse, why don't you stay in England, and try to make the profession what it ought to be, instead of shutting yourself up with a deadly disease in Russia? You're brave, you're downright, you're a challenger – and you're never afraid of consequences. It's people like you who could reform a great profession, if anyone could do it.'

Virginia smiled a little as she answered her.

'Your approbation's as whole-hearted as your hostility used to be, but it's considerably less justified. I can't be a reformer yet, because I'm not ready.'

Almost regardless of Daphne she went on, absorbed in her subject:

'When I was nursing in the war I did have visions of acquiring a great influence somehow, and putting an end to some of those pettinesses and restrictions which make work that's already hard enough almost intolerable for most people. But I'm not the right person – at any rate not yet. The nursing profession can never be reformed by someone intolerant; it's too full of prejudices and Victorianisms and unreasonableness. It wants someone patient and pitiful, who'll try to understand the limitations of the half educated. I've had too good an intellectual training to know what it means to struggle blindly, half equipped, towards an ideal of service which exists only in one's better moments – moments that get fewer and fewer as one's youth departs, and one becomes more tired, and one's sordid experiences increase. I've no patience yet with the people I have to work with; I'm too well educated, and too aggressive. I shall have to earn my right to speak in hard places.'

She turned again to Daphne.

'Meanwhile, my views on nursing won't get you any nearer to a decision about Mr Sylvester. Won't you let me see you with a chance of happiness and freedom before I go?'

Daphne did not reply. She sat for a long time in silence, thinking, unable to face all at once the prospect of utter loss.

At last she said reluctantly: 'I'll wait for another week and see if anything happens. If I don't hear anything from him by then I'll start proceedings against him.'

And with that Virginia had to be content.

The week was barely over when another paragraph in *The Times* brought Daphne's failing hopes to an end. She had watched its pages carefully for any mention of Raymond, and at last was rewarded by a few lines headed 'Ellswich By-Election':

'We understand that Mr Raymond Sylvester, who recently consented to stand as Liberal Constitutional candidate for Ellswich, is now in that city, making preparations for his campaign, which will begin immediately.'

It was over, then – the possibility of a recreated past. He had been in London, and had left it to fight his election without seeing her. She held Jack in her arms as she read the words which told her that Raymond had eliminated her from his life. But he could not eliminate Jack, who had kept her up all night with one of his periodic attacks of pain. His querulous fretful whining helped Daphne to her decision. Virginia was right; she had suffered too much on Raymond's account, but she would not suffer any more. There was no longer an alternative for honour and self-respect.

But whatever he might deserve of her, she would not strike a blow at Raymond in the dark. He was probably unaware how good her case was; he must know her decision, must be prepared for the unwelcome publicity which scandal would bring to the name of a rising politician. Of course he would not take any notice of her letter, but that too would be all for the best.

So after tearing up several sheets of note-paper, which could not be posted because they were blotted with her tears, Daphne sent a brief note to Sylvester in Ellswich to tell him that she had made up her mind to begin divorce proceedings against him.

Chapter XXII

The Last Problem

Daphne's first visit to her solicitors confirmed her belief that she would have no difficulty in getting rid of Sylvester. And when she came back from Markham & Lyles' office she realised again that Virginia had been right. The knowledge that in a few months' time she could put Raymond out of her life for ever came as an immense relief after the purposeless expectation of the past year. She had found the interview trying, but now that it was over she sat down to rest, with her mind more at peace than it had been for many weeks. Once this business was over she would sell the flat and go down into the country for good. She would be glad to see the last of it; the very room where she was sitting held the memory of that final quarrel, whose mere recollection was an outrage. Soon she could put away from her all heritage of the past except Jack, and he would be so entirely hers that she would almost forget that he had ever been Raymond's as well.

Her growing satisfaction at the prospect was interrupted by a ring at the front-door bell and the entrance of her maid to say that a lady wanted to see her. Social callers had long ceased to trouble Daphne, and she roused herself with an effort from her drowsy fatigue.

'Did she say what she wanted, Ethel?'

'Only that she must see you, ma'am, and that it was important.'

'And she didn't give you any name?'

'She did give it, but I couldn't catch it,' the maid replied. 'It was a queer sort of name; sounded foreign to me.'

'Foreign?' Daphne repeated mechanically, turning over in her mind the list of her acquaintances. 'Oh, well, you'd better show her up. I suppose I must see what she wants.'

Ethel obeyed, and in a few moments, after a valiant and successful effort to master the strange name, she opened the door and announced: 'Signorina Farretti.'

Daphne saw a small dark woman, whose slender figure was clad in exquisite garments which only Paris could have produced. Neither the name nor the face were immediately familiar to her. The evening spent in listening to *Carmen* had long ago faded into the grey background of occasions when Raymond had found her inadequate.

'You are Mrs Sylvester?' The soft, musical voice with its slight foreign accent seemed to caress her name.

'Yes, I am Mrs Sylvester. Why do you wish to see me?' inquired Daphne, drawing forward a chair for the stranger.

Lucia Farretti seated herself and unfastened the jewelled clasp of her white cloak before she replied: 'I have come to plead with you on behalf of your husbánd.'

'My husband!' A surge of passionate emotion flooded Daphne's heart. What plea could there be but that he might be permitted to return to her – what explanation but that he would have come before if he had not doubted her forgiveness? Joy and pain almost choked her for a moment, but she was impelled by a sudden misgiving to ask: 'Who are you that you should come to plead for my husband?'

The direct question did not appear to disturb Lucia. She

replied serenely and without hesitation: 'I am his mistress. Often since he left you I have been with him. I spent much time with him in Japan.'

There was a long pause. Daphne averted her head, unable to find words, until at last Lucia spoke again.

'I suppose that now I have told you this, you will wish to send me out of your house.'

Daphne turned again and met her visitor's eyes without flinching.

'No, I don't think so,' she said slowly. 'I don't think I feel any the worse towards you for knowing you are his mistress. I don't suppose it's much easier to be his mistress than it was to be his wife. Won't you tell me who you are? If I have seen you before, I don't remember you.'

'It is not likely that you will remember. Your husband told me that you had seen me only once, more than a year ago. I used to sing some of the leading parts in the Verdi Company at the Orpheum.'

Recollection suddenly flashed across Daphne's mind.

'I remember now – you were Carmen on the night I was there. So it *was* to the opera he used to go – and to see you,' she added, half to herself.

'Yes. It was to see me.'

Daphne looked intently at Lucia, with a genuine desire to know what manner of woman had kept Raymond's allegiance longer than she had kept it. And as she looked her thoughts were illumined by yet another memory. That night at the opera she had caught in the expression of Carmen a fleeting likeness to someone whom she could not name. But since those days the face of which Lucia Farretti reminded her had grown pale in fighting on her behalf that grim enemy who had seemed at one time to be her only friend. Small wonder that those dark, sad eyes and delicate features had seemed so strangely familiar! It was Virginia's image that had been with Sylvester in Japan, and as Daphne realised this her heart was torn with sudden pity for her husband.

'Tell me what you want to say to me,' she demanded gently of Lucia.

Lucia reflected for a moment, seeking for words in which to put Sylvester's case before Daphne. Her gold-embroidered purse-bag contained the letter she had received from him that morning, with its unstudied imprecations and its desperate appeal for advice:

'It's just my damnable luck that this should happen at the very crisis of my career. It's Daphne all over to leave me alone till I begin to count on being safe, and then trip me up just when I see my way towards getting through this campaign successfully. And it's not as if it were only this election business. I might get that over before she could do anything much, but I shall be simply ruined with Wintermere if my name's dragged into the papers in connection with a divorce case. As if it wasn't bad enough for a man to live a cat-and-dog life for a year, without having the whole tale of it flaunted on the front page of every penny rag! I don't think for a moment she's got any sort of case against me, but whether she wins or loses she'll get me into the devil of a mess. It's the damned publicity that will do for me, both in the Ministry and with my constituents. The whole beastly business kept me awake all last night, and I've got such an infernal headache this morning that I haven't the vaguest notion what to do for the best. Would it be any good going to see her, do you think, and explaining what a frightful upset she'll make if she tries to get her own back? It's the last thing in the world I want to do. I don't feel as if I could stand a scene in the middle of all the worry and strain of this election. But anything would be better than having my whole career ruined just when everything is beginning to look so promising. For God's sake tell me what you think I ought to do; as it is, I'm simply at my wits' end.'

This outburst of self-commiseration did not reveal Sylvester to Lucia in his most attractive aspect, but, unlike Daphne, she knew men too well to expect from them any sense of proportion when anything that they held dear was at stake. The last quality that she looked for in Sylvester was sufficient humour to save him from sometimes appearing ridiculous in her eyes.

She realised, as she recalled the words of Sylvester's letter, that she could explain her business most directly by reading to Daphne part of what he had written. She decided, however, that she would try to manage without doing this, not for Sylvester's sake, but for Daphne's. She evidently still loved him, poor thing; her violent start at the first mention of his name had made that quite obvious. And it would be a pity to destroy the last few illusions which she probably had concerning him. She had doubtless been through a very hard time – like most women who expected men to be reasonable, instead of treating them as the spoilt children that they were.

So instead of quoting Sylvester's words she began gently to explain.

'This morning I had a letter from your husband telling me that you are about to begin divorce proceedings against him. He is terribly distressed at the news, for it appears that, if you really intend to do as you have said, you will absolutely ruin his career.'

Daphne looked startled, but a little incredulous.

'I'm afraid I don't understand. What can my husband's private affairs have to do with his public life?'

'In one moment I will explain to you,' said Lucia. 'It is partly on account of his election that he is distressed. It seems that he has begun to fight it on – what did he call it? – a basis of opposition to some new Divorce Bill which is causing much excitement in this country. Your Ellswich appears to be a town with a cathedral, where there is still much respect for the morals of Queen Victoria.'

Daphne laughed a little bitterly.

'And Raymond is supporting them with all his might! I see. It's a curious position for him, isn't it? Of course I've heard of the Bill,' she continued. 'In fact I've studied it, because it will probably help me. And I quite understand that there would be a good deal of opposition to it in a place like Ellswich; Raymond's chosen his ground just as well as one would expect of him. But electioneering campaigns don't last very long, do they? Surely it will be over long before his own connection with a divorce case is realised?'

'That is true,' Lucia answered serenely. 'But he says that the people who elect him will never trust him any more if they discover, after he has opposed divorce for moral reasons, that he was expecting to be divorced himself. They will not return him again, he says, when there is a general election. And there is more than this. It appears that Lord Wintermere, his Minister, is himself leading the opposition to the Bill, and has made up his mind to allow no divorced man to serve him. So if you divorce your husband he will lose the Minister's favour, and that will do him greater harm than anything in the world. At present he has before him very wonderful opportunities, but you, if you do as you have said, will take them all away from him.'

Enlightenment had dawned upon Daphne now, and the moments in which Jack's pitifulness had smitten her, had made her cry out for retaliation against her husband, came back to urge her passionately to take this supreme opportunity. She would not meet Lucia's eyes, which implored so much more eloquently than her words, but once again averted her head and said bitterly: 'Why should I care what becomes of him, when once I have made my decision? What did it matter to him what became of me when he left me for you just before my son was born – my son whom he—' She stopped suddenly. Not to Lucia Farretti would she acknowledge the injury which Raymond had done to Jack through her.

Lucia answered her as calmly as ever, though her eyes continued to plead.

'We were cruel. But people are often cruel when they love.'

'And yet you expect me to be merciful?'

The reply came without hesitation:

'I expect nothing. But I ask you to be merciful. Your husband has the ability to be a famous diplomatist; he may do great service to your country. Will you prevent him from doing that service for the sake of your own satisfaction?'

Daphne locked her fingers tightly together.

'Did *he* ask you to come to me?' she asked abruptly.

'No. I came of my own accord. I know him well, and I thought perhaps I could explain things to you better than he could himself.'

'But don't you realise that you give him away absolutely by coming here? If my case against him was strong before, it is infallible after all you have admitted to-day.'

Lucia shrugged her shoulders indifferently.

'I know nothing of your divorce law. I only know that you are like me – a woman who loves him in spite of everything.'

Another question arose to confront Daphne from the depths of her distress.

'Is his career so much to you,' she asked slowly, 'that

you are ready to sacrifice your certainty of keeping him? You ask me not to divorce him, when you know that if I divorced him he could marry you. Isn't it strange that you of all people should come to ask me this?'

Lucia smiled a little pitifully as she replied: 'No, it is not strange, for he does not ever want to marry me, and I would not marry him if he wished. He is not the first I have loved, and perhaps he will not be the last. One day I shall tire of him, just as I expect he will tire of me. I will love as it pleases me, but I will not lose my freedom.'

Daphne could only look at her, silent in her perplexity, and Lucia continued: 'You are not a child of the world, Mrs Sylvester, and you do not understand. We who are children of the world find our joy in the moment as it passes. The hour is sweet – why should we spoil it by thinking of to-morrow?'

'No, I don't understand,' Daphne said slowly. 'If only I had understood, perhaps I should have known better how to keep him.'

She could not hate this woman who had stolen from her a love that had never really been hers, and on a sudden passionate impulse she turned imploringly to Lucia.

'Signorina – you don't think he will ever come back to me?'

Lucia shook her head.

'No, he will never come back,' she said very gently, 'for he will never trouble to learn you enough to love you. He does not know what you are, but he cannot forget something that you are not. I expected to find you stupid, awkward, perhaps hysterical – I thought very likely you would not listen to what I had to say. And instead you have been none of those things, and you have heard me as though I had been your friend and not your enemy. You deserved a better fate, Mrs Sylvester, but it is not often that men such as your husband are satisfied with the women who love them.'

'But you love him,' Daphne exclaimed, 'and yet you know him so well! Did you know him as well when he first took you away with him?'

'Almost as well,' Lucia admitted calmly. 'But he is beautiful, and he loves my music. I am not so unreasonable that I expect more from a man.'

For some moments Daphne could say nothing, for as the immensity of this last perplexity dawned upon her, the world which she seemed to have settled so satisfactorily for herself an hour ago began to sway about her in a darkness of wild confusion. And like a flicker of fire the sudden fierce longing to see Raymond again pierced through the chaos – just once again, even though he were to receive ruin at her hands. She rose at length and going across to Lucia looked down into her dark troubled eyes.

'It is a great thing you have asked, and I must have time to think it over. I can't make my decision now, but if I could I wouldn't tell it to anyone but him. If he cares to come here within the next few days I will let him know what I have decided. Will you tell him this when you answer his letter?'

'Thank you, I will,' replied Lucia, realising instantly that further entreaty would be inopportune.

Daphne, still haunted by that strange likeness to Virginia, accompanied her to the door. She knew that Lucia had supplied her with the last weapon against failure, had proved a witness more definite and authoritative than any hotel chamber-maid. But Daphne realised that she was evidence of even more than her husband's infidelity. That undeniable resemblance was the proof of an enduring faithfulness in Sylvester – the faithfulness to an earlier love for which both she and Lucia Farretti had equally to pay the price.

Chapter XXIII

The Last Loneliness

Two days later Daphne and Virginia sat waiting in suspense for the ring of the front-door bell. It was about half-past eight in the evening, and the supper that they had scarcely touched had just been cleared away. Though July was not yet over, the evening was cold, and a small fire was burning in the grate. Daphne, tense with anticipation, moved restlessly about the room.

'I'm so glad you came to-night, Virginia. I don't believe I could have faced it without you.'

'Yes,' answered Virginia, 'it's lucky my orders didn't come this morning. I don't think they'll be later than to-morrow.'

'I can hardly believe that it may be the last time you'll come here – and to-night of all nights too. What time exactly did I tell you his letter said he'd come? I tried to make myself look at it again, but I couldn't.'

'Soon after half-past eight, you said,' replied Virginia.

Daphne altered the cushions in the arm-chair for about the twentieth time.

'It was so strange seeing his writing on the envelope,' she said. 'Even now I can't believe he's really coming. I wish I had the least idea what I'm going to do. But as soon as I was sure I was going to see him I knew I couldn't make up my mind till I did.'

'You do realise, don't you,' urged Virginia, 'that if you promise not to divorce him you're making it almost impossible for yourself to do it in the future if you wish? You'd be regarded as having condoned his offence, perhaps even as having connived at it. Sparing him now practically means giving up your freedom for always.'

Daphne winced perceptibly, and replied with unaccustomed bitterness:

'I know. I haven't forgotten that. I quite realise that if I let him off I shall be responsible for my own misfortunes. I always am.'

Virginia made no further attempt to influence Daphne's decision, nor did she express by any word or look her inward opinion of Sylvester for bringing himself to ask so much of Daphne. The sudden sharp ring at the front-door bell struck like a bomb into the quiet, expectant room.

Daphne sprang agitatedly to her feet.

'Virginia – I can't see him yet! I can't – I don't know what I'm going to do; I must go to Jack again first. It's a great deal to ask, I know, but will you see him for me – just for a few minutes?'

'Of course I will,' Virginia replied, forcing back her reluctance, and abruptly Daphne disappeared.

She had scarcely gone when the bell was answered and Sylvester announced. Virginia felt almost sorry for him as he came into the room, he looked so apprehensive and embarrassed. He started violently when he saw her.

'Good Lord!' he exclaimed. 'You!'

Virginia bowed, with a ghost of the mocking smile that he remembered so well.

'Yes,' she said, 'even I.'

'But what are you doing here? I came to see Daphne, and it's urgent.'

'I know. But she didn't feel able to see you just at once.

I suppose that surprises you? As for my being here, it's nothing out of the common. I still come often to see Daphne, and she likes having me. You can't grudge her a little thing like that, you know. You didn't leave her much to live for when you went off in that unceremonious manner.'

'I see you haven't changed,' he remarked. 'You're exactly the same as ever.'

Virginia smiled derisively.

'There you're wrong,' she said. 'But no matter. It doesn't concern you at all.'

'Doesn't it? Do you know that ever since I last saw you at Oxford your image has been continually in my mind?'

'Well, you can put it out now. I'm a hospital nurse, and I'm nearly thirty – neither of them things which appeal to you much, I should imagine.'

'I remember now,' he said, 'I heard that you were nursing. But why in the world are you doing it?'

'That's my affair,' answered Virginia.

'What a damned silly waste of a fine intelligence! As for your being thirty, it's absurd; you always looked a child, and you do still. And anyhow it wouldn't matter to me if you were fifty, and you know it. I suppose you've better reason than ever for reminding me of my reputation, though – as you did once before. I suppose you've forgotten that, but I haven't – for I loved you differently from the others. I did, Virginia. Of course I cared like that too – tremendously – but not only like that. You stimulated my intellect, and I wanted your mind as well as other things. I loved you for it – I always have, and I do still.'

Virginia moved away from him to the fireplace.

'It's a great pity,' she said, 'for it's because of that that we've managed between us to make a pretty thorough mess of Daphne's life. Oh, I admit the fault was much more yours than mine; all the same, I'm not going to shirk my share of the blame.'

'I don't see how you're to blame for my mistake.'

'For your deliberate attempt to humiliate me at Daphne's expense? No, I'm not responsible for that. But I oughtn't to have let her marry you. I realised the kind of person you were long before she did, and it was my business to warn her.'

'Well, anyhow,' he said bitterly, 'whatever I've done to her, she's got the means to pay me out now – or at any rate she seems to think she has.'

'She has. I know all about that. But I'm not going to forestall her. She must tell you as much or as little as she likes – it isn't for me to interfere. But I only hope she'll make you pay to the utmost.'

'You're hard, Virginia. You don't seem to realise that if I hadn't loved you I shouldn't be standing here to-night, obliged to humble myself before the woman I despise, or else lose everything.'

Virginia stopped him with a gesture of impatient contempt.

'I quite expected you to say that; to forget, though you may despise Daphne, that you're quite ready to ask her to make a tremendous, incredible sacrifice for you. But *I* don't forget; I don't forget how she's paid for your faults all along – your faults and my ridiculous pride. Do you think I wouldn't have suffered any shame to save her from it all, if only it hadn't been too late? For I'm sorry – sorry – sorry—'

Her voice broke; angrily she dashed away the inconvenient tears. But Sylvester had seen them, and they had roused again into fierce life the old unsleeping passion.

With hands outstretched imploringly he moved towards her.

'Virginia, you say Daphne's paid, but you don't realise how I've paid too. You don't know how I've tried to imagine you with me when I've had to put up with her – how, ever since I last saw you in Oxford, I've longed just once to touch you – Virginia – just for one kiss—'

She moved rapidly to the door.

'You're forgetting yourself worse than ever,' she said with cold emphasis. 'But I suppose it's hopeless to try to make you realise the kind of person you are. I think it's time you saw Daphne; I'll go and tell her.'

She disappeared. His hands fell to his sides, and he gazed blankly, hopelessly, at the open door.

As he had travelled up to London from Ellswich he had contemplated many possible attitudes which he might adopt towards Daphne, without being able to decide upon one of them. The unexpected interview with Virginia had gone far towards robbing him of his self-possession, and as Daphne came into the room the little that remained completely departed, so startled was he by the unfamiliar fragility of her appearance. She was white as a ghost, and tense as the string of a violin, but her resolution was practically made. She went straight to the point as he stood hesitating before her.

'So you thought your reputation worth saving? You even thought it worth while to come and see me?'

'You see – it's my whole career,' he stammered. 'As things stand, I may have a chance to be Minister of Arbitration some day, but the Secretaryship's the first step, and for that a seat in the House is almost essential. This by-election's an unexpectedly good opportunity, and now I've begun to fight it one way I can't possibly change—'

'I know. Signorina Farretti told me all that; you needn't

explain. And now that you've begun your campaign,' she continued, 'do you really think you've a reasonable chance of winning it?'

'I do. There's a great deal of feeling against my opponent. A good many people whose political opinions aren't violent will vote for me because of their objection to him personally.'

'Which you emphasise,' she said unexpectedly, 'by the contrast of your own infallibility?'

He bit his lip, but did not answer, and she went on at once:

'Then you're fairly certain of success?'

'Yes, unless – anything unforeseen – hinders me now, my success is practically assured.'

'I see. And you really hope one day to be Minister of Arbitration?'

'The chances are in favour of it – unless I lose Lord Wintermere's goodwill.'

'And why do you want that position so much?' she inquired.

'It's one of the finest jobs going, where international relations are concerned,' Sylvester replied. 'As far as any single individual can, the British Minister of Arbitration holds the peace of the world in his hands.'

'And do you really care a great deal about the peace of the world?'

'I care very much,' he said. 'Any thinking man would.'

She looked at him steadily, standing before him in silence as though meditating upon her decision. He had come prepared for a scene, and her unexpected quietness had restored to him his own self-possession. He took up the conversation at the point vital to himself:

'I understand you propose to divorce me for cruelty and misconduct?'

'Yes. Those are the grounds,' she replied. 'But I may not need them both if the new Bill goes through.'

'I think you'll find it rather difficult to prove either.'

'On the contrary,' she said, 'I have adequate proof of both.'

He looked a little startled.

'Perhaps,' he said, 'you'll be good enough to explain.'

'Certainly. The night before you left England you stayed at the Clarence Hotel, Folkestone. Signorina Farretti was with you as your wife. The address of the hotel was on the note you sent me before you crossed, and a friend of mine looked up your names in the register. The chamber-maid remembered you too. Besides, you know, Signorina Farretti admitted her relations with you quite frankly.'

The completeness of her information placed him at an unforeseen disadvantage. He had entirely forgotten that his note had been written at Folkestone. He was only able to falter shamefacedly:

'I see. I suppose it's no use my trying to deny anything when you've got proofs like that. But,' he collected himself again, 'you can't prove cruelty. You can't make a charge like that out of a mere loss of temper.'

'Can't I?' In quiet, expressionless tones she described the result of that mere loss of temper. 'You don't perhaps remember flinging me aside? Because your violence took me unawares I couldn't stand up against the shock, and in consequence I fell against this fender here and hurt myself severely. Your son was born that night, and afterwards I had to have a serious operation. And then—' She checked herself suddenly. She could not bring herself to tell him even now of Jack's condition.

'I have adequate proof of all this,' she continued. 'You can ask Dr Mackintosh, who was with me when Jack was born, or the surgeon who operated on me afterwards. Or

Virginia Dennison, who found me almost unconscious an hour after you'd gone. If the law wouldn't call that cruelty, then there's no cruelty in the world.'

This time he turned away from her in growing agitation. His last hope of release seemed to have departed; moreover, he was genuinely shocked at the consequences of his act.

'Daphne – you mayn't believe me, but I didn't know. Even though I felt towards you as I did then, I couldn't have left England like that if I'd known. I'm not quite a savage, and what you've told me makes me horrified and ashamed. I haven't even the right to say I'm sorry. But,' his voice shook, 'I do apologise for having expected you to spare me what I deserve.'

'You needn't,' she interrupted him, 'for I've made up my mind already. I'm not going to divorce you.'

'Not – going – to – divorce me!' The suddenness of the relief almost unnerved him. 'You mean you're going to let me go on as I am, and take no action?'

'Yes, Raymond. That's what I mean.'

'In spite of everything that was – and is? Can you possibly have forgiven me for all that I did to you – forgiven me enough to let me go on with my work unhindered?'

'That's a different matter,' she said. 'I'm not at all sure that I've forgiven you. I don't really think I have – but my decision didn't depend upon that.'

Fearful of showing him the slightest sign of all that her resolution had cost her, she again became severely practical.

'I suppose a voluntary separation is what you'd like – for I don't imagine you ever intend to come back to me, Raymond?'

Her hands were clenched behind her back as she asked the question, and her fingers tightened as he slowly shook his head.

'You needn't be afraid,' she went on. 'I'm not going to ask you to come back in return for what I've promised you. Signorina Farretti makes you far happier than I ever could.'

There was no reproach in her tone; she simply stated a fact which had become as obvious to her as it was to him.

'Besides,' she continued, 'I wouldn't have you back now even if you wanted to come.'

'I know,' he said almost humbly. 'Much less than I've done to you could be enough to kill any woman's love.'

'You haven't,' Daphne broke in. 'I'm as much of a fool as most women, and there's one part of me that loves you and wants you as badly as ever. That's just it. If I didn't love you I might ask you to come back and let us try to begin again together for Jack's sake. But because I do love you I couldn't endure it. I wasn't quite sure of that until you came tonight, but I do realise it now. I couldn't bear to have you, knowing that you never cared for me – that you only asked me to marry you because Virginia refused you and hurt your pride. Oh yes, I know that now; I can even be sorry because she made you miserable. It was wrong of you to marry me, but it was my fault I wasn't as suitable a wife as you expected. So only one thing remains, and that's to give you up altogether. I know as well as you do that it's best for us both.'

She turned to him abruptly. 'Have you anything else you want to say to me?'

'There's just one thing.' He hesitated. 'I hardly like to ask you any more, Daphne – but will you allow me to see the boy before I go?'

She turned away from him in sudden fierce reluctance.

'I – I'm not sure. I don't think you'd really care to see him.'

'You don't even credit me with the ordinary feelings of a father, then?'

'I don't know. They weren't much in evidence before Jack was born, but it wasn't that I meant. You see – Jack's not quite the same as other children.'

'Not quite the same! Daphne – how isn't he?'

She did not reply, and he pressed the question more urgently:

'What in heaven's name do you mean?'

'Well – for one thing, he'll never be able to walk, your son.'

There was a long silence. Sylvester's face had become very pale. Suddenly he turned to her and faltered: 'Daphne, you don't mean – that I – that afternoon—'

She bowed her head, and before her quiet dignity his spirit touched its utmost depths of self-abasement. In the woman standing before him, nothing remained of the immature girl whose physical awkwardness and mental confusions had so often irritated and bored him. That moment was the worst that he had ever experienced, for in it he saw himself not only as he was, but as she saw him.

'You understand now,' she said at last, 'why I told you that I didn't think I forgave you. Forgiving always seems to me to imply forgetting – putting a thing entirely out of one's life as if it hadn't happened. But I can't put Jack out of my life, and every time I see him I can't help remembering – that afternoon.'

He could endure no longer the unreproachful gaze of her sad eyes; suddenly turning, he gripped the edge of the mantelpiece and bowed his head upon his hands. His shoulders shook with the unavailing sobs of belated remorse.

Daphne watched him, struggling with her emotion, fighting down the fierce desire to put her arms round him and comfort him, to tell him, so pitifully and so vainly, that she would forgive everything and banish the past if only he would come back to her and try to begin again. She knew that her yearning love could never hold him and that his passionate regret would not last, nor did she desire to handicap him by binding upon his shoulders a perpetual burden of remorse. She knew that while Jack lived the past could not be banished; clearest of all she knew that their life together ought not to have been, and must never have another beginning. She had worn herself out in hoping to restore a relation that had never existed. So she stood beside him in silence, and at last Sylvester spoke:

'Daphne, I didn't know – I never guessed. I scarcely remembered afterwards what I'd done. I could never have asked anything of you if I'd known. How could you spare me as you've done and never tell me—? Daphne, take my life and make of it what you will. I can't ask you to remain tied to me now. Let the divorce go on – I'll make it as easy as I can for you. I've ruined your life – and his; it's only fair that in return you should ruin mine.'

'What would be the good of that?' asked Daphne. 'It may be your fault that there'll be one useless citizen in the world, but will it make things better if I turn you into another? Would it be fair, just because you've done a great deal of harm, that I should spoil your one chance of doing good? I'm not going to. I want to see you a great statesman and a great peacemaker. I want your public life to make up for your life with me. It can, Raymond, and it shall.'

She touched his arm gently.

'After all, Jack's partly yours – I can never forget that. Come and see him if you like before you go.'

Like a man walking dazedly in a dream, he followed her into the next room to see his child. Jack lay sleeping in his cot beside Daphne's bed, the saddest victim of their disastrous mistake. His tiny pinched face already wore an expression of suffering almost uncanny on such baby features. Sylvester could not speak. With pale face and bowed head he stood motionless beside the baby's cot. As he looked at the fragile atom of humanity that was his son, he realised to the full the wreck that he had made of the lives of both wife and child. Daphne had been right; to those who had endured so much at his hands he could make no reparation. Only, perhaps, in the service of his race could he atone for the injury that he had done to them.

They left the sleeping baby in silence, and in silence stood looking mournfully at one another. Then Daphne put out her hand in token of farewell. Sylvester took it and held it for a moment; then he dropped it and went out hurriedly. Daphne heard the door close, and going to the window listened to his footsteps as they died away down the street.

Virginia waited for a little while after the shutting of the door; then she came back to Daphne, who stood beside the window, with no expression on her face, and no light in her eyes.

'Well?' Virginia inquired.

Daphne said dully: 'I'm not going to divorce him.'

'Indeed! And why not?'

'He's done so little good so far. I couldn't deprive him of his one chance to do it.'

'You mean he's got no sense of responsibility as a man, but he might have as a national representative?'

'Yes. Something like that.'

'And is he ever coming back to you?'

'No. He's never coming back.'

'Did you ask him to come?' inquired Virginia.

'No, I didn't. I told him that I wouldn't have him even if he wished – and he doesn't wish. I couldn't really have him back after all that has happened, especially as I still love him. You always knew that, Virginia.'

'Yes,' said Virginia, 'I always knew that.'

For a long time they sat on either side of the hearth without speaking. Virginia's thoughts went back into the past, back through her hospital days to Oxford and beyond. They wandered in the fields of battle with vanished loves who had long been dust; they strayed with Patricia in the darkness of Drayton garden after the heat of an acrimonious debate. They lingered with Daphne along Oxford Street in May; they hovered above her as she lay moaning and half-conscious where she had fallen beneath Sylvester's hand. Finally they came back to the present and remained there; the future was too dark and uncertain to visualise in dreams.

There was, after all, a greater love, Virginia thought, than to lay down one's life for a friend who had always been a friend, and that was to forego a just retribution, lying ready to one's hand, against a friend who had become an enemy, and had done one an irremediable wrong. It was still strange to her to realise that it was of Daphne that she was thinking this – of Daphne who only two years ago had still been an unformed girl, less lacking in heart than in discretion, and with a mind as amorphous as her style. The same contrast struck her that had impressed Sylvester half-an-hour ago. In the woman before her with sorrowful eyes and firm, grave mouth, she scarcely recognised the Daphne Lethbridge of the Oxford days.

Daphne at last broke the silence:

'I don't know if this is an end or a beginning, Virginia. Everything I have cared for much seems to be going away. Raymond's gone, and this time for always. Pat will soon marry Mr Stephanoff; they'll be very happy, and there won't be any room in their joy for a depressing person like me. And in a little while you'll be gone too, and I shall be left alone – all alone with Jack in an empty world.'

'Yes, you'll be lonely, Daphne, lonelier, I suppose, than you've ever been before. But solitude's no reason for despair. You're in splendid company in your loneliness; the Messiahs of the world will be with you, and all the saints and martyrs who ever toiled and died, all the men of genius, the thinkers and explorers and inventors, who thought that their supreme effort was in vain, but still went on.'

'I know. Some people seem to have been able to find victory in the deepest depths of all. But I – what am I to do?'

'You're to find victory too, of course.'

'I? But how?'

'Write,' answered Virginia promptly. 'Pat told me the other day that when you were in Sussex you thought of the beginning of a novel. Why don't you begin it at once? You'll be able to create people then, and when you've done that you'll never be really lonely again.'

'Write!' Daphne smiled a little sadly. 'Perhaps I might, if Elijah's mantle were still able to fall upon Elisha.'

'It isn't necessary, Daphne. Elisha has quite a good mantle of his own. Your book won't be brilliant, and it mayn't even be very clever, but that won't matter so long as you tell as much of the truth as you've learnt from life. And it's when everything seems to be at an end that the time has come to tell it.'

Daphne turned and looked meditatively at the fire. 'What shall I write about?' she asked.

The smile that had always puzzled her appeared for a moment upon Virginia's lips and then vanished away.

'Write the same thing that's always being written and always being forgotten – the thing that people need to be told again and again and again.' She sprang suddenly to her feet and stood beside the mantelpiece, looking down at Daphne.

'Write that the apparently truest love is not always worthy of trust, that the grandest human life is often the most mortal, and that amid all these transitory things success is the most worthless, most transitory of all. Tell them that one's plans may crash and one's loves fail and one's idols be shattered, but that this is only the beginning of the things that are worth while. Tell them that the struggle with that despair which lies waiting to storm the defences of every human soul is the only war worth winning, that in this victory alone is triumph over circumstances to be found. Write that peace is not to be looked for in the serene shelter of a man's love or on the summit of that mountain of ambition which is climbed by trampling on the hearts of other people, but only in the dusty highways of the world. Only a few will understand, and most of them will forget, but one or two will remember, and that makes it all worth doing.'

Daphne looked up at Virginia, and as she looked the faintest flicker of life, of expectation, illumined for a moment the hopeless weariness of her expression.

'But, Virginia, do I know all this?'

'You didn't always. But now you do. You know better than I, Daphne – far, far better than I. Pat once said to me, while we were both at Drayton, that all you needed was to believe in yourself, and that if you ever did, you'd become a fine person. I disagreed with her at the time, but I know now that she was right. And in a little while you'll know it too. You'll always be able to believe in yourself henceforward, just because you've done a great thing and a good thing, whatever people may say about it. For some day they may get to know your story, and they'll criticise what you've done, and say it was weak or immoral or absurd. It doesn't matter what they say; they only understand the world's wisdom, but you know a better wisdom than that. . . . I'm not sure that I even profess to be a Christian, so I suppose there are some things I haven't any right to talk about. But it has always seemed significant to me that when it was "found to be expedient that one man should die for the people," there was no sort of distinction made between one kind of people and another. He hadn't to die for the worthy people, or the people who tried to be noble, or the people who understood – but just for the people. Because if the best had been carefully chosen out, the ones who were left would have been more in need of a Saviour than ever. It's never for the people who deserve it that we're called upon to sacrifice ourselves; they don't need to have sacrifices made for them. No, it's for the weak and the wicked and the undeserving that we have to give things up. Look at the lives of people like doctors and nurses; more than half their days are spent on patients whose diseases are due to their own sins and follies. Look at the teachers of boys and girls in schools; they don't wear out their gifts and their energy on the brilliant and the ambitious, who'd get along all right without any teachers at all. No; they give their best work to the lazy and the backward and the stupid, who either can't or won't learn. Just in the same way the clergyman in a slum parish spends all his time and thought on the people who drink and swear, and beat their wives, or are unfaithful to their husbands. Just in the same way the soldier fights and dies to save some foolish politician from the fruit of his mistakes. You're one of them now, Daphne, one of the children of the Kingdom, who because they save others lose the chance to save themselves. You're giving up a great deal for Raymond – your just retribution for the many wrongs he's done you, your hopes for the future, even in a way your own honour. He isn't worth it – and that's what makes your sacrifice a splendid thing.'

She ceased, and stood looking into the fire. Then the clock on the mantelpiece struck eleven, and she turned suddenly to Daphne.

'Look!' she exclaimed, 'how late it's getting! I must really go – I've been talking so much that I never noticed the time.

I expect I shall find my orders waiting for me when I get back. I'll come in again if I can before I go, but if I don't it'll mean that I had to leave at once. You'll understand that, won't you?'

'Oh yes,' replied Daphne. 'Of course I shall understand.'

'I think I'll walk back,' said Virginia. 'It's quite fine, isn't it?'

Daphne lifted the curtain and looked out of the window. 'Yes, it's quite fine. But it's a very dark night.'

'I know it's dark. But there are a few stars shining; there generally are a few if you look for them, though sometimes they're very hard to find.'

She smiled up at Daphne as they left the room together. 'There's no good-bye, is there, for people like us?'

'No,' answered Daphne. 'We won't say good-bye.'

She stood at the door of the flat and watched Virginia as she went down the stairs. At the bottom Virginia turned and waved her hand. The light above the porch shone radiantly upon her upturned face. Then once again the door closed.

Daphne went back to the empty room and sat thinking, hour after hour, beside the fire. How could there be anything splendid in what she had done, she who had acquiesced meekly in a sordid compromise, who had allowed love's jewels to be trampled in the dust? She would never wear them again, but life without them would have to be faced; it would go on the same always – for ever and ever the same.

The last smouldering coal collapsed, and the ashes fell through the bars with a dull crash. From the half-open door of her bedroom came a faint, plaintive sound; her crippled child was moaning a little in his sleep. Long after the fire was dead and the room had grown cold she still sat there thinking – thinking of the words that Virginia had spoken, and hearing again the sound of Sylvester's footsteps, echoing away into the night.

VIRAGO MODERN CLASSICS
&
CLASSIC NON-FICTION

The first Virago Modern Classic, *Frost in May* by Antonia White, was published in 1978. It launched a list dedicated to the celebration of women writers and to the rediscovery and reprinting of their works. Its aim was, and is, to demonstrate the existence of a female tradition in fiction, and to broaden the sometimes narrow definition of a 'classic' which has often led to the neglect of interesting novels and short stories. Published with new introductions by some of today's best writers, the books are chosen for many reasons: they may be great works of fiction; they may be wonderful period pieces; they may reveal particular aspects of women's lives; they may be classics of comedy or storytelling.

The companion series, Virago Classic Non-Fiction, includes diaries, letters, literary criticism, and biographies – often by and about authors published in the Virago Modern Classics.

'Good news for everyone writing and reading today' – *Hilary Mantel*

'A continuingly magnificent imprint' – *Joanna Trollope*

'The Virago Modern Classics have reshaped literary history and enriched the reading of us all. No library is complete without them' – *Margaret Drabble*